Prolo

C000176895

I WAKE UP, NAKED, *in a large bed in a pokey room. There are no curtains, and light streams in through the slats of the blinds. My whole body itches. There don't seem to be any sheets: I've been sleeping under an uncovered duvet, on a bare mattress. The room smells of stale beer and mouldy food. Outside there are the sounds of traffic: horns hooting and engines revving and people shouting. Rubbing my sore eyes, I look around this room that I have never seen before. I'm still wearing last night's eye make-up. The mascara sticks my lashes together and as I rub my eyes the glitter comes off on my hand.*

As I sit up I can feel that my thighs are bruised and sore. This is not a place where I want to be. There are jaws closing round my brain, crushing it. My brain pounds against my skull. Energy courses through me as if I'm coming up on a pill. I'm lying in this strange bed but I'm rushing and my jaw is going and my blood is pulsing. I chew the elastic of my star bead bracelet to calm myself down, but as my teeth grind against each other electricity shoots through my brain. Blue lightning flashes across the room.

My clothes are on the floor – tangled up with crushed beer cans, Chinese takeout cartons, overflowing ashtrays. Wrapping the duvet round me, I lean forward and pick up my clothes from the floor. My hands shake as I pull on my underwear and dress. There are stains all over my dress, like it's got mixed up with some soy sauce from one of the ageing takeaways. My hair smells of smoke, and so do my clothes, and this smell makes me feel sick.

IN
BLOOM

IN
BLOOM

CORDELIA
FELDMAN

First published 2021 by Dandelion Digital, an imprint of Paper Lion Ltd
13 Grayham Road, New Malden, Surrey, KT3 5HR, UK
www.paperlionltd.com
info@paperlion.co.uk

A catalogue record for this book is available from the British Library

ISBN
Paperback: 978-1-908706-34-8
eBook: 978-1-908706-35-5
Audiobook: 978-1-908706-36-2

Design: cover by Two Associates, interior by seagulls.net

For my mother, father, brother and Spitfire.

Chapter 1

I'M LYING ON MY BED watching my two fantail goldfish, Richard and Judy, circle round and round their tank. My favourite album – *Sliding Gliding Worlds* – is playing as I think about what I'm going to wear out clubbing this evening. I settle on the dark purple tie-dyed mini-dress and throw it into a bag with my overnight stuff.

"Mum, can I have a lift to Lily's?" I yell down the stairs.

"*May* I, Tanya." Mum corrects me. "If we leave *this minute*. And why haven't you put away your clean clothes?"

"I've been finishing my *King Lear* essay." I reply in a triumphant tone.

"You are a good girl." Mum says, beaming at me, her voice softening. "You work so hard. I'm proud of you."

Mum's wearing fuchsia lipstick today with amethyst eye shadow and chocolate eyeliner. Her hair is styled in the same chin-length dark brown bob that she sports in photos taken thirty years ago.

"Put your clothes away now, I'll just put your father's dinner in the oven," Mum says.

A few minutes later, I pull on my knee-high boots and clamber into the car, climbing over Mum's tennis bag and avoiding the tube of tennis balls on the floor. I feel the Thursday night excitement bubbling in my throat: I'm going to Magic Realms nightclub with Emily and Lily, which we try to do as often as possible on Thursday nights; whatever we tell our parents we're doing.

"What are you girls up to tonight then?" Mum asks, keeping a deliberately casual note in her voice.

"Oh we're just going to the cinema."

"Why are you wearing that outfit? Isn't it a bit over-the-top?" Mum's interrogation continues, but I'm a step ahead.

"The boys are coming: Ben and his mates." My pre-prepared answer slides out.

"Oh I see." Mum smiles. "That's nice."

She likes Ben because he's Jewish like our family, goes to private school and his dad's a barrister. Basically, he's the sort of boy she'd like me to go out with.

When we draw up at Lily's, Emily is already there and they're both also wearing Spank mini-dresses: Lily's is emerald green and Emily's is shocking pink. They've been dyeing their hair, I notice with envy. Lily has pink streaks running through her blonde bob and Emily's got blonde stripes in her brown curls.

I guess this means that they haven't touched the English coursework that I've now finished: I pat myself on the back for being organised enough to write my essays before I go out partying.

"Good evening, Mrs Marshall." Lily greets my mum in her best talking-to-grown-ups voice. "How are you and Mr Marshall and Carl?"

Lily fancies my brother, of course. She must never, ever be allowed to get her claws into him though. She smiles at my mum. Mum adores Lily. She kisses her on the pink-stained cheek.

Lily looks beautiful as usual. She's shorter than me, petite, perfect hourglass figure. Her skin's flawless and it's this gorgeous golden brown colour. She's got huge cornflower blue eyes and silky blonde hair that she hates because it gets greasy quickly.

"We're fine sweetie. How are your family?" Mum asks her voice softening as she throws Lily her most indulgent smile.

4

"Very well, thank you, Mrs Marshall."

Mum gives me a hug goodbye. "Be sensible girls." She instructs. "Stick together."

I feel the familiar wrench of guilt, but ignore it. Lily and I look at each other, sharing a moment.

We escape upstairs to the sanctuary of Lily's room; tripping over shoes and exercise books and glittery scarves on the stairs.

"Do you think Neil and James are going to be there?" Lily asks.

Her mouth is open like a fish as she applies violet eyeliner to her lower lids. She's nabbed the best spot: sitting on the chair positioned in the middle of the dressing table, right in front of the mirror.

Lily's seeing Neil, sort of casually, just at Magic really. I'm sort of dating his mate James, like Lily and Neil though, only on Thursdays at Magic. His real girlfriend is only fifteen and apparently she's already had an abortion – according to the regulars at Magic. The boys are older than us. They're already working in London; we're in our first year of sixth form.

"Hope so or how are we going to get sweeties?" Emily replies. "Can you move over a bit, Lily?" She asks her, squeezing into the tiny gap between Lily and the window, trying to catch a glimpse of herself in the mirror.

"Those dolphins we had last week were fab, weren't they?" I say, placing a turquoise bindi in the middle of my forehead and checking that it's straight using the little mirror in my handbag. I'm not going to try to fight my way to the big mirror.

"Yeah, they were wicked. I hope the boys have got dolphins for us this week," Emily says.

"Or swans," Lily says, placing a butterfly sticker on her cheekbone.

"You got any silver glitter?" Emily asks Lily.

"Yeah. Loose glitter dust or pressed silver eye shadow?"

"Eye shadow I think.

"T, can you just hold this a minute?" Lily says, handing me an empty plastic bottle. She pulls out a bottle of Smirnoff vodka and starts to pour it into the little bottle that I'm holding. "Hold still, T. The parentals won't miss a little bit of this, will they?"

On the walk to the station we drink the vodka with Diet Coke, taking a mouthful of the neat spirit and then washing it down with a mouthful of the soft drink. It tastes horrible, and still of bubble bath, which was the previous occupant of the little bottle, but we haven't got much time to get wasted.

We run, giggling, down the road to the train station – from King's Cross it's only fifteen minutes to Magic Realms on the tube. As we approach the club down the cobbled alleyway under the station arches I can hear the trance music pumping out into the street. I recognise a few people in the queue – other Magic regulars: friends of Neil and James; boys from other schools near us; the same bouncers who are here every week.

Everyone is wearing fluorescent or tie-dyed clothes, with reflective patches or bright Indian-inspired patterns. There's a bit of a space age look to some of the outfits – the Crasher kid thing from up north is making its way here. Some people are wearing Acid House-style smiley face T-shirts. We push to the front of the queue – regulars get certain privileges – and with a wink to the doorman we hurtle inside like drunken fairies, and set off in search of adventure.

Inside, the club is a cross between a souk, an enchanted forest and a music festival. I imagine Glastonbury must be quite like this, although I haven't been there yet. Fluorescent drapes hang from the ceilings; the walls are daubed with forests and mythical landscapes.

Entering the club, we turn left to the cloakrooms, which are on an outer circle, next to the bar while the dance floor and market place are inside the circle.

We enter the market place, purchase some lollies and candy bracelets; and mooch around looking at the fluorescent fimo jewellery on sale. The next-door stall is selling slime, and we smear it on each other's hair and clothes, chasing each other around the club with handfuls of glowing green gunk, and giggling.

"Hey, T. Where's Lily?" a voice says behind me.

It grates that the first question – quite often the only question – any boy ever asks me is 'Where's Lily?' or 'How's Lily?' or 'How's your mate, you know, the fit one.' I can't imagine anyone asking Lily or Emily "Where's Tanya?"

I turn round to see who's talking. It's our friend Ben. He's wearing baggy jeans and a red Spliffy T-shirt and I see that he's had his ear pierced with a big fake diamond stud. It doesn't suit him – his ears are too big and stick out and it just draws attention to them. His thick black wavy hair is gelled into curtains.

"Hi, Ben. She's probably off snogging one of her many admirers." I tell Ben and his face drops, his big blue eyes widen and his mouth turns down at the corners. He's been unrequitedly mooning after Lily since he met us both on Israel Tour last summer. He worships her so much and follows her around in such a pathetic way that we call him 'Moonboy' behind his back.

" Benjy, have you got any sweeties?" I ask.

"Maybe," he says in a hushed voice, looking around, anxious. He must have some. Ben likes to think he's a dealer. Generally he just buys a few pills and the odd gram of speed at any one time to sell on to his mates.

"What've you got?"

"Christmas trees and green tulips."

"Which ones are better?"

"The green tulips are uplifting, giggly and floaty. The Christmas trees are heavier and more intense, people say they have heroin in them. What d'you reckon?"

I think about it for a minute.

"Let's have three of the green tulips." I decide, sliding some money into his hand.

I don't want to be so wasted that I can't move, not tonight. Tonight, I want to dance and giggle and float around the club like a butterfly.

"Hi Ben." Lily's materialised. She throws him one of her dazzling smiles and he blushes.

"Hi Lily," he says. "You look nice."

"Thanks Ben," she replies. "We'll catch you later," she says. "Come on, T, let's go and get mashed."

Ben looks after her helplessly as she walks off, and I shrug at him and turn to follow her.

The two of us squeeze into one toilet cubicle and bolt the door, huddling together in excited anticipation.

"Shit, Lily, I think I've...oh no, here they are." I extract the bag of pills from where I've stashed them inside my bra. "Thought I'd lost them for a second there."

"What are they? Show me." Lily demands.

We examine them. They're a lurid emerald green colour with tulips imprinted on them.

They taste disgusting. I always forget how bitter they are. It's when they *don't* taste bad that you have to watch out though – there are lots of dodgy dealers who'll try and skank us with fakes which can be anything from aspirin to dog worming pills.

We wash the pills down with water and run off to dance. As we're leaving the loo I catch sight of myself in the mirror. My eyeliner has smudged a bit, my dark curls have softened. As always, I look prettier once I'm in here and I've got some pills and I can relax a bit. I smile at my reflection. This is going to be a brilliant night.

On the way to the dance floor someone pinches my bum, I swerve round: it's Neil.

"Hi gorgeous, Lily here?" He asks. His pupils are massive and his T-shirt reads 'I said NO to drugs but they didn't listen'.

"Yeah, course. James around?" Neil shakes his head.

"Nah sweetheart, not tonight. He's going to Wonderland tomorrow." I bite my lip, trying not to show my disappointment that James is not here. 'Adventures in Wonderland' is another trance night that happens every Friday at the Cellar in Farringdon. If you're really hardcore you go to both, back to back, but our group tend not to go out on Fridays because we're all Jewish and have to stay in on Friday night for dinner with our parentals.

Lily runs off somewhere with Neil, and Emily snuggles up in a cage in the chill-out room with Neil's mate, Skipper. The cages are round the walls and I snogged James in one of them a few weeks ago. I can't believe he's not here tonight. I've been building up to seeing him all week: what a let-down.

"You coming up?" Lily mouths at me later, after we've been dancing for a while – the sound of her voice drowned out by the thumping beats.

I elbow a wasted boy out of the way. He's got his shirt off and sweat dripping down his hairless chest. He's got a Mitsubishi sign painted on his cheeks in yellow UV paint and he's wearing one white glove, blowing a whistle. He's got crasher kid written all over him. He's holding a piece of paper which says "Tune" on it.

"Not yet. You?" I mouth back, wiping glow stick boy's sweat off my arm.

"No. When did we take them?"

It feels like we've been dancing for ages. I look at my watch, tilting it towards the UV light.

"About 40 minutes ago," I shout to her.

"Should be soon then." Lily calls.

I watch the circles that all the glow sticks are making in the air. I look around the packed dance floor. Lots of the kids are blowing whistles slung on fluorescent shoelaces round their necks. Most have UV sun block stripes diagonally on their cheeks and whited-out lips. Then I feel a muscle spasm running up from my feet to my thighs, and I clutch Lily's arm.

"I'm coming up," I say. "Here we go."

I look into her eyes and her pupils are huge and her jaw's just starting to grind.

"You know I love you T," she mouths.

"I love you too," I say.

We hug each other. I stroke her hair which is as soft as a chinchilla's coat. She runs her hand down my arm and it tingles and…

"You up yet?" Emily runs up to us. "We're getting old," she says, pointing to the glowstick boys.

"Yeah, really up. You?"

"Yeah. Great pills. Looks like we should get some of those Mitsubishis next," she says, pointing at the boys who are jumping up and down and hugging each other, their eyes wide and jaws grinding. "Look." Emily thrusts her arm at me. She's got a gorgeous fairy painted on her shoulder in fluorescent pinks and greens and yellow. "D'you like it? I've just had it done, for free coz one of the face-painters fancies me."

The music thumps: the beats build in fours. This is ecstasy – my mood rises higher, crashes through the glass ceiling, thrusting up and up, through the earth's atmosphere, through the hole in the ozone layer, into the heavens.

I grip Lily's hand, she's grinding her teeth, and the music pumps through us. We are a conduit for the fours and fours and fours that thud up through the floor and up our thighs and up and up. The three of us plus Ecstasy makes four. This is what it is all for – this now, at one at three with each other and the beats and the pills turning and tumbling on the screens in front of us.

A little later we troop off to the Well where we lounge around on beanbags and smoke and listen to the chilled music and the bongo drums.

"I wish we didn't have to go to school." Lily says.

"Yeah, I know. I wish we could just go clubbing all the time and all live together in a huge house in…"

"Holland Park?" Emily suggests.

"Primrose Hill. It's nearer Camden market." Lily says.

"It'd be cool if we could take a year off between now and the Upper Sixth, and just go clubbing and meet interesting people and experience stuff." Emily says, blowing a smoke ring, her mouth a perfect O, her curls tighter and springier than mine.

"Well, we can have a year off after next year." I say.

"Yeah, I know you love school, T, and you always get top marks for everything, but I want it now. I might not feel like this next year. It's just ages away anyway; we'll have to do all our A-levels before then." Lily says.

"Euggghhhhhhhhhh."

I don't want to think about A-levels though, not now. I look up at the painted ceiling where dragons and fairies are frolicking in a magenta and periwinkle sky, and concentrate on just feeling the pill. Everything is amazing, I think. Nothing can touch me. I'm here with my best friends, in our favourite place where everyone looks out for us. I love them. I love everyone. Everything is connected and I understand it all. I smile with my whole body, every single one of my muscles.

I look at the tableau of my friends laid out before me. Lily is blowing smoke rings, her brow furrowed in concentration. I love that owl face she does when she's thinking. Emily is rolling a joint in her usual professional way. I want to stay here at Magic Realms forever, I think. I never want anything to change.

"Lily, we'll always be best friends, us three, won't we?" I ask

"Yeah, of course." She puts an arm round my shoulders, tucks the label of my dress back in. "Always. Shall we get some more sweeties?"

"Yeah, I want to be more battered than this." I say. I don't want to lose this feeling. I hold onto it, clutch it to me. We've still got the whole night and there's so much to do still, so many people to chat to and rooms we haven't yet explored.

Chapter 2

THE MUSIC STOPS DEAD and the lights come on, flooding the club with a too-harsh whiteness. I blink and rub my eyes, and so does everyone else in the club, muttering and grumbling. With the UV tubes turned off it doesn't look bright and fluorescent and magical anymore but tawdry, messy, trashed.

Empty water bottles on the floor, crushed cans, empty fag packets. The floor is dirty. In the bright light people look fucked, spotty, older than they did in the dark. There are some ancient fossils here. Old people should have some dignity and stay at home, they certainly shouldn't be out clubbing, thinking they're still 'down with the kids', I think.

I check my watch: it's 3am. I don't know why Magic has to finish so early. Actually, it's probably because most people who come here have got school later today, I realise.

We join the cloakroom queue behind about 50 people: other girls from our school, boys from Ben's school, grown-ups who work at the club, European university students with plastic-framed glasses and bum-bags, kids wearing fluoro lime-green, yellow and orange jackets with reflector strips.

"Shit, should've come earlier." Lily whispers, rubbing her cheek where her silver star stickers have fallen off, leaving a sticky trail. The cloakroom queue's massive.

"We going to Paul's cafe?" she asks.

Her jaw is grinding too, pupils huge, eyeliner smudged, make-up sweated off. I bet I've sweated off and smudged all my make-up too. I push my bra-strap back up my arm and feed the silver hoop back through the side of my dress where it's detached itself. I notice that my tights have ripped and torn.

"You want to?" I ask.

"Yeah. I'm still mashed. So are you, your pupils are massive," Lily says. "Let's go, it'll be fun."

"You gonna make it to the cafe, ladies?" Neil says, coming up behind Lily and putting his arms around her.

She turns towards him and lets him nuzzle her neck, or at any rate she doesn't stop him. I envy her ability to flirt and not show if something or someone pisses her off, her lack of awkwardness, her ability to hide her feelings, her… I don't know what it is.

Neil does not look so attractive in this light where I can see his pristine white Reebok classics have been dirtied by the floor. One of his front teeth is missing and he's got a pierced eyebrow.

"If you've got any more stuff." Lily says.

"Of course, for my favourite girls." Neil says.

"Ok, everyone, this way out. No, the front door is closed. Out this way." A bouncer says, pointing us towards the back door that leads into the alleyway behind the club.

Coats retrieved, we tumble onto the street, and walk down the cobbled alley – past the people giving out packs of glossy bright flyers. I rip the clear plastic packet open, discard any that are South or East London, or cheaply produced and not shiny, saving the best, prettiest, brightest ones to put up on my wall. The flyers promise freedom: *Escape From Samsara, Adventures in Wonderland, Apocalypse, Kundalini, Biology.*

We start walking, following the crowd towards the cafe. The pavement springs under my feet, it moves slowly like I'm tripping, my legs wobble; my steps time-lapse as we move towards the café in a gaggle of ravers. The air is crisp and cool. My jaw aches and my eyes itch where the weight of blobs of mascara force my eyelashes down: boulders flopping onto my cheeks.

Reality begins to creep in under my ecstasy blanket. I need to get to Paul's cafe, have a nice cup of tea and a sit down. I'm glad we don't have to go to school in 3 hours like we usually do on a Friday. I'm tired and I want to go to bed. The wind lashes my face. I pull my coat around me: relieved that I've changed into my trainers and pulled a pair of Adidas tracksuit bottoms on under my mini-dress.

Rain starts to fall out of a dark sky. This is not a warm Balearic night. We are not coming out of Pacha onto the beach in Ibiza. We haven't yet even been to Ibiza.

"Shit, T, you got an umbrella?" Emily asks me, putting her packet of flyers on the top of her head to shield her hair from the drizzle.

"No, but I've got a hood, ner ner ner ner ner." I pull my hood up over my hair; it catches in my butterfly hair clip. I have to hold the hood on the top of my head because of the wind.

At the cafe we pull up a few chairs, get our free cups of tea, and I think about the possibility of getting involved with the chocolate biscuit cake. I'm not hungry but don't want to turn down free cake.

"Dance, babe?" Neil asks Lily. The sound system is pumping and some bongo players have set up and are drumming.

"Go away." She says, throwing him an icy, unwelcoming stare. "I'm eating my cake."

I rub my foot where a blister has come up. I want to go home. I have a headache that is coming now that the effects of the pills are wearing off. The thumping techno and thuds of the bongo drums are starting to grate. I need to wash my itchy face. I stare at the floor and watch the glow-stick boys from earlier who are dancing and flailing their arms. The floor looks sticky.

There's not much space and despite the cold outside it's steamy in the room. I see that Emily and Lily are sweating and look ashen and peaky. The cakes sit in their towers: chocolate crunch cake in its oblongs dusted with sugar and shot through with nuts; mooncake – a chocolate fudge cake; chocolate caramel squares – shortbread topped with a layer of caramel and a topping of chocolate. Looking at the cakes make me feel sick: I'm so not hungry.

"Everything is spirals, man." Neil says as he rolls a spliff. His fingernails are grimy.

"What does that mean?" I ask him, putting my hands over my ears as Glowstick boy and his friends blow their whistles and shout 'Tune'.

"It's all spirals." He repeats. "Spirals in nature: fractals…"

He waves his arms with disproportionate enthusiasm, sending his tea flying over my tie-dye dress which runs all over my legs.

"Owwwwwwwwwwwwww you absolute fool!" I shriek as the scalding liquid sears my legs.

If I was still fucked I wouldn't care but now the pill's starting to wear off I'm so so so cross that this has happened right at the end of the night as well.

"What are you talking about anyway?" I can't keep the irritation out of my voice.

I don't even want to know really. I have absolutely zero interest in Neil's topics of conversation now that my thoughts are returning to normal from their pilled-up haze.

"It's the spirals in nature…" he starts to explain, tapping his joint on the ashtray and looking at me.

"Oh, the Fibonacci sequence?" I ask.

"The what?" He obviously hasn't heard of it.

"The pattern that petals are arranged in. It's a mathematical sequence." I explain.

"Nah mate, it's all spirals. Fractals man. And the ley lines. Follow the ley lines along the Thames and they... and crop circles. The aliens are coming."

"Really?"

"Yeah, man. The aliens are coming for us. They are going to land on the plains, you know what I mean?" Neil is getting into his subject. He sounds excited.

"Oh, you mean Erich von Daniken and the Chariots of the G-ds on the Nazca lines?" I say. That's what my brother Carl told me.

"Yeah, man, that's the dude. Far out." Neil says

"But surely that has been proven to be absolute bollocks."

He shakes his head, his blond dreadlocks swing around his face. "Nah it is the truth. The government just don't want us to know, but the revolution is coming. We are going to reclaim the earth, with the help of the aliens."

But the revolution is not coming, I think. I don't believe in anarchy, changing the world through drugs, squatting, that the aliens used the Nazca lines as a landing strips or make crop circles. I have nothing in common with these people except drugs and music.

"Time to go, girls?" Emily asks me and Lily, as if reading my mind.

"What's the time?"

"6 o'clock. The tubes should've started running by now."

I pull on my coat; pick up my flyers and my rucksack. My eyes are itching – I need to take my lenses out but I'm too vain to put my glasses on in front of boys, even boys I don't fancy.

We leave Paul's and walk down the steps to the tube. The diamond-shaped metal grill, has just been pulled open and the escalators have whirred on. We're first down the escalators, first on the platform, first on the trains apart from a couple of poor suckers going to work in their suits who cast us disapproving looks as they push past us with their briefcases and comb-overs.

Back at Lily's we lie on the floor of the living-room in sleeping bags, resting on cushions we've stripped from the sofas. We're safe from scrutiny as her parents are off on a cruise. There are ashtrays all over the floor and the glass tables have been pushed to the side of the room. We're listening to Massive Attack while the room fills with the smell of spliff and the acrid tang of my own Marlborough light.

A children's programme, Teletubbies is playing. Brightly coloured creatures in baby-gros with TVs in their tummies and different shaped aerials on their heads gurgle and roll around the screen. They live in a weird land where they eat special toast and custard made for them by their vacuum cleaner Noo-Noo who is like Peter Pan's Nana, but a hoover rather than a St Bernard. The strange land is green, covered in rabbits and multicoloured flowers and windmills and exotic animals: a psychedelic *Watership Down* where nothing bad can happen.

"Tea, anyone?" Lily asks.

"Oh yes please." Nothing could be better after clubbing than a nice cup of tea, but not biscuits because we're not hungry from the pills: they take your appetite away until the next evening. It's awful having to have family lunch on a Sunday when you've been out clubbing on Saturday night, and your parents are going:

"Why aren't you eating? Are you anorexic?"

At school on a Friday it's de rigeur to skip lunch. No- one eats lunch, unless they're obese, or not Jewish. Mum makes me packed lunch but I just throw it away on a Friday.

"Here, T." Lily thrusts a mug of tea under my nose.

"Mmm thanks Lily." I sip the tea. It is milky and nice and hot.

Chapter 3

"TIME TO GET UP." Mum twitters, wrenching my curtains open. "Mum, stop it, it's the middle of the night, go away." I open my eyes and see that in fact it's light outside. That's so weird though: I'm exhausted, the tiredness fills my head and seeps into my bones, as if I've been dancing all night rather than sleeping for nine hours. It's a week after our last trip to Magic Realms and…

"It's nine o'clock, if you want to come shopping with me I'm leaving in fifteen minutes. You are not going to make me late. Get up immediately." She starts pulling my covers off me and it's cold with my feet exposed. I pull the covers back from her and bury my face in my pillow.

"No, leave me alone." I mutter, my words muffled by the pillow.

"I'm going to feed the birds now, if you're not ready in ten minutes I'm leaving without you." Mum stomps out of my room, her heels clicking down the stairs.

"Alright, I heard you the first time." I mumble after her receding form.

I close my eyes and pull my covers up over my head. I want to go back to sleep and wake up feeling normal. This must be a comedown, I realise. I've been lucky enough to have avoided them so far, but this is blatantly my first come-down. I lie in bed listening to my own breathing, the roaring in my head and my thoughts that scream 'I want to die'.

"Tanya, I said I was leaving at nine fifteen, it's nine twenty and you're still in bed, get up right now."

Mum has reappeared and is hovering in my doorway, a peregrine falcon about to dive. I don't know what's got into her; it must be the menopause kicking in. "Here, wear this."

She picks up a fluorescent orange T-shirt with 'I blame the parents' emblazoned across the chest in black glittery letters and thrusts it towards me without bothering to read the slogan.

"I can't, I'll look too…"

I can't possibly wear that, I don't want people to look at me. I fumble around in my underwear drawer next to my bed for some knickers, socks and a bra. I pull out a pair of scarlet cotton knickers which say 'Robbie' on them – a present from my ex-boyfriend Robbie – sigh and put them back.

I miss Robbie so much at the moment, even more than usual. Sometimes I don't even think about him, but lately I have a lot. He's always there, just in the corner of my eye, loping down the road with his record bag slung over his shoulder, drawing on a Camel light with his mane of blond hair tumbling over his shoulders.

It takes me what feels like an hour to get dressed. I keep forgetting where I'm up to in the getting-dressed saga, stopping to catch my breath and stare vacantly into space and listen to my breathing. Somehow I've only succeeded in getting some underwear on and I have to hunt around for ages to find my deodorant which has fallen down the side of my bed.

I sit up in bed, and fish around on the floor for something to wear; locating a pair of black Adidas tracksuit bottoms and an old grey Reform Synagogue Youth T-shirt with a toothpaste stain down the front. I pull these over my underwear and haul myself out of bed and into the bathroom next door. The thought of splashing cold, wet water onto my face is unbearable, so I wipe it with a cleansing wipe and brush my teeth. The dull metallic taste in my mouth doesn't disappear though. The roaring in my ears is the sound our prehistoric boiler makes when it's fired up.

"At last." Mum says as I descend the stairs slowly.

My stacked trainers are making my feet too heavy to lift, which is weird because usually I don't even feel the weight of these shoes.

"Careful, sweetie pie, those stairs are dangerous, there's a bit of carpet coming up there." She points to the edge of a step.

I look down, and as I'm staring at the carpet I catch it with my shoe and trip over it, tumbling down the stairs. I sit in a heap at the bottom of the stairs, feeling the scratchy carpet under my bum and leaning back against the bottom stair, trying to pull the strands of my mind and body back together so I can get up.

"Oh, Tanya, darling, have you hurt yourself?" Mum rushes over and puts her arms round me and strokes my cheek. "I told you you'd break your neck wearing those shoes." Mum says, sighing and helping me up. I lean against her, feeling her sinewy strength and hoping it will waft into me.

"Not really." I reply, rubbing my aching bum that I can tell is going to be bruised in a severe and permanent way.

"Come on, let's go." Mum says, unlocking the door and shepherding me out to the car.

Mum witters on about…I don't know, I'm not listening, and I interject "Yes" or "No" or "Oh I see" at various points and stare out of the window at the oak, sycamore and poplar leaves turning gold and copper and bronze, the autumn day far softer and brighter than my mood which is flat and grey as the road itself.

We leave the main road and amble along country lanes to the farm shop. A strange thing is happening to the sky.

"Mum?"

"Yes sweetie-pie?" Mum replies, turning her head towards me.

"Is there about to be a storm?" I ask her.

"I don't imagine so, sweetie. Why do you think that?"

"The sky is closing in on us and pushing down." I explain. "The air is crackling."

"Maybe, then." Mum says sounding unsure. "I hadn't noticed this though. Don't worry; we'll be home before it starts raining", Mum reassures me, glancing at the sky and then back at the road ahead.

"How do you know?"

"Because I am your mother." She retorts, with a sense of finality. This is the only answer she ever gives to a question like that – to which I suspect that she doesn't know the answer.

We pull into the farm entrance, behind a horrible lurid blue Freelander. Mum swings the car into a too-narrow space. There is a clatter and then a crunch as she knocks a terracotta urn, and drives over it.

"Shit" mum says, slamming the handbrake on and switching the ignition off. "You didn't hear that rude word, did you sweetie pie? Don't ever use that sort of language yourself, will you?"

She opens the door and we get out of the car and walk past the furniture shop, the Aga shop and the delicatessen to our first destination – the fishmonger's.

Ted lifts a rainbow trout, whacks his cleaver down its spine, removes the guts, slices its head off, and docks its tail. I shudder: feeling the metal flaying my own skin, crunching my bones and severing my flesh.

"What can I get you today, Mrs Marshall? I've got some lovely halibut, and salmon steaks, look." Ted lifts a slab of salmon, lurid orange with silver scales, and a piece of halibut, white as Carrara marble.

"Any cod?" Mum asks with a hint of hope.

Ted shakes his head. " 'Fraid not. You can't get cod for love nor money these days Mrs Marshall."

"When I was a child, growing up in Grimsby, we used to feed cod to the cats." Mum sighs and I can hear the rusty old cogs in her brain turning as she gets into her storytelling stride.

"Cod used to be so plentiful that people wouldn't eat it. I can hardly believe that it's such a delicacy nowadays." Mum tells Ted.

"It's a funny old world, that's for sure." Ted says, humouring Mum, letting her pontificate.

"It's terrible, all this over-fishing in the North Sea." Mum says. "When I think about all those poor little codlings being caught when they're too young to breed – it's just wrong." She shakes her head and looks all sad about this severe fish abuse.

"Will you take the salmon steaks then, Mrs Marshall?" Ted asks.

"Yes, thank you Ted, that will be lovely. Your father and I can have salmon teriyaki for dinner." Mum says to me.

Ted nods, turning the slabs of fish in the scales, lifting them out in his plastic-gloved hands.

I stare at the pebbledash lino and at the ice that the fish nestle in, mingled with emerald green plastic grass and shells. Their sightless eyes gaze back at me. The light hits their glistening skin: yellow, pink, blue, rainbow.

"Mum, can I go to the Destiny shop?" I ask. I need to get away from the dead fish.

"All right sweetie, but don't spend any money."

"£35 for a day workshop to connect with the angels all around us," reads the sign above the counter of the Destiny New Age shop. The writing is gold and silver stars and glitter are scattered over the lilac paper.

"Do you get lunch for £35 though?"

"No, you have to bring your own. You might get free tea or coffee though." Amber Rose, the manager of Destiny, tells me.

She has long black nails, and wears a huge turquoise pendant, which is set off by her black corset. Her fingers jangle with silver rings.

"So, how do you connect with your angel then?"

"You may not know it, but they are all around us. Have you ever had a near miss, like when you almost get run over?"

I mull this over. A series of my accidents, both of the body and of the heart, slash through my mind: shattered glass, blood, the broken segments of my heart flapping and bleeding. I shake my head.

"Umm, no, I tend to have real accidents"

"Anyway, I never would have thought this, but angels are everywhere. We just can't see them for looking." Amber Rose says, smiling at me.

I purchase an amethyst and peridot rough-cut stone bracelet to ward off the evil eye, avert pregnancy and increase concentration, and a chart of the properties of different minerals and gemstones.

A few minutes later I'm back in the car with Mum, perusing my chart.

" 'Onyx is a leveller, calming the mind, and increasing openness to love. Quartz is the love stone, calming the heart. Peridot increases contemplation, wear it during meditation. Tiger's Eye enhances memory, wear it in an exam.' If they worked, I'd have the best health, the amount of jewellery I wear." I tell Mum.

"It's all rubbish." Mum sniffs. "People shouldn't be allowed to write such rubbish."

We drive on to Tesco, out of our village towards the next town where the supermarket has been built on an old industrial estate.

The lights in the supermarket give me a headache. They're too bright and it's freezing in the kosher section, among the Tivall veggie burgers and Osem soups.

"Mum, I've got to go to the loo."

"Why didn't you go at the farm shop?" Mum says, looking cross. "How many times have I said – always go to the toilet before you leave anywhere because…"

"Yes Mum, alright, I know…" I don't understand why she's making such a fuss. I could have been to the toilet in the time we've been arguing about it.

"We'll be home in half an hour. Can't you wait till then?"

I shake my head. I can't wait for a single minute. I have to get away from these lights.

I run to the loo, collapse onto the toilet and stare at the walls and floor. The lines between the tiles dance and the floor bubbles like a prehistoric tar pit. I'm getting acid visuals even though I haven't taken anything. Orange bursts of light dart out of the walls towards me. Time slows down. My heart thuds. The sound of my wee is deafening, and when I attempt to get up, I don't have the strength. Waves roar through my head and I feel nauseous. I know something terrible is about to happen, but I've got no idea what. I don't know why I'm feeling like this and it terrifies me.

It feels like hours that I'm on the toilet, unable to move, barely able to breathe but when I look at my watch it's only been five minutes. I should return to Mum, but I'm welded to the toilet seat, paralysed by my fear of something, I'm not sure what. My headache throbs and pounds. I try to count tiles on the floor but they're moving away from me and making me dizzy. 'If I close my eyes it will stop,' I tell myself, but it doesn't. The silence thuds. I'm not strong enough to sit up so I sink to the floor.

The tiles are freezing through my tracksuit bottoms. I stare at the floor and the tiles begin to slide and shift amongst themselves, and if I live for a hundred years I'm not going to build up enough energy to walk back to the biscuit aisle again. My face itches, there are hundreds of parasites crawling all over it, eating my skin. I'm shaking, I glance up at the ceiling and it's sagging, it's going to drop down and I flinch, the room starts spinning, revolving and I shut my eyes because I can't look anywhere, nowhere's safe. I want to die, please let me die and the white noise roars in my head.

"Are you alright sweetie?" Mum queries on my return, grabbing my arm. "You were gone for ages."

I nod, although I'm not. Profound exhaustion sweeps over me: I can barely keep my eyes open.

"Period pains." I mumble.

"You look terrible. Have you got a temperature?" She puts one hand on my forehead and one on her own.

"No, I'm fine."

We trundle round Tesco. I hold tight to the trolley: terrified that I'll become separated from Mum and I'll never be able to find her again. I feel about five years old, gripping Mum's arm, leaning against her. I resolve to never go to the supermarket again. It must be something to do with the supermarket, I've never felt like this before. As soon as we're out of Tesco I'll be fine.

At the Monterey Bay Aquarium – where I went with Mum and Dad and my brother Carl a few years ago – the tanks are enormous, several storeys high, and the sea otters and turtles swam far above us, diving amongst the streaming kelp. I'm there now – I'm in a tank, my senses muffled by the water, while everyone else is outside, I can see them but I can't reach them.

"How would you know if something's a phase?" I ask Emily. It's a week after the supermarket trauma, a week after my supposed come-down started. I don't see how it can be a come-down though, because they only last a day and I'm still enveloped in it. We're sitting on Emily's window sill so we can smoke out of the window. Unfortunately it's cold, windy and has just started to drizzle.

"How do you mean?" Em asks, her blue eyes wide with interest.

"Like, if you felt miserable," I say. "And then it went away but it kept coming back. How would you know if it's a phase?"

"Or if it's always going to be like that?"

"Yeah."

Emily furrows her brow, thinking of the correct answer, because in Emily's mind there is always a perfect solution to any problem. She's sensible, calm, logical; the balanced one of our group. Emily is skinny, with brown curly hair like mine but hers always looks neater somehow, and she can wear anything because she's got small boobs and brilliant posture from years of ballet. She's just got a lovely natural style. I wish I was more like her.

"Can we close the window, Em?"

"Yeah sure. You cold?"

"Freezing."

"It seems quite mild to me."

We clamber off the windowsill and sit cross-legged on the floor which is totally uncluttered and bare except for a blue and grey Persian carpet. Emily's bedroom feels so different from the disorder of my own room. Neat photo montages of Emily and her friends and family at various stages of her life line the walls, her bed sports a white duvet cover and one teddy bear sits with his back to the pillow. A framed photograph of an arctic landscape hangs on one wall and her ballet prizes crowd the bookcases.

"Well you wouldn't know, would you, until it stopped happening." She answers my original question finally. "Are we talking about Lily?"

I groan inside. Lily's always been really emotional and histrionic, ever since we were toddlers: alternately bursting into tears, or laughing hysterically. But I haven't. I've always been happy, confident, grounded, normal.

"No. Not like Lily. I mean, that's just the way she is, isn't it? She's always been like that." I say.

"Tanya, maybe you should see someone about it."

"About what?"

"Whatever it is you're worried about. It's really hard with you, because you keep things so bottled up, but there's obviously something wrong, isn't there?" Emily says, looking concerned, placing a hand on my arm.

"I don't know. Maybe it's just a phase. Maybe it's just growing pains or whatever?"

"Well, if it is, they'll tell you. And then you'll be able to stop worrying about it." In her eyes, Emily has solved the problem, drawn a line under it and already moved on to other topics. "Have you heard the new Orbital album? It's really fab." She asks.

I haven't moved on to other concerns in my own mind though. Walking home from Emily's, in the fading light, I know that I can't go on like this, I'm barely alive anymore. The leaves are turning brown and curling, ready to fall.

I miss Robbie. I miss having someone who I knew had chosen me, someone who put me first. Not that he did put me first of course, or not first before football anyway. I might never meet anyone else. I might shrivel up and die alone whilst all my friends are happily married. I've felt like this for a whole week. I might feel like this for the rest of my life. I want to die. I don't want to kill myself, I'm scared that I wouldn't do it properly and wake up maimed or paralysed. But every night as I fall asleep I hope I won't wake up in the morning.

Chapter 4

"Look, sweetie." Mum says, pointing out of the car window at the sky.

I glance upwards in time to see a soaring hawk with a red underbelly and a forked tail.

"Do you know what that is?" Mum asks me. It's three days after my conversation with Emily and Mum, Dad and I are on the way to Oxford to see my brother Carl.

"Red kite?" Of course I know what it is. We see them over the motorway every time we drive this route and Mum points them out every time.

"Yes. Isn't he beautiful?" Mum says in a soppy voice. "Isn't he the most beautiful bird you've ever seen? Look how he coasts on the thermals."

"Yeah. I can't really see the bird now, he's gone."

"You know, they've come back from the brink of extinction. Their numbers were down to just twelve birds, but now there are 430 breeding pairs in England and Scotland." Mum informs me, pulling her teacher hat on and setting it at a jaunty angle.

"Is that right? I've never heard that before, Mum, thank you for telling me." It comes out with a heavier tint of sarcasm than I intend. It's not that I'm not interested in Mum's pearls of wisdom, but every time we drive to Oxford we see red kites and she trots out this nugget of information. I must've heard it fifty times.

"Don't speak to your Mother like that." Dad says. We are having the rare treat of my Dad's company for a whole day. He spends about twelve hours a day at his office in the City doing whatever stockbrokers do, and he spends a lot of the weekend working too.

"Shut up! It's none of your business."

"Don't you dare speak to your father like that, Tanya. Apologise immediately." Mum hisses.

"No. It is none of his business. I'm talking to you, aren't I?

"Say sorry to your father. I insist." Mum says, in her stern teacher voice, turning round to give me a threatening look.

"Sorry," I mumble.

"Now say it as if you mean it."

"Sorry," I repeat, as if I don't mean it at all. Mum is obviously bored with telling me off now.

"Look at those sheep, Tanya. Look at their black faces. Do you know what they are?" Mum is off again on her own M40 Safari.

"Black faced sheep?" I guess.

My brother has been at Oxford University studying English Literature for the past two years. I'm looking forward to seeing him so much: it's dreadful being stuck at home with just my ancient senile parents for company. I know that if Carl was around I'd be able to tell him about what's been happening to me, in Tesco and stuff, about how I feel a lot of the time these days. It isn't really possible to talk about it over the phone though.

"Are we nearly there yet? I need a wee."

"Well you'll just have to wait. I told you to go before we…"

"I did. But I need another one."

"For God's sake, Tanya. Hold it in. That's why you've got a bladder sphincter." Mum says.

I wriggle in my seat. "Look, Dad, services 2 miles."

"OK dear, we'll come off the motorway." Dad says.

Dad doesn't want me to wee on the seat of the new Mercedes. He's wary of such incidents after being scarred for life by the time I puked all over the cream upholstery of one of his company cars when I was six. That car smelled of vomit for the rest of the time we had it. I'm not a good traveller, which is a shame, because I'd rather get back to reading *Mrs Dalloway* than listen to the parental selection of *Classic FM*, *Moneybox* and *The Archers*.

As we approach Oxford through the chalk hills of the Chilterns, it starts pouring with rain, as it always does, which makes me even more desperate for the loo. It's always wet in Oxford. I don't know how Carl stands it really. I don't think he notices the weather much.

"I think we should leave the car at the park and ride and get the bus into Oxford, you know there's never anywhere to park in the city centre." Dad is saying.

"But Cuddles might give us some books to take home, or some sheets to wash. We need to have the car with us." Cuddles is my mother's name for my 6 foot 2, 20 year old brother, who, in the two years he's been up at Oxford has coped with his laundry with aplomb.

"Alright, darling, whatever you think is best, I don't mind what we do." Dad defers to Mum, as always.

We park about a million miles away from where my brother lives, and tramp in the rain over Magdalen Bridge, along the High Street. The dreaming spires come into view, the Queen's College cupola, Carfax tower, the church with the spiral pillars. The dome of the Radcliffe Camera peeks out from behind the clouds. We stumble over the cobbles in Radcliffe Square and there he is: on the steps of the library, his college scarf round his neck, surrounded by girls. He breaks away from them and strides towards us: a smile on his face, as if he'd really rather be going out to lunch with his family than hanging out with his student mates.

"Mum, Dad, Tanya. Hello. How lovely to see you."

He looks so gorgeous, my brother, with his lustrous caramel wavy hair tumbling over one of his grey eyes, stubble just breaking through his olive skin. It's not fair that he should've inherited the tanned skin, pale eyes and blond hair of Mum's family whilst I've inherited the ghostly pallor, hazel eyes and corkscrew dark curls of Dad's ancestors. Mum throws her arms around his neck, I hold his hand and breathe in his smell of beer and sweat and smoky clothes that could do with a wash.

"How's my Cuddles?" Mum says, in her most full-of-love voice which she reserves for him.

"Mum." He hugs her back.

"How's my boy?" Mum strokes his hair.

"Yeah, fine, Mum. How are you lot?" He looks at me, and then at Dad. As my brother looks at me with his soft eyes I wish that he could be with me all the time.

"We're fine." Mum replies, in a voice that is not going to convince my almost telepathic brother.

I force a smile.

"You look nice, T."

I don't, of course. I haven't had a bath for days because the thought of taking all my clothes off, getting wet, drying myself and putting clothes back on again seems too exhausting.

"Where would you like to go for lunch, Cuddlekins?" Mum asks.

"The Pike? I could do with a good fish and chips." My brother suggests. This is a gastro pub in a nearby village, a popular destination for families to treat their student offspring to lunch.

"Of course, sweetie." Mum threads her fingers through my brother's ones and leans against his shoulder with a contented smile on her face.

"How's school Mum?" My brother asks over lunch. The Pike is packed, as always. Everyone is in parent and student trios; parent and student couples; or larger groups of parents, siblings and new student. Most of the students look miserable as they pick at their food. I can't tell whether they're sad that their parents are about to leave them at university, or whether they want their parents to leave them alone in their student lives. Maybe they're just not hungry because they went out drinking or taking drugs last night and now they can't force any food down and don't want to have to make conversation and would rather be in bed.

"We did that experiment, with eggshells and acid… Do you remember what happens?" Mum asks my brother.

Everything seems OK when we're with Carl and we're a whole family again. He smooths all the rough edges, fills the gaps in conversation, makes Mum laugh, talks to Dad about skiing and radiates his golden aura-of-Cuddles. A few years ago Mum's brother – Uncle Harry – went to a fortune teller who told him that Carl was going to be the saviour of the family. He is, just by existing. If he could live with us all the time I know things wouldn't be so bad. We should be able to stretch lunch out quite a bit, the service here is very slow and Carl can usually be prevailed upon to have three courses and coffee. My brother has a healthy appetite.

"What are you thinking about so seriously, T?" He asks me, as he tucks into his mozzarella in carozza. However much fried stuff he eats, he never puts any weight on.

"Nothing." I prod my salad with a fork. I'm really not hungry but I know if I don't eat some of it Mum will be cross with me.

"Nothing will come of nothing, speak again." Mum pipes in.

She has eaten a tiny bit of her smoked salmon and put her knife and fork down. No-one is telling her to eat up and finish what's on her plate. I hate it when she gets like this: competing with me for Carl's attention, trotting out quotes to impress him. He's my brother, let me have him to myself for a bit. I nudge Mum's glass of Shiraz towards her elbow and she knocks it over.

"Look what you've made me do you half-wit." She hisses at Dad as she dabs at the tablecloth with her napkin.

The wine-fall has already begun though: tumbling over the edge of the table into Mum's lap and over her dusky pink suede shoes.

"I'm going to the toilet to get some of this out, you pour some salt over the stain on the tablecloth." Mum instructs Dad.

I look at my Dad: he looks very old, there's more grey hairs than he used to have and his face is as wrinkled as a Shar Pei puppy's.

"How's school?" My brother asks me.

"S'alright." I mumble.. "I got an A for my last English essay."

"That's brilliant, T. Well done. What are you reading in English?" He asks, tucking into his fish and chips which have just arrived.

My mind empties. I look down into my goat's cheese salad and pick out the artichoke hearts and start to eat them first.

"Have you started *King Lear* yet?" He asks, spooning mayonnaise on his chips.

Oh, let me not be mad, I think. "Yeah," I reply.

"How are you enjoying it then?" He is trying to get me to say a bit more I think. He is looking a bit worried that I am not saying much. As I realise this I clam up even more.

"It's horrible."

The spilled wine reminds me of the blood as Gloucester's eyeballs are removed. I know I must be making my brother concerned, and I really don't want to upset him, but I can't think of anything to say that isn't miserable, boring or negative.

"Yes, I suppose it is."

'As flies to wanton boys are we to the g-ds
They kill us for their sport,' I think.

"Are you coming home soon?" I ask Carl, a pleading note creeping into my voice despite my attempt to sound casual.

"Well, T, you see the thing is I really need to hang around here for a week or so, at least until the end of tenth week It's just been crazy here, I'm not getting any work done." He pats my arm to console me, but my stomach clenches.

"What have you been doing then?" Dad asks Carl.

"Oh, you know. Rowing, table-tennis, directing *Equus* for Cuppers.'

"What's Cuppers?" Dad asks.

"Intercollegiate drama competition." Carl explains.

Mum returns from the loo and sits next to my brother, gazing at him with a soppy expression, moving her chair closer to his. I spoon the froth from my cappuccino into my mouth. I'm already feeling the loss of my brother, picturing him waving us off and returning to his golden, blessed Cuddles-life of success and enjoyment in all spheres.

Dad is absorbed in the details of the bill, reading and rereading it just to check that they haven't overcharged him by 2p or anything. Carl tells us stories of what happens in his life here and it's another world. I hold on to this precious time with my brother, dreading the minute when it will be over and he will leave us again.

Eventually he looks at his watch and says, "Great to see you, you lot, but I've got to dash, I've got a production meeting for *Equus*."

A handshake for Dad, a kiss for Mum and a grin at me, and he picks his coat up from the back of his chair, swinging it over his shoulders and striding out of the restaurant. I watch his receding form, and then he's gone, leaving a trail of gold Cuddles-dust and a vacuum. I grasp Mum's hand, she's crying too.

Chapter 5

"Look, T." Lily whispers, and lifts her vest-top up exposing her midriff. It is now pierced by a metal bar and there is a crusty wound there.

I shudder and turn away from her, lighting a Camel Light and taking a drag on it, blowing the smoke out in a seductive way channelling Ingrid Bergman in 'Casablanca'.

"It's infected." I point out, coughing because the smoke has gone up my nose. "You should take it out before you get blood-poisoning or whatever." I take a sip of my fresh mint tea to wash away the taste of the cigarette.

It's five days after my trip to Oxford and I feel great, normal in fact. I can't believe I ever felt miserable. It must have been a come-down. We're sitting in Rick's cafe in West Hampstead. They love us at Rick's and always give us free chocolate cake. Rick's Israeli. There are tiles round the walls – green, turquoise, azure, and strings of fairy lights and candles everywhere. It's a mermaid's grotto – starfish climb the walls, plastic tuna hang from the ceiling and there is sand in tanks round the walls where crabs and lobsters live.

"Nah, it's fine. It'll look like that for a bit, but as long as I keep using my saline it'll be OK." Lily says, chuffed with herself at being the first of us to dare to get a body-piercing.

I peer more closely at it. There's a stainless steel curved banana bar going vertically downwards through the skin just above her belly button. On the top end of the bar is a ball with an aquamarine crystal in, and a large fuchsia crystal nestles in the bottom of the bar that rests in the hollow of her belly button. If it wasn't red, puffy and oozing pus it would look really good. As it is, it looks horribly painful. I'm both envious and relieved that my own belly button is not in pain. Her Mum is going to freak out though.

"Where'd you get it done?"

"Metal Mayhem in Camden. Em came with me."

"Why wasn't I invited? When?" My stomach plummets with the awful feeling of being-left-out.

"Yesterday. Em got her nose pierced."

"No way!"

Em's Mum is going to screw as well. I can't believe they didn't ask me to come with though. They're only friends through me. Before she came to our school this year Emily was my friend from out of school, and Lily only even met her when we all went on tour to Israel together last summer. "So, how long before it looks…"

"It's fine, stoppit. It will look perfect in, like, a week or something."

It won't, I think. I hope it goes toxic and you get gangrene and you have to have your whole body amputated from the midriff down, you two-faced sneaky double-crossing, self-obsessed bitch. It's Lily I'm cross with, not Emily. Lily would have set it up, I bet…

….Lily would have called Emily and said:

"Come with me to get piercings, just the two of us."

Emily would have been flattered to have been asked to be Lily's accomplice. They would have wandered round Camden together, looking at the bell-bottomed jeans in the market, dancing under the UV lights in the cyber-chic clothes shops. They would have bought chips wrapped in newspaper and falafel and sat out by the canal –

eating their lunch and talking about Greg and Ian and arranging double dates.

So, Lily would have persuaded Emily that it would be great if they got piercings together and flirted with the piercer: batting her lashes at him and consequently getting a massive discount. She'd have made Emily go first, of course, and then she'd have got hers done and then they would have bonded over coffee, bought by Emily because of course Lily would have spent all her money by then. Sometimes Lily really upsets me. I know I'm overreacting and that Em and Lily are friends with each other and, as such, can do things without me, but I still feel hurt and left out.

… "T, can I borrow £5? Please?"

No, I think. Use your own money. "Yeah, OK." I say, opening my purse.

A passport photo flutters out and I see that it's one of me and Robbie that we took in the photo booth at the station last summer. We're sticking our tongues out at the camera and we look happy. Robbie Robbie Robbie. I miss him. I slide the photo back into my purse and hand Lily my only crumpled fiver without a protest, as usual. I'm livid with her though.

I wish I could put my money where my mouth is and actually blow up and tell her what I think of her. But I'm unable to get the words out, unable to deal with the inevitable outcome of crying, shouting hysteria.

"Have you done your English homework?" Lily asks, lighting one of my fags, which of course she's taken without asking me.

"No," I tell her, even though I have.

No way is she copying off me. The homework is an empathy exercise: pretend you are King Lear on the moor, and write the story of the play so far, as if you are narrating it to someone from another country who has just arrived in England. I find it easy to imagine this, and I'm very proud of it. Lily is absolutely not seeing it, which means I have to pretend I haven't done it or she'll worm it out of me and force me to lend it to her, and copy it.

"I bet you have," she says. "You always do your essays early and get As for them. You're such a swot."

I look over to the door, wishing I could just make a run for it and get away from Lily, who's pissing me off even more than usual, when, oh bollocks…

"Lily, Tanya, hey, what're you doing here?"

Ben strides through the door and almost runs over to us in his eagerness to get close to Lily as quickly as possible, tossing his head in what he must think is a nonchalant sexy way but in fact makes him look like he's got Tourette's. I can so not deal with chatting shit to him right now and watching him fawn over Lily.

"What're you doing here?" I retort.

Obviously he has come here because he thought he might 'bump into' Lily, he knows this is one of her favourite haunts. Since when has Ben started going out for tea like a middle-aged hairdresser, anyway. He should be out playing football and drinking White Lightning and puking with the other boys.

"Well, there's a new boy at my school who I thought you'd like to meet." He says, somewhat surprisingly.

And indeed, a boy who I've never seen before turns round from the bar and saunters towards us, drinks in hand.

"Hi Tanya, hi Lily, I've heard so much about you." He says, smiling at *me*: at me, not at Lily. "I'm Sebastian." He says, kissing me first on one cheek, then the other, like a sophisticated European person.

An electrical pulse surges through my whole body. He is gorgeous: tall, I guess about 6 foot 2 or so, with broad shoulders and thick but straight sandy-brown hair streaked with blond; big yellow-green almond-shaped eyes, like a lion's, and a rather unrealistic tan for winter in England. He reminds me of Aslan the lion from the Narnia books: I loved those so much when I was little. Seb has the same nobility of bearing and aura of power and rippling muscles and gold fur.

I look away – suddenly aware that I've been staring at him very hard since the moment he walked over – and watch Ben pull up a chair as far away from Lily as possible and position it at an angle where he can watch her without her seeing him gazing at her.

I sneak a glance back at Sebastian under my lashes. He's wearing a Smiley T-shirt and a string of brown beads round his neck and khaki combats and looks much much much better than Ben. Ben's hair is wavy and almost black. He's deathly pale but he's got lovely big blue eyes and an expression that makes you want to hug him.

Lily makes the transition to there-are-boys-watching-me mode and it makes me want to hit her. She leans forward with her elbows on the table and her arms pressed against the sides of her body so the boys are treated to a full view of her cleavage, pinpointed by her gold-plated 'Sex Kitten' necklace. She's got so much make-up on as well: blusher, eyeliner, midnight blue mascara, iridescent eye shadow, coral lipstick with gloss over the top. I bet she curled her eyelashes this morning too. I mean, it's only 11.20 am, I don't know what she's playing at.

I catch a glimpse of myself in the mirror: no make-up, not even concealer, greasy hair, a spot on my cheek, ugh.

"How are you doing, T?" Ben asks.

Across the table Sebastian is telling Lily about what records he's been buying.

"Yeah, like, all I need now is some decks yeah?" I can hear Seb telling her. "If I save £20 a week, I'll get them in like 4 years."

He's got a great voice: deep, a bit husky: a confident, slow, drawl. His voice is full of money and breeding. He is probably not of the faith, or as my Mum would say: 'He's not suitable, Tanya.'

"OK. " I reply to Ben, wishing that I was talking to Seb and that Ben was talking to Lily.

"How's work?" He means schoolwork, presumably.

"Good,"

"What subjects are you doing?"

"English, Biology, History and Maths AS."

"I'm doing English, History and Latin."

"Cool, I loved Latin GCSE. I would've done it at A-Level but Mum thought it'd be better for me to do a science – make me seem more versatile. I love Biology anyway, especially the evolution stuff."

"I want to study Classics at Oxford." He says, somewhat surprisingly.

I'd just assumed that he probably wanted to study music technology and be a DJ.

"Really? I want to go to Oxford too. My brother's there."

"It'll be cool if we both get in." He says, smiling.

I must make more effort with Ben, I tell myself. He is an intelligent and interesting boy and is better company for me than my stupid girly mates. And of course, if he's now going to be hanging out with this new boy it could be useful for me to spend a lot of time with Ben.

"You coming to Lee's party on Saturday?" He asks quietly, meaning, of course, will Lily be there.

"Yeah, definitely," I reply, remembering that Lily has her cousin's wedding that weekend and will be in Manchester.

She'll be so pissed off that we'll all be at Lee's without her. I must make a real effort to have the best time ever so I can tell her all about it afterwards.

"Should be good. I'm playing, so's Seb."

"Is there a dress code?"

So Seb is coming. So I can see him again. So I must make an effort to look as beautiful as possible.

"It's a '60s theme. Wear whatever you want, whatever they used to wear then. Has your Mum saved any of her clothes from when she was a teenager?"

Yeah, right. My Mum is a size 8 even now and she used to be a size 6 then. I've seen pictures of her from the 60s: a wood nymph with ironed dark brown hair falling to her waist: her eyes ringed with kohl, endless tanned legs stretching down from a Mondrian-print mini-dress ending in white ankle boots. Obviously I would not fit into any of Mum's clothes. I wish I resembled Mum at my age, rather than a teenage version of my Dad with huge boobs.

"I'll ask her." I say to Ben, knowing I won't, but I'm smiling inside anyway.

I'm going to become friends with Seb and then he is going to fall in love with me, and I'll be really pleased that Robbie split up with me because I'm going to be much happier with Seb.

Chapter 6

W E'VE BEEN STANDING on the doorstep of Lee's house for ten minutes, shivering in our thin cotton dresses. The dye in them is starting to run in the rain. I make a mental note that tie-dye clothes are not suitable for wearing in December in England.

I stare at the mahogany double doors with frosted glass inserts and brass doorknobs. They are ostentatious doors. Lee's parents are obviously loaded though, even if their taste in doors is questionable. There is a green Bentley in the drive with a number-plate which reads GARY56. If I was called Gary I would not advertise the fact.

At long last there's a banging noise, a scuffle, the door is pushed open. We scatter down the outside steps as the doors swing towards us.

"Fuck off. You're not friends of Josh Levy and Aaron Goldstein from Reform Synagogue Youth!" Lee is saying to two spotty youths wearing Kappa tracksuits and Nike Air trainers as he throws them out of the house.

"Nah mate, I'm Josh Levy's mate, innit." One of the boys protests as they amble off down the street, swigging Diamond White cider from a 4 litre bottle and smoking full strength Benson and Hedges.

"Shit, girls, how long have you been waiting?" Lee does a double take as he spots us. He's wearing purple velvet flares and a white shirt with a ruffle down the front that hang down to expose the waistband of his Calvin Klein boxer shorts – a mix of Jim Morrison and Adam

Ant. "I'm so sorry, the doorbell's broken. Dad didn't have time to get the electrician out to fix it before they went away." Lee says.

"Oh, we've just arrived." Emily lies: unwilling, as always, to make a fuss or to make anyone feel uncomfortable.

I feel a surge of love towards her and quash my own irritation and sulkiness and desire to go home before we've even gone into the party.

"Gosh, it's raining." Lee sounds surprised, wiping a few drops off his violet afro.

"Oh, it's only drizzling." Emily says.

"Let's get in, shall we?" Caitlin says, wiping her leg, which is covered in stripes which could be varicose veins, but are in fact blue streaks from her dress.

I hover on the doorstep. I just can't go in there, it'll be horrible: I'll hate it. I'm just feeling a normal amount of anxiety I tell myself. It will be OK and if it's not I can just go home.

The sounds of the party drift towards us – laughter, thumping beats, corks popping, glasses being dropped.

I've been so pleased about having a night off from Lily, but now we're here and she's absent I miss her – the buzz she creates, the way we get drink and drugs showered upon us when she's here, the way we become the centre of attention when we're with her. Without Lily I feel even more invisible than when I'm her shadow.

I glance around the room to see if I can spot anyone I want to see, and I can't, there's just loads of people I don't know, or half-recognise, the sort of people I'll have one of those 'Hi, how are you?' 'Fine, how are you?' conversations with, and then be stuck for anything else to say to.

"Hey, Tanya." Ben says. He's appeared and of course he's looking over my shoulder for Lily. He's not looking his best tonight.

"Where's…"

"She's in Manchester." I watch his face fall, and then he tries to gather up his disappointment and put it back in its box.

"What's she doing there?" He asks. "Why isn't she here?"

"She and her boyfriend Greg are there: at her cousin's wedding." I stress Greg's name, but at the same time I feel sad for Ben, because I know he loves Lily. Also, I like Ben a lot whereas I think Greg is a complete dork and a total loser.

"Oh, well." Ben says, resigning himself to Lily's absence.

"Where's Seb?" I ask, trying not to sound too desperate, but at the same time my heart is thudding against the walls of my chest because I really want to see Seb now.

"There." Ben says: pointing to the decks over the other side of the room. I haven't seen Seb on the decks before, he looks really cool: holding his headphones to one ear, leaning over the decks, spinning the record, brow furrowed in concentration, big hands moving deftly, thick blond hair falling over one green eye.

"He's coming off in a minute: I'm headlining." Ben says. I smile at the description -'headlining' – when there haven't been any flyers or posters and there are about fifty people here. Anyway – it's only 9.30pm, the headline slot will be 12 – 2am.

"I'd better go and warm up." He says, as if he's about to star in *Don Giovanni* at Covent Garden. He turns from me and disappears, cutting a swathe through the crowd.

"Here, T, drink this." Emily appears at my shoulder with a glass of something raspberry-coloured. She is smiling and I can see the purple and blue glitter dusting her brow-bone sparkle in the UV light.

"What is it?"

"GHB tea."

"Seriously?" I don't really know what GHB is and I'm sure Em doesn't either.

"Nah, it's Sangria silly, it's nice." Emily says, reassuring me.

I sip it. It doesn't taste of alcohol at all but of orange juice. There are strawberries and apple and orange slices floating in it.

"Have you bumped into anyone selling any…"

"Yeah, here, do a half with me?"

"What are they?"

"Swans." Emily says sounding pleased with herself at having scored Swans, as well she might.

"Yay, they're my absolute faves."

She bites half the pill off and spits the other half into my hand. I wash it down with the sangria, and as I lift my arm up I realise there are pink streaks snaking down it from my dress. I spit on my hand and try to rub the pink away, but it won't budge.

I sip my drink and scan the room. I guess I should see about mingling a bit. My friends are all sitting in one corner of the room with each other as usual.

"Going to the loo." I say to Em and Caitlin. I'm not though. I'm going to talk to some randoms in the other room.

I walk through the kitchen to the lounge, which is packed with people. There are bin liners all over the floor, to protect it from spillages. I notice spaces on the wall where the wallpaper looks like new, where the family photos and paintings must have been taken down. All the cupboards and surfaces are bare of ornaments: Lee isn't taking any chances.

I pass several groups of people who I don't recognise – ravers and metallers, rock chicks and indie boys. They must be Lee's friends from football and his youth movement – he goes to a different Jewish youth movement from us and went on a different tour round Israel last summer.

The back door is open so I sneak out into the garden. There's someone sitting on the wall: smoking, blowing smoke rings out into the night air, which is now crisp and less heavy after the rain. I catch my heel on a loose paving stone, trip and grab his arm. I turn my head up and find myself looking into Seb's big green eyes. He smiles.

"You okay?" He asks as he helps me to my feet.

I lean on him. He smells of Hugo Boss which is what my brother uses. Weakened by my fall, my stomach flips over and a warm fuzzy feeling spreads up my calves and into my thighs. I'm not sure if it's just the pill.

"Yeah, fine, sorry. Cool party." I say, even though it I'm not enjoying the party at all and would rather be at home snuggled up with Mum on the sofa, watching David Attenborough's *The Life Of Mammals* which is being repeated tonight on BBC2.

"Yeah, isn't it? D'you catch any of my set?" He looks me right in the eyes with those huge green cat's eyes of his.

"Yeah, we turned up during 'Binary Finery', great tune."

"You sorted for pills?" he asks.

"Have you got any?" I try.

"Open wide." He slips a pill into my mouth. I can feel the first one starting to kick in at last now, anyway. He puts his arm round me and pulls me towards him. I close my eyes, thinking he's about to kiss me, but he doesn't. We just sit there. Something brushes my hair and I start.

"What was that?" I say, touching my hair.

"Bats," He whispers. "I've been out here watching them."

My eyes adjust to the light and I can make out the little dark shapes swooping low and hear the soft rustle of beating wings. I wouldn't have thought Seb was the sort of person who sits outside in the middle of parties watching bats, but then I don't really know him. I haven't ever even spoken to him, except in a group situation.

Then he bends his head and kisses me. I try not to think about Robbie. I give up, and sort of think wistfully about Robbie underneath, but enjoy it anyway. It feels nice to be kissed and he tastes good – minty with a hint of sangria – his tongue is strong and, surprisingly, pierced. It feels strange but not uncomfortable. The balls on the ends of the bar must be plastic, they aren't cold, and he seems to know what he's doing, following my tongue, nibbling my lips, but then when he tries to slide his hand up my skirt I get nervous and want to find the others and tell them what has happened. Before the moment is quite over I am already reworking it in my head, thinking about how I'm going to relate it to my friends in a few minutes.

"Look, I'll catch you later." I tell him, moving his hand off my thigh.

"What's this pink stuff?" He asks me, holding his hand up to the light that trickles out from the windows of the house, and the little lamps that are dotted around the flowerbeds.

"Oh, I spilt some sangria on my leg. I say.

I don't want him to know that my tie-dye has run.

"Gotta find Cait and Em."

I totter back into the house, watching my step and smiling on the inside. I glance back and he's watching me and smiling a sort of secret smile, and looking out into the dark. Or maybe he's just mashed.

"Where you been, T?" Em collars me as I return to the party via the kitchen, where they're all gulping sangria.

"Oh, nowhere," I say. I decide suddenly that I don't want to share it with her, not yet, not unless stuff happens.

"Heh, but I saw you snogging Sebastian outside." She grins. I am touched that she seems genuinely excited and happy for me rather than what I know Lily would be like: pissed off that someone who, I realise, is a bit of a catch, like Seb, has not chosen her.

"Do you like him?" Em asks me.

I pause to think about this. He's definitely cute. I haven't been with anyone since Robbie though, apart from James at Magic, which doesn't really count. Seb's got a nice tongue as well.

"I don't know." I say. "I haven't really talked to him. He gave me a pill though."

I am protecting myself. I am protecting Seb, and myself.

"What, for free?" Em asks.

"Yeah." I am smiling inside and my lips are still tingling. Seb.

"Chocolate?" Em offers: holding out a packet of Rolos. "Here, T. Have my last Rolo."

"No thanks."

The fact that they're eating anything means that they haven't done enough drugs yet to have lost their appetites. No one's pupils are large yet anyway. I feel a glow of being special, that Seb chose me: he chose to kiss me and not any of them.

Caitlin is rolling a joint and Em is crushing up something that might be either coke or speed with her school library card. Our library cards are thin card laminated with clear sticky back plastic, and not really suitable for crushing drugs. The card is fraying and coming apart at the edges.

Chapter 7

"**H**AS HE CALLED YET?" Lily asks.

We're sitting on the radiator in front of the bay window in our form room, just before assembly. No one else comes near our patch.

"Yeah." I say, although he hasn't.

It irritates me that she's got to be so nosy about the situation with Seb when she wasn't even at Lee's party, and it's none of her business. It's unkind of her to ask if he's called. If he had I would obviously have told her, so she could guess that he hasn't. No need for her to rub it in.

"What'd he say, then?" She sounds surprised and even a bit annoyed that he's called: that there might be a boy in the world who prefers me to her.

I don't understand why she's such a bitch really, she's got about fifteen hundred boys trailing around after her. She's had her hair streaked with platinum blonde, caramel and copper for the wedding at the weekend and feathered round her face so now she looks like a hair model. Her nails, which have never been as good as mine, are now French manicured and square-cut and she looks polished, perfect and a hundred times better than me.

"Oh, you know, he wants to take me to the cinema tomorrow night." I improvise, making a note to ask Mum to take me to the cinema so Lily won't know that I wasn't with Seb.

If he just calls me then everything will be OK. I just have to get through today at school, and then survive the whole evening that stretches ahead – the Sahara desert: barren, relentless, dull, dry and no doubt silent without the phone call. I have convinced myself that he is not going to call now.

He didn't call on Sunday: one wouldn't expect a call that soon anyway as that would signal that the boy is a loser and too keen, possibly stalker material. He didn't call Monday or Tuesday, and it's now Wednesday morning, which means that this evening is really when he should call, according to *The Rules* and *How to Make Anyone Fall in Love With You*. In fact, if he was going to he would've called anyway. Boys don't read dating manuals. If they're interested they just call when they remember which is unlikely to be a whole 5 days after the incident. When I got together with Robbie he called the next day and he said…

…"Tanya?" Mrs Jones's voice breaks into my thoughts. We're in form assembly discussing some current issue although, since I haven't been listening, I've got no idea which one.

"Yes, Mrs Jones?"

"Well? What do you think about these National Drugs Helpline posters?"

I think they're a load of sensationalist, scaremongering, misleading rubbish, I think to myself.

"I imagine that they're a very effective deterrent," I reply.

"I don't think anyone would be put off taking drugs by these posters, if they really wanted to take them." Clara says.

She can get away with making a comment like this as she's never taken any illegal substances as far as I know. I look around the class, wondering who Mrs Jones assumes takes Class As, and wondering if she reckons that I do. Lily's always been naughty, Mrs Jones might suspect her, or maybe our teachers assume none of us do because we're not the sort of girls who do that and we're too busy doing our biology homework.

Of course, if we understand the first thing about biology we'll realise how bad drugs are for us, and how we're going to have lowered serotonin levels and be miserable, unhappy and forgetful in thirty years, if we manage to avoid the more immediate pitfalls of dehydration, unprotected sex, heart failure and coma. Oh, I almost forgot about the strychnine, powdered glass and dog worming tablets that might be in our pills, which will cause agony and death.

We can't seriously worry about thirty years on though. I can't imagine ever being older than about twenty two. I look at Mrs Jones who must be about nine million years old, and have no idea about what her thoughts and world view and stuff might be. It must be awful to have grey hair and, eugh, even worse, grey pubes, and wrinkles. No wonder my Mum keeps having face-lifts and shrink-wraps and dyes her roots and borrows my clothes.

I watch Lily doodling in her notebook – the infinite spirals and garlands that are the trademark motifs of Magic Realms blossom on her page in blue biro. Our parents and teachers don't consider how much fun drugs are though. That's why girls like us do them. We're not escaping dead-end jobs, abuse, hopeless lives: we're looking for novelty. Magic is a place where we fit in, where we're not the private-school-girls-who-go-to-Jewish-youth-clubs that we are the rest of the time, but part of the fluorescent sparkly Magic tribe.

The door of the secret garden that drugs have led me to swings open and its tropical flowers glow amber, scarlet and turquoise. I am no longer in the classroom but surrounded by the heady scent of hibiscus and poppy; hummingbirds and toucans fly around this sudden jungle, okapis and tapirs snuffle in the undergrowth, jaguars and ocelots slink in the shadows, and they speak in tongues I can understand. Treasures can be found here if you just wait for them to show themselves to you: new friends, further understanding of everything, huge maturity.

There is another way from the Jewish middle class life of parentals, bridge and dinner parties, tennis clubs and Radio 4. I would never ever not have done it, I think. If I had every single evening back when I've done pills, I'd do it all over again every time.

"So, Tanya, what do you think?" Mrs Jones asks. The door of Eden slams shut.

I look at the poster 'What Ecstasy Does to You' and the staring eyes bulge out of the skull in the photo, which is stripped of skin and flesh. The bloodshot eyes lock with mine and I know Mrs Jones must know all about me. I haven't got the faintest idea what she's just asked me but now my mind isn't just blank, it stings.

I look back at Mrs Jones and a switch flicks in my head. It is no longer possible for me to be here: the walls are breathing, the ceiling sways, the desks move away from me on a conveyor belt. The stares of my classmates are the lines of longbows and spikes at Agincourt: sharp, relentless, hostile.

"I've got to go." I tell Mrs Jones: stumbling out of the classroom, passing the astonished gazes of Clara and Helena.

I don't know where I'm running to, only that I have to get out, but I pick up speed as I pass along the corridor, past the displays of Anne Boleyn's execution, past the burning of heretics under Bloody Mary and slaves crowded on ships on their way to America. I turn down the stairs, descend four flights and then I'm out of school – away from my prison and into the park.

The park passes by in a blur as I run to the tube station, jump on the first train and start to think about what to do, what's happening. Thoughts buzz around my head – a swarm of angry bees. I can't go

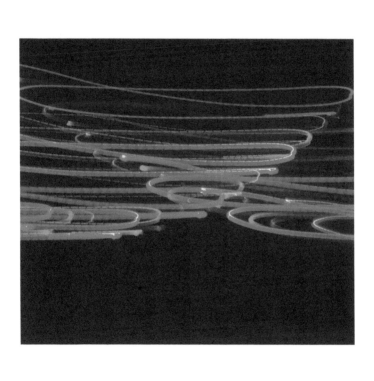

home – Mum will kill me if I turn up a mere two hours after I've gone to school, especially today when she knows I've got lessons all day. My timetable's up in the kitchen so she can look at it. I can't go to Oxford to see Carl, it's too far. If only I could go to Robbie's, in fact, that's what I'll do: I'll go to Robbie's. He'll know what to say, what to do, he always has an answer for everything.

Walking up his street, the street I used to be on intimate terms with, tears run down my face. It seems like a lifetime ago that it was the night before my sixteenth birthday and I was walking down this street with Robbie and his liver and white springer spaniel Fred.

"I really should shag someone before tomorrow." I remember saying as Fred wrapped his paws round my leg and rubbed his tummy against my knee and buried his face in my crotch. Fred always fancied me more than Robbie did.

"Well, you know, I would if you really want to but I'm worried you might fall in love with me or something." Robbie said. "Girls usually do."

This was rubbish of course. Robbie at this point had had sex precisely once with a girl called Sharon who he met on holiday, and looking back on it he probably made her up.

"Piss off," I said, and that was it, the moment passed, leaving me with the embarrassing burden of my virginity which unbelievably I still haven't managed to get rid of.

House martins swoop and bomb up into the eaves of the house next door to Robbie's, even though it's winter and they should be in Africa. Telegraph wires cut across the sky – zebra stripes.

But are they white stripes on black or black stripes on white, and if you peel the black is it white underneath or dripping flesh and what if its internal organs fall out through the gashes where the stripes have been. It's possible that the stripes are a lattice holding the whole animal together.

Robbie's house looms into view, the lilac house. Robbie's Dad told Robbie's Mum to paint the house 'whatever colour you like darling' and when he came home from work that day the house was lilac. He could never bring himself to broach the subject of the colour of the house again, a colour it's remained ever since, for the past sixteen years: for almost our whole lives in fact.

The monkey puzzle tree in their front garden obscures most of the lilac but behind it I can see Robbie's window's open and I can hear music coming from his room and as I draw closer I hear two voices – Robbie's and a girl's – and they're laughing and no doubt talking about normal stuff and they don't run out of lessons for no reason and they don't worry about whether someone they've snogged once has called, or is going to call and I bet Robbie's thinking 'I'm so glad I split up with Tanya and met Michelle who's…' and by the time I've finished this thought I've walked past the house and I can't turn back now because I've missed my chance and the moment's gone and there'd be no point anyway because it's all over and there's no going back to the way things were before.

Chapter 8

"She's just got no fucking clue, my Mum, you know." Wendy says, staring me hard in the eye and waving her arms around to emphasise her point.

It's Lily's seventeenth birthday and we're all at Luigi's, our favourite Italian restaurant.

"It's like I'll be in my room, yeah, and she'll storm in screeching: 'It's a pigsty in here, why can't you put those plates in the dishwasher, I am not clearing up after you. You are absolutely not setting a foot out of this house until you have handed in all your coursework. I've had it up to here with you and your friends going out drinking and heaven knows what else. You should never have got entangled with that crowd. Why don't you see Rachel and Hannah anymore, they were nice girls and they…'"

"Eugh! No way, they're absolute losers." I say.

Rachel and Hannah are religious Jewish girls who only go out with boys of our faith who they don't touch. They don't go shopping on Saturdays, don't drink, don't smoke, don't take drugs. Basically they're totally sad.

"Exactly." Wendy nods in agreement, her asymmetric fringe falling over one brown eye.

"I don't get why she can't see that." Wendy continues. "I mean, it's blatantly obvious, right? But Mum goes on and on, like: 'Your father and I are working ourselves to the bone to pay for you to go to that school. You have no comprehension of how lucky you are. We would have killed for your advantages,' blah blah blah. It pisses me off. I'm handing in all my work, I'm getting good grades."

"Yeah, you are."

"Well, I'm getting OK grades anyway. Not As like you, but mostly Bs. So I'm not headed for Oxford like you are. So what? It's not as if I wanted to go to our school anyway, I'd have been totally happy at the comprehensive. They don't understand anything, they don't even try. Why are they so dim?"

Wendy's Mum is actually quite nice though. I wish Wendy's Mum was my Mum sometimes. I'd quite like to swap Mums I think.

We like it here at Luigi's because it's cheap, the waiters are all cute, and they make a fuss of us. Tonight I'm not hungry though and I've ordered a baked potato. *Put one o, put two o, put three o, put four o, put five o, put six o, put seven o, put eight o, POTATO!* The playground chant runs through my mind on a loop.

I stare at the baked potato in front of me which reclines on a bed of lollo rosso lettuce and is split open to spill its guts of cottage cheese. I've chosen this fat-free meal as I'm worried about putting on weight but I feel sick even contemplating it, let alone eating it.

I try to focus on what Wendy is talking about but I just can't. She's still going on about her problems with her mum and as her friend I should be listening but it's screamingly dull and I want something else to occupy myself with, like eating my dinner, but I just can't bring myself to get entangled with the potato. I spear some lettuce on the fork. Shit, they've put dressing on it. I visualise the oil in the dressing coalescing in my bloodstream. I push the lettuce to the far side of the plate. I sprinkle pepper over the cottage cheese, coal in the snow, spots on a Dalmatian. I sip my water slowly. Wendy halts her monologue and stares at me.

"What's wrong with you, Tanya? Why aren't you eating?"

"I feel sick. Big night last night."

She cocks her head: a dim owl regarding me. My mother's anorexic and all my friends have been itching to jump down my throat about this for years, just waiting for the warning signs.

"Eat something, you'll feel better." Wendy says.

I'm not convinced, but I clean the cottage cheese from the left cheek of the potato and decide to eat it. It's fluffy and warm, and I'd love it if I was feeling better, if I was feeling different. I concentrate on the potato essence of it; the solidity and firmness, but it tastes of nothing. It doesn't taste of potato but of, I don't quite know how to describe it, metal or sand or something that isn't meant to be eaten. It tastes off-key, it tastes how I feel.

"How does that taste to you?" I ask Wendy, offering her a forkful of the potato.

She chews it, swallows and considers for a minute.

"Fine." She says. "Actually it's really good."

It must be me then. I must have a vitamin deficiency or something which is why my sense of taste has gone funny and why I'm so tired all the time. Tomorrow I'm going to the doctor to have some blood tests and get it sorted out. That's what it must be.

"Can I have a glass of the Rioja, please." I say to the waiter, who is hovering behind my shoulder: a hummingbird with a notepad.

Wendy looks concerned, cross, worried, and something else that I can't quite place. The glass arrives. It's a 250ml one and I gulp it down. The wine warms me up and even encourages me to attack the potato with renewed energy. The mass of potato diminishes.

Ask me what's wrong, I plead in my head. Enquire as to why I'm behaving in such an odd way. Maybe she's so wrapped up in herself that she hasn't noticed my peculiar behaviour. Normally I love going out for dinner with my friends and chatting to everyone but tonight I just want to fade into the background and not talk at all.

I gaze under my eyelashes towards the other end of the table, the top end I would much prefer to be sitting at, where Lily, Emily and Caitlin are. I do not want to be at this end with Wendy.

Lily's already drunk, and Greg's dancing attendance on her in his goofy way: gazing into her eyes, grasping her hand in his clammy paw. His greasy hair flops over his acne-pitted forehead. She has this effect on all the boys. They don't seem to notice how needy she is. I thought boys were meant to be put off by that, but they don't seem to be.

Barry, Caitlin's boyfriend is over from Dublin and he and Caitlin are wrapped round each other in a corner, whispering and giggling, he's stroking her hair, which can't be that pleasant for him as it's caked in gel and glitter spray. Emily's just started seeing Ian, who's so silent we call him Interesting Ian, but she's not bothered about what we think of him. Which leaves me: single, alone.

Maybe if I had a boyfriend I wouldn't feel so lonely. Maybe that's what this is all about and if I had someone who wanted to be with me I'd feel better about myself. I think about Seb who still hasn't called me after ten days. I wish he was here. Well, I wish he'd called me and we'd been out on a date already and we were here together.

I always used to like being on my own and reading and writing essays and stuff, I used to think it was pathetic that Lily always had to be surrounded by loads of disciples fawning over her. What's wrong with me? I think.

"Huh?" Wendy looks at me.

"What?"

"You just said: 'What's wrong with me?'"

"Did I?"

Whoops, I didn't realise I'd said it out loud. She looks at me as if I'm insane, which I probably am. Talking to yourself is meant to be the first sign of madness isn't it. That and hairy palms, or is that werewolves. I'm probably turning into a wolf. That'd be cool though. I'd like a long furry tail and fangs and…

"Anyway, what is wrong with you Tanya?"

"What do you mean?"

"You used to be really chatty and bubbly and outgoing and now you're in another world a lot of the time and you seem quiet and like you've got no energy."

"Do I?"

Shit, I didn't realise it was so obvious. I hardly even know Wendy.

"Is it about Lily and Greg, and Emily and Ian, and Caitlin and Barry?"

"Well, yeah, I guess, sort of."

"I think that sometimes. Like: 'What's wrong with me? Why can't I get a boyfriend?' and stuff. At least you've had a relationship with Robbie who's really fit. I've never had a boyfriend. Do you miss Robbie?"

"Yeah. Especially at something like this."

"Is anything happening with you and Seb?" she asks, her nose twitching, sniffing for information.

"I don't know," I say.

It irritates me that my one snog with Seb is public information. It's also really annoying when people ask me what's happening with him. As if I know what's happening with him. But her attention's started to wander anyway.

"Sorry, T, I've got to go," she says, looking over my shoulder where she seems to have spotted someone better than me to talk to because she disappears down the other end of the table to join the A-list.

I watch as Wendy is swallowed into the group of our friends: laughing and joking with them, lighting Lily's cigarette for her, downing shots of tequila with Emily and Ian. A minute ago she was telling me that she's unhappy, that she feels left out, but now that's all forgotten and she's lost in the group, enjoying herself. I used to be able to do that, I used to be able to just switch my problems off and have fun, but I can't do it at the moment. The day Robbie broke up with me pushes to the front of my mind…

…"Your Mum hates me anyway." Robbie says with an air of finality, moving away from me so that our thighs aren't touching anymore.

We're sitting looking over the cricket pitches near my house, in the park. It's the end of summer and it's getting dark.

"No she doesn't." I protest. "Why are we talking about my Mum anyway? What's it got to do with her?"

"Because it's more aggro that I can't be fucked with. She thinks I'm not good enough for you because I screwed up my GCSEs."

I look at Robbie's profile, silhouetted against the dusk light as he takes a drag on his Silk Cut ultra. He looks effortlessly cool as he smokes. He's half-turned away from me, blond hair flopping over one eye. He's got beautiful thick shiny dead-straight hair. He looks across the cricket pitches, turning away from me. I am losing him. I have lost him. I would do anything to get him back.

"Robbie." He turns back to me.

"Yes, what?"

He sounds bored. He is bored with me.

"Is there anything I can do that would change your mind?"

"We've been through this already, Tanya, a thousand times. I don't want to be in a relationship. I want to be getting battered with my mates, not…I dunno, trying to make conversation with your mother on Friday night."

I love him and this might be my last ever chance to have sex, I think. It isn't right that I still haven't done it with anyone yet by this age.

"Anyway, she'll be happy now."

She will, yes. I can hear her already, triumphant.

"You should have listened to your mother. I know more about the world than you do Tanya. He's too weak to fight for you…."

… I miss Robbie so much. I don't want to be here in this restaurant with these people. They're not my real friends; they don't know anything about me. I feel so distant from them all. They're glossy tropical fish in a tank and I'm standing outside the glass, looking in.

I down a glass of champagne, and everything shifts even further away from me. My thoughts cycle from fear and dread to a longing to get out of this situation to fear and dread and back again, with an undercurrent of: I can't be here, I have to get out, I have to go home and finally – I can't stay here for a minute longer. Lily's wasted by now, she doesn't care whether I'm here or not. I ambush Emily who's on her way to the loo.

"Em,"

"Hey, T, I came to look for you. Where've you been?"

"Um, just talking to Wendy." Well, about half an hour ago I was, for ten minutes.

"Em, I've got to go. Can you tell Lily that, um, I've got a headache, and I'm sorry but…oh, whatever, make something up."

"Yeah, sure."

She looks at me, but she's too drunk to focus properly. She still looks great though, as usual.

I make a swift exit, before Lily can accost me and berate me for leaving her, my best friend, on her birthday, with only all her other friends and her boyfriend to look after her.

It's raining, of course, and I've forgotten to bring an umbrella. I walk as quickly as I can to the station, hoping that no-one is going to come running after me and begging me to come back to the party. I don't want to go home but I can't go anywhere else on my own in the rain. I sit at the train station and bite the skin around my nails.

I used to bite my nails but I stopped when I was twelve so they'd be long for Robbie's Barmitzvah and he'd fall in love with me. He didn't – he got together with someone else that night – but I've still got the nails and take great care of them. Recently I've started biting and peeling the skin at the sides of my nails though. I don't want to draw blood. My aim is to stop just short of drawing blood, but quite often I go too far and the blood spurts out and I can't stop it and then I focus on the pain which helps.

There's a paper napkin in my pocket from the restaurant. I tear strips from it and wrap them around my bleeding fingers and pull my gloves on so Mum won't see.

The sense of relief I felt for a few minutes when I left the restaurant evaporates as I approach my house and is replaced by anger with myself for leaving Lily's birthday early. It's only 10 o'clock on a Saturday night which is much too early to be getting home from my best friend's birthday. If my parents are in I'll have to explain to them why I'm home at this ridiculous time, if they're out I'll be alone with my more and more alarming thoughts. Both alternatives are as bad as each other. I linger a few metres up the road and smoke a final cigarette in the yew coppice behind the laurel hedge while I work out what I'm going to say.

Chapter 9

IN THE KITCHEN WITH MUM, I watch her feeding the avocados into the liquidiser. They spin round and spatter and it makes a loud whirring noise. Mum adds yoghurt to the mixture which spreads through the avocado and turns it a pale but intense green. The phone rings.

"It'll be one of your friends." Mum says. "You answer it. I've got avocado all over my hands."

I pick up the phone. "Hello, Tanya speaking. Who is it please?"

"T, something terrible's happened," a voice whines.

I sigh. It's Lily of course. In Lily's view, something terrible happens to her every day. Sometimes it seems that Lily's life is just one long succession of disasters punctuated by tantrums and narrow escapes. I just don't have the energy to deal with this at the moment though.

"Hang on a second."

I leave the kitchen. I don't want Mum to hear this conversation. I take the phone up to my room, kick the door shut and make myself comfortable on my bed

"Go on, Lily, what is it?" I feign concern.

"No, it is really awful." She says.

"Come on, Lily, what's happened?" I attempt to keep the irritation out of my voice.

"I can't tell you over the phone, I just can't. Meet me at the park in ten minutes."

But I've got homework, I think. I'm in my bedroom, it's warm. As soon as I get off the phone I can go back into the kitchen and be with my Mum, and it's nearly supper time and I'm starving. I don't want to be out in the freezing cold and rain with Lily moaning at me. But I don't say this. "See you in ten minutes," is what I say instead.

As I close my bedroom door the photo of me and Robbie tumbles off the bookcase. I pick it up and gaze at it for a moment. We're sitting in my garden. He's lying with his head in my lap, looking up at me. I'm cradling his head. It's an intimate moment. Lily must've taken it. A brief pang of loss pulls at my heart and then I put the photo face down on my dressing table, and leave the room, pushing all thoughts of Robbie to the back of my mind.

"I'm just going out to meet Lily." I shout to Mum as I leave the house, pulling my coat on and feeling so irritated with Lily for making me go out in this weather. I can hear the rain thudding against the roof.

"OK sweetie. Just make sure you're home for dinner," Mum calls after me.

Outside it's freezing cold and, of course, raining. I start running to warm myself up and to shorten the journey. I don't stop running until I'm at the park. It's only five minutes away but it feels much further on this cold, dark night. I head for our favourite tree, an ancient oak, and she's sitting huddled at its base. She's not even wearing a coat and she's shivering.

"Lily?" I say, with a questioning note in my voice. "What's happened?"

She throws her arms round me. She looks awful. Her face is blotchy and puffy, her mascara's run. She presses something into my hand, and it takes me a few seconds to realise what it is. It's a pregnancy test. Shit, she's pregnant. Her parents are going to screw. I can't believe she's been so stupid.

"It's OK," I tell her.

It isn't OK though. It couldn't be much worse. A ghastly tableau hurtles through my mind: Lily mountainously pregnant in a Maths lesson, pushing a pram, leaving the baby on a train by mistake, living in a dirty council flat with a screaming toddler – if it survives that long. I quash these images; I've got to focus on how I'm going to salvage this situation.

The next day after school I pop into the chemist for some curl reviver mousse and some facial wash. I spot the pregnancy tests. Shit, they're £10. I pick one up and realise the two shop assistants are both busy serving customers. With a quick glance to my left and right I slip the pregnancy test up my jumper and stalk out, trying not to look guilty.

I find Lily in the park, smoking.

"Marlboro Light, T? I think it's better for the baby. Less tar and everything." She sighs. "I just wanted to see what it was like."

"Haven't you and Greg done it before then?"

"No. How can I have got pregnant after doing it once? It's so unfair."

"Lily," I pause. "You're not pregnant."

"How do you know?"

I pull out the pregnancy test I've just nicked from Boots. "Listen: 'A blue line in one window means the test has worked. A blue line in both windows means you're pregnant.' Show me yours again."

She pulls her own pregnancy test out of her satchel where she's been carrying it around all day. It's got bits of gum and blue tac stuck to it now, but I can see clearly what I thought I'd glimpsed earlier: one blue line and one blank window. The bar that would have severed Lily's childhood is left unlocked, the window's left open so she can climb out of this mess.

"Oh, yeah. Sorry T, didn't read it properly."

"Dipstick."

She looks a bit embarrassed and then she breaks into one of her dazzling smiles, and I can't be cross with her anymore, she's just too silly, it's just such a typical thing to happen to Lily but everything's going to be fine. She starts giggling, and then we're laughing hysterically, because Lily's got away with it again.

I'm still cross with Lily about the her-and-Em-getting-piercings-without-me situation. And the her-copying-all-my-marks situation. And the all-boys-have-to-choose-her situation. I think she's a bitch to Ben, and she's a bitch to Greg too. They're poor blind fools coming after her. It's not just this pregnancy test incident – this is just the latest in a long line of things.

I resent her. I resent her draining all my energy and always making herself the centre of attention. I resent her using me as an emotional buffer. I don't know how I've put up with her for so long. She always makes me sort out her problems and she never says thank you properly. She snaps at me and shouts at me as well, partly because she can't be bothered to behave nicely and partly because she knows I won't react.

A week after the pregnancy test incident she collars me in the corridor at school, standing on a radiator to catch my attention. I walk over and she clambers down, sending her books flying.

"Why didn't you wait for me?" She demands. "I was going to pick you up and drive us both to school."

"I went on the coach."

"You've got Mia on the coach, you've got Clara and Helena at school, you've got Ben and Lee out of school. Where does that leave me? Us?"

Well, maybe you should look inside yourself Lily and ask yourself why I am building up different friendship groups that don't revolve around you I think.

"T, why are you ignoring me?" She asks.

I don't look at her. I stare at the lilac wall behind her.

"I'm not." I say.

"I know you're cross with me. You've been avoiding me." She says in an accusatory tone, pushing loose strands of hair behind her double-pierced ears, which is what she always does when she's nervous.

I don't say anything. Maybe for once you should figure it out for yourself. I think.

"I'm an amazing friend to you." She says.

"You're not. You only ever think about yourself." I can't believe I said that but it just slipped out.

"That's not true." She says, her voice shaking and her lips quivering.

"It is. When was the last time you asked me how I am? You only ever want to talk about yourself and…"

"What have I done?" she pleads.

"It's not just one thing. It's a build up of things. You always shout at me because you know I won't react. It's horrible."

"Well if that's what you think, let's not be friends anymore." She shouts, stamping her foot and gritting her teeth.

"Yeah. Let's not be friends anymore." I say. "You're shouting now."

"I am not." she yells.

"Fine." She says, "Let's not be friends anymore, I don't care," and stalks off.

This is when I should beg her to forgive me, and apologize for upsetting her, but I don't. I just watch her go.

After my argument with Lily I walk to the car park at the back of school on my own. I pass the horse chestnut trees and I start crying. I hate myself for being so pathetic. This is not me.

As I approach the car park, I can see Mum's car. I must stop crying before Mum sees me: I don't want her to know that I've had a fight with Lily because she'll be cross with me. Wiping my eyes, I open the passenger door. It's not Mum driving though: it's my brother. He must be home from Oxford for the holidays.

"Hi Tanya," Carl says. "What's the matter? Why are you crying?"

He looks so gorgeous and the warmth that he radiates wraps around me.

"I had an argument with Lily." I say, looking into his huge grey eyes. Nothing seems as bad when I can tell Carl and he can absorb my pain and make everything better.

"About what?" He pushes his caramel hair away from his face.

"About her being selfish. And other stuff."

He puts his arms round me. "It will be alright. You'll make up."

"We might not though. She just uses me to sort out her problems and…" I am crying again. I put my head on my brother's shoulder.

"Please don't cry, T." Carl says. "Just try not to think about it for the moment, OK? It will blow over. I'm sure you and Lily will make up. We're going to have a good time over the holidays, aren't we?"

I nod. It will be so good to have my brother at home and for us all to be together like a proper family. Everything is so much better when he's around.

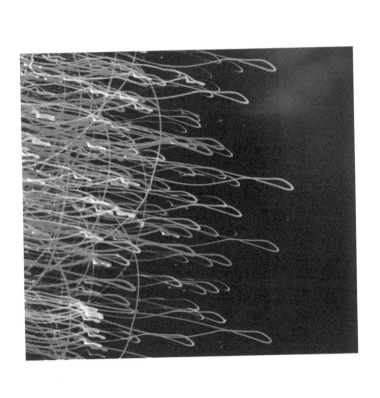

Chapter 10

"Your young man's here, Tanya." Mum calls up the stairs to me: as if we've been waiting for my date to show up to take me to my high school prom in an American teen movie.

My first feeling of excitement about this evening bubbles up. It's going to be a brilliant night – I can just feel it somehow. My fantail goldfish Richard and Judy swim around their tank, their orange feathery fins and tails waving behind them: beautiful tangerine streamers to herald in the New Year. I drop in some flakes for them; adjust the sunken pirate ship and its attendant pondweed.

"Happy New Year darlings," I tell them.

I'm in no rush to leave yet though – I've only just started my make-up and I've changed my outfit three times. I'm still not sure that I'm wearing the right thing. The lilac eye-shadow that seemed to harmonise so perfectly with this top when I tried it out in the shop looks too garish. I wipe it off and apply my trademark silver, adding a dust of hologram glitter particles over my cheekbones and a raspberry bindi in the middle of my forehead to bring out the green of my eyes. I'm having an OK hair day: my dark brown hair has formed into largely frizz-free ringlets.

It's New Year's Eve, which I've been dreading as it's twice as expensive to go clubbing compared to every other night of the year and loaded with ten times the pressure to have fun. I would so much rather not be going clubbing. A couple of years ago when we were fifteen we all went to a house party in our village on New Year's Eve – about 100 of us, all the Jewish boys and girls of our age. It was brilliant – we sat around drinking vodka and all our friends were there – it was the place to be and people still talk about it as the best New Year's Eve ever. Three girls drank so much that an ambulance was called to take them to hospital. When the parents of the boy who was having the party got home, his Mum saw the scenes of devastation and just fainted in the hallway. Afterwards we all walked back home, we didn't have to worry about transport or anything. I wish we were doing something like that tonight, but we're not.

We're going to a club night called 'Elysian Fields' at Alexandra Palace, having already parted with £35 each for the privilege of attending this intimate gathering of 2,000 people. We're meeting our other friends in there. Ben's come round to pick me up, no doubt to ask me if he's got a chance with Lily now she's single. This is fine by me because I might just be able to find out from Ben whether Seb likes me before I bump into him later this evening.

When I emerge downstairs, Ben is sitting next to Mum on the sofa, looking through old photo albums of me and my brother Carl.

"And this was when we all went skiing" Mum says, pointing at a photo. Ben's eyes follow her finger. "And Tanya did a wee in the car because we couldn't find a service station with a toilet, well, we could but you know those French service stations, they just do it into…"

Mum's already tipsy and enjoying making a fuss of Ben in the absence of having my brother here to fawn over.

"Where's Lily?" Ben asks me.

"Lily's in Israel with her family," I tell him.

I'm relieved Lily's not in the country: we haven't spoken since our bust-up at school at the end of term. Ben looks so disappointed though: those big spaniel eyes fall, his mouth turns down and his whole aspect droops.

Mum butts in. "Would you like a glass of champagne, Benjamin?"

"Yes please, Mrs Marshall, how kind of you, oh thank you Mrs Marshall, Veuve Clicquot, how wonderful."

Mum beams at him. I can almost hear the cogs in her brain turning: *What a great catch for my girl, his dad's a barrister, he knows about champagne*. What she doesn't know is that he's got twenty ecstasy pills and two grams of coke in his wallet, or at least I hope he has because I've already paid him for my stuff.

Ben sips his champagne; I drain my glass in one mouthful and slam it down onto the table.

"Come on, Ben, we're leaving. I'm sure Mum will tell you about the time Carl puked in the car on the way to Toledo another day."

"You got ID?" The bouncer at *Elysian Fields* asks me. He's a big, brawny chap with a thick neck that is as wide as his head and a ring through his nose like a bull.

"Here," I thrust my fake student card into his hand.

"Date of birth?" He demands, staring into my eyes as if he's daring me to stumble over the numbers or even just hesitate.

I tell him my made-up date of birth, realising with a jolt that soon I'll be old enough to go clubbing legally and then it probably won't be fun anymore, without the adrenalin rush of having to lie about my age and get away with it.

We enter the club, ascend the stairs: it opens its jaws to swallow us. There are flocks of doves hanging on wires from the ceiling mingled with silver and gold balloons emblazoned with 'Elysian Fields New Year's Eve'. The venue is cavernous and it's a lot colder than I thought it would be inside. We squeeze past sweaty and already trashed revellers, stepping through the fake snow that covers the floor. The club's full of really wasted trance heads dancing their Hello Kitty socks off, and waving glow-sticks. None of our friends seem to be here, although the venue's huge and we've got a few rooms left to search still.

I'm waiting in the cloakroom queue on my own when someone pinches my bum. I swerve round: it's Seb. He pulls me behind a pillar and I'm shaking, just his presence is enough to make me feel weak and faint. He puts his arms around me and I just melt into him, breathing in his now familiar scent of Hugo Boss aftershave. He looks so cute in the dark – the whites of his eyes glow in the ultraviolet light and when he starts to kiss me he tastes of toothpaste and chips.

"Have you seen any of the others?" I ask him.

"Caitlin's kicking about somewhere, Lee's not here yet, Emily's around." He says, stroking my hair back from my face as if he actually likes me, as if he's been waiting to see me.

"Sorry I didn't call you," he says. "Been busy."

You could have made a phone call, you wanker, it would only have taken a few seconds. I'm not sure whether that's a good enough excuse, but whatever: it's New Year's Eve and he's here now with me and I really really like him, so so much. He puts his hand behind my head and pulls me towards him and we're kissing again and…

"I've been looking everywhere for you two," Ben's voice says, right behind my ear.

Seb springs away from me with the guilty demeanour of a small boy who's been caught with his hand in the sweetie jar. It unsettles me that he doesn't want Ben to see us together. Ben however looks extremely pleased with himself at having caught us touching each other.

"Alright mate, you sorted?" Ben asks Seb, and grins at me as if to congratulate me for getting Seb to snog me.

"Yeah, yeah, it's good shit." Seb says, tossing his head and turning away from me and towards Ben.

"Yeah, those Christmas Trees are safe," Ben agrees.

He looks completely wasted already: his pupils massive, his teeth grinding.

Go away, Benjamin, leave me with Seb, go and try it on with someone else, I mutter to myself. Now that the me and Seb dynamic is placed under the lens of Benjamin's interpretation I feel awkward, and Seb obviously does as well, because he's let go of my hand and has thrust his hands into his own pockets.

"Alright, I'll catch you guys later then," Ben says, and slopes off, winking at me in the most annoying, unsubtle way as he disappears through an archway which is covered in clematis, passionflowers and roses.

Chapter 11

I SIT IN THE KITCHEN IN MY DRESSING GOWN, tracksuit bottoms, furry slippers and scarf examining the day's TV listings. It's still dark outside, and the rain thuds against the windows. If it would at least snow it wouldn't be so miserable out there. It's New Year's Day 1997: the morning after.

Emily has stayed over and is still asleep in my room and I don't want to wake her because we got home late last night and no-one normal would've woken at 6am, heart hammering, breathless and full of foreboding. If only I had an idea of what this terrible thing is that it seems is bound to happen to me, if only it would just happen so I could deal with it and move on. I sip my coffee which is now lukewarm.

A slide show of images from last night whirrs and clicks in behind my eyes: hugging all my friends at midnight; starting to shiver when the pills begin to wear off about 2am and borrowing a sweater from a random boy and being teased by my mates; snogging Sebastian in the Garden of Eden room; leaning against the Tree of Life; waiting in the freezing cold for a cab with Em and Caitlin and longing to be tucked up in bed already as the snowflakes settle on our clothes and hair…

The year stretches ahead with nothing to look forward to now until the summer – Christmas and New Year are over, and the Easter term is starting in a week and I'll be going into school in the dark, and coming out of school in the dark, and not seeing any daylight except for a few minutes at lunchtime. I'm dreading going back to school – groping for an un-laddered pair of opaque tights in the early pitch-black mornings; the situation with Lily that's bound to pan out: her blanking me in such an obvious way that no-one can ignore it or not notice that we're not speaking; our friends splitting off into different groups: Emily and Caitlin and Clara and Helena and Wendy having either to take sides or stay friends with both of us but see us separately. The whispering, backbiting, bitchiness – just the thought of it does my head in.

"I don't want to go back to school in three days." I tell Ben as we sit at the pond later that day.

A mallard launches himself into the pond, kicking up spray with his big paddle feet, the curve of his breast plump. Water slides off his back: water off a duck's back. He turns his emerald green face towards me and smiles, his bill open.

"Why not?" Ben asks, his head cocked to one side like the duck's. "I thought you liked school."

"I dunno. Bored of it I guess. I want to do something else, travel, I dunno, work…" Of course I do not want to do either of these things. I don't know why I just said that.

"Well we'll be going to uni soon. You could do a Gap year, anyway. I'm going to go to Israel." His eyes light up. "Those girl soldiers are hot. I'd like a tanned, red-haired Israeli chick in an army uniform, carrying a rifle and…"

"I'm so not going to Israel- can't think of anything worse. It'll be exactly the same as being here, just with bombs and mosquitoes. I'm going to Madagascar to study lemurs." I decide on the spur of the moment, and then I remember that I'd have to sleep in a tent for a year there. "How's Lee? I haven't seen him for ages. Where was he over the holidays?" I ask, carefully not mentioning Seb.

"Lee was in Mustique with his family. Seb's OK too" he replies, "He's um, really busy with coursework and stuff."

We both know this is not the case – Seb never does any homework. Ben could have come up with something a bit more convincing about why Seb has not called me.

"Look, T," Ben says in an avuncular compassionate chat show host voice whilst looking into my eyes with a soulful and yet resigned expression. "I think he does like you but…"

"He's gay?" I try.

"No, he…um… split up with his last girlfriend quite recently and…er… he doesn't want to get involved with anyone else right now."

I feel crushed: a car in one of those big pincer things. I had sort of guessed, but at the same time I've been making up so many excuses for him – everything from he's gay to he's lost my number to he's scared I'm not interested to he's been abducted by aliens.

"How long ago?"

"'Bout six weeks?"

I suppose that is not that long ago, although I've never seen Seb with anyone in all the time I've known him.

"Who was she and why did we never meet her?"

"A friend of his cousin Imogen. She's a bit older, she split up with him because she wanted to get married and have kids and stuff. Anyway, they split up before we met Seb, before he came to my school and…"

"How much older?"

"She's 27."

"That is a lot older," I say.

"She's really hot though, she's…"

"OK, I don't want to know, shut up."

Reluctantly, I feel a surge of respect for Seb, that he has been out with a significantly older woman, if Ben is telling the truth. He is Experienced With Girls, which makes him even more attractive to me.

"Why are you being so edgy?" Ben asks. "I'm only trying to help."

"Just shut up alright? If it was you moaning about your great love for Lily, do you think I'd be going on and on about how much better Greg is than you?"

"Well what would you say? He's got deeper acne scars? He's got a more fetching lisp? He's got a more spazzy walk? He's more stupid and dull?" Ben sniggers and a bit of his Diet Coke comes out through his nose.

I laugh – more at the bubbles coming out of Ben's right nostril than his description of Greg. "But do you think Seb does like me though, or can he just not be arsed unless we're wasted and I'm there?"

"Well sort of a bit of both. He likes you enough to snog you when you're wasted and you're there, but he doesn't want to be in a relationship now."

"But would he ever or not?"

"I don't know. He hasn't said anything to me at all about you."

"I don't believe you though."

"Swear on my Grandma's life." Both Ben's grandmothers are dead.

"But hasn't it come up, you know, in conversation?"

"We don't have those sorts of conversations."

"What do you talk about then?"

"Tunes and football and pills and politics."

"Politics?"

"Yeah, the situation in the Middle East, Northern Ireland, Cuba…"

Clearly I'm not missing much conversation-wise. "What's he actually like?"

"He's quite uncomplicated really – relaxed, easily pleased, positive. He's not really right for you, T; you'd get bored of him so quickly."

We sip our cans of Diet Coke and stare out into the pond which is black and deep and holds its secrets.

The phone doesn't ring. My heart is in my throat the whole time. I need to get out more, I know I do, but I am trapped – trapped. I loll around the house just in case the phone rings.

"Saying that Fifi won't sleep in the car is completely untrue, of course she will, all babies sleep in the car." Mum is telling someone over the phone. "She doesn't have behavioural problems – if a child that age is badly behaved it's their parents who need to see a therapist, not them. Oh yes, I quite agree Olivia, if Carl cried in the middle of the night we never picked him up. No, I know you always left your two to cry as well… you know they let Fi get into bed with them? Yes, I know, a child needs boundaries."

Mum is obviously talking to Aunty Olivia about their brother's child-rearing techniques. Uncle Harry and his fiancée Alexis have just had their first baby Fifi who they are raising according to some modern method that Mum and Aunty Olivia don't hold with, although what it's got to do with either of them I just don't know. Nor do I understand why the whole thing is a matter of such trauma to the ladies of the family. Nor do I have any interest in the whole thing.

But it does strike me as richly ironic that for all Mum's parenting wisdom there is something terrible wrong with me and she hasn't even noticed. Stop criticising your brother and his fiancée – if they wanted your advice they'd ask you. But, I think *I* might have a brain tumour or some form of inoperable brain cancer.

I call Carl and after three rings the answering machine clicks in.

"Hi Carl, hope Oxford is fun, missing you. Why do you never answer your…"

"T?" It's so calming to hear my brother's voice.

"Carl, I was just…"

"I know. You OK."

"Yeah." No.

"Look, I'm just on my way to formal hall, can I call you tomorrow, I'm a bit late to meet Immi and… oh she's here now…" The line goes dead.

My brain tumour might have removed my powers of speech by then though. Anyway, who's Immi? He's never mentioned her before. I don't want my brother to have a girlfriend who he prefers to me anyway.

"Yeah, OK," I reply to the turned-off phone and slide the handset back into its cradle, staring at it resting there lifeless when a moment ago it had transmitted Carl's words and aura to me.

Everything is so bleak and hopeless, I think as I lie on my bed, unable to muster up the energy to do my Biology homework, read *King Lear* or even watch my fish. I stare at my legs and I can see all the sleeping cat hairs that lie just under the skin, curled round with their tails under their bodies.

I do exfoliate between waxes like I'm meant to but my skin grows over the hairs too thick, or my exfoliator isn't strong enough or something. Exfoliating needs to be done in the bath and I haven't had the energy lately to take my clothes off, get wet, wash my hair, get dry and then start all over again.

I rummage around in the drawer next to my bed for the special tweezers with the pointed ends which I can dig under the skin with and tease the hairs out. After a few minutes of this – during which time I've turned my calves into a mass of bleeding holes – I collapse into bed, close my eyes, pull my covers up round my ears and listen to the lonely stutter of my breathing – in, out, in, out – droning on and on hopeless and unchanged.

Chapter 12

"YOU'VE GOT NOTHING TO BE MISERABLE ABOUT. Go and get dressed. You've been wearing that disgusting dressing-gown for days. " Mum hisses at me.

I sigh and turn the volume up on the TV. It's the second week of January. Two blubbery mountainous women are screaming at each other about one of them having swiped the other one's husband. The husband looks about my age and has that pallor caused by a diet of junk food and beer. His skin is dusted with a coating of acne. He's skinny and dressed in a tracksuit and has one ear pierced with a small gold hoop. I have no idea why he is such a catch.

"So? I'm miserable. Why do I need to have something to be miserable about? Why can't I wear my dressing-gown for watching Trisha?"

"You have a family who love you." Mum says, sounding weary, "You have everything you want, you're brilliant at your school work, you're heading for Oxford. When I was your age…"

I've heard it all before.

"Turn that thing off when I'm talking to you, Tanya."

"I'm not coming."

"You are. It's your uncle's wedding. You are going to make yourself look pretty and you are going to be ready and you are going to come up to me at the party and say 'What can I do to help, Mum?' before I ask you. You are not going to make us wait for you." Mum says. "And why haven't you had a bath or washed your hair?"

"Why are you wearing such atrocious lipstick? Fuchsia is really not your colour." I tell her.

"Actually, the *Colour Me Beautiful* lady told me that fuchsia *is* one of my colours actually, as is black." Mum says, triumphant. "I'm the only season that can wear black. It doesn't suit you."

"What is meant to suit me then?"

"You're a Spring, so definitely not black or all those dull neutrals like navy, grey, aubergine and khaki you're so fond of." Mum answers triumphantly. "You should be wearing peach and powder pink, coral and watermelon. Look," She picks up a book off the living room table and flicks to a page.

There is the most vile photo of an '80s American housewife with huge clip-on earrings, too much blusher, over-plucked eyebrows, bouffant side-parted hair and an open-toothed grin. She is wearing a disgusting outfit as well.

"What is this book anyway?"

"I went to a 'Colour Me Beautiful' evening with your Auntie Olivia and Lily's Mum."

My chest constricts. So she must know. Lily's mum must have told her that Lily and I have fallen out.

Mum looks at me with an inquiring gaze.

"Do you want to tell me something, sweetie? Are you upset about arguing with Lily? Sharon says Lily is distraught."

Here we go again, I think.

"Friends can be horrible sometimes." Mum says, somewhat surprisingly, coming over to sit next to me on the sofa and putting her arm round me.

I'm expecting her to tell me off for upsetting Lily, as she normally does, but she doesn't.

"Do you want to tell me what happened?"

"No."

"Well, come on, stop moping about it. You and Lily will make it up, sweetie."

"I hope we don't. I hope she gets killed in a horrible accident, or maimed, or paralysed or facially disfigured."

"Stop it, Tanya. Don't say things like that."

I'm obviously not just upset about having a fight with Lily, I think. I actually don't want to be friends with her anymore. In eighteen months' time I won't have to see or speak to her again, ever. My life will be a Lily-free zone.

"Come on sweetie, get dressed. We have to leave soon."

"Where's my brother?" The only bit of this whole event that I will be able to deal with is seeing Carl and sitting next to him while his solid bulk absorbs some of my pain.

"He'll be here in a minute. Go and get dressed now and by the time you're ready he'll be here."

I drag myself into my room and stare at the outfit Mum has set out on my bed: the bright hues jump out at me. I can't wear this, it is imperative that I wear something that won't make me stand out: I want to wear black and grey and no make-up.

But I pull on the vest top, the skirt and my black lace-up velvet pointy boots. I scrape my hair up into a high pony-tail and loosen some strands at the front of my face, clipping back the sections with sparkly hologram silver butterfly hairclips. I tie a hair-band with a turquoise fabric rose sewn onto it round the base of my ponytail.

"Bye bye kids," I say to Richard and Judy. "I wish I was coming swimming with you amongst the drowned pirate wreck and the fluoro ferns. Richard lifts his head up, flutters his long lashes and blows me a haughty bubble.

"Put some lipstick on." Mum says, as I emerge. "Come on, you'll feel better if you make a bit more effort to look pretty."

"No I won't."

"Stop complaining. We're going to have a lovely time." Mum says.

We do not have a lovely time. The synagogue is freezing cold and I'm shivering in my thin cotton cardigan, skirt and bare legs. There are no attractive men, of course, only several etiolated youths dressed for the Polish ghettos of the 1880s in hats, long coats…actually, they've got the right idea: at least they're probably not cold.

The service is completely in Hebrew as it's a United shul, and so I can't even attempt to keep up. Dad and Carl are on one side of the room with the men, whilst we're on the other side of the room with the rest of the women, who pay no attention to the service, and simply chat about various religious friends who I don't know and attend to all their vile children running around and screaming and crying.

"Mum, my train, Shoshanna took my train." A small boy screams and bursts into tears.

You just wait, I think. Things are going to get so much worse. You just wait till your Mum can't kiss it better any more and she thinks you've got nothing to be unhappy about and you can't bear school and you wake up every morning thinking 'I can't believe I'm still alive.'

"Stop it, Tanya, you're embarrassing me." Mum hisses, elbowing me in the ribs. "What are you crying about?"

"I'm not crying, leave me alone." I say, but when I reach up to my cheek I can feel the tears trickling down it.

"Here." Mum hands me a tissue from up her sleeve. "Just try and behave normally can't you, for once. Stop thinking about yourself all the time and try to behave appropriately. It doesn't matter how you feel. No one cares how you feel; they just care how you behave." I wipe my tears away, blow my nose noisily and bite my tongue.

After the service Kiddush segues into lunch at the hotel down the road from the synagogue. This is exactly the sort of food I don't like. It has a horrible metallic aftertaste. There is only sweet, boiled kosher wine here – as I predicted – and not even that on the children's table where I'm seated with my brother and various cousins ranging between 1 and 14. It seems extraordinary that there are no male members of the family of my age, but there aren't. The trapped sensation rises in my throat. I have to get out before…before….

"I've got to go." I tell my brother Carl.

"Tanya, what's going on?" Carl grabs my arm, trying to stop me leaving.

"I can't be here."

How could I describe it, it's just a sense that I have to get out, that I can't possibly survive the event, that I'm welded to my seat and that if I don't run a terrible thing will happen.

"That's just not a proper answer. You have to be here."

"I've got an essay I need to finish. Mum knows about it."

I heave myself out of my seat, my legs are lead and I've got pins and needles so I slip as I shuffle away from the table knocking over a tower of cakes which tumble off their stand and splatter on the floor. As I make a break for the exit, slipping in a puddle of chocolate sauce from the profiteroles, I glance over to Mum's table and see that she is engaged in conversation with 93 year old partially blind Auntie Henny. Luckily she doesn't look up and see the mess I've made, or that I'm running out of the wedding.

Only once I'm outside the hotel do I realise that it's on the edge of the motorway and there's no way of getting anywhere else. I sit on a wall in the car park watching the cars roar past and hoping that one of them will veer off the road and crash into the wall, killing me instantly. Once I can drive it will be totally different, I'll be able to go anywhere I want. I think of where I might want to go now if there was any transport to anywhere and can only come up with home, back to bed, back to sleep. I'm going to feel OK tomorrow; it's just these events, these family things. My family don't understand my life or my problems.

This is the most miserable that I've ever felt. Everything is dark and the slate grey clouds press down on me. A black shape appears out of the clouds of gloom. Suddenly, out of the corner of my eyes, I see that there is a black panther sitting on the wall swishing his tail and watching me. I know that there are wild big cats in the countryside, even if the government try to cover it up. People let them out after the Exotic Animals Act came in and you weren't allowed to keep them as pets anymore.

I've never seen a wild big cat before near Watford on the A41, but here he is. He must have come in from the woods at the side of the motorway.

"Hello," I say to him and I reach my hand out so he will come over to me.

I hold my breath, willing him to approach me. He stares at me with huge amber eyes and swishes his tail. I smile at him and it's the first time I've smiled in ages.

At last he begins to stalk along the top of the wall towards me, his tail held vertical in the air. He sits down right next to me and puts his paw out, patting my leg. I edge closer to him, I'm sure he used to be someone's pet after all, he's not dangerous. He is warm and soft and solid, his muscles ripple along his shoulders. He rests his head on my knee and closes his eyes. I stroke the top of his head, it is velvety and smooth. His chin presses down on my knee and I am so privileged that he is choosing to be here with me. He soaks up all my pain, or at least some of it and I breathe in his big-cat calm.

After a few minutes he stretches and slopes off back into the bushes from whence he came. I hold my secret close to my chest. I have seen him and touched him, I know he is here, I know that wild big cats roam the A41. And then I see my mother flouncing towards me, her aubergine skirt billowing in the wind, exposing her taut calves. She looks very angry: her eyes are narrowed and her mouth set in a grimace.

"I thought you'd be here." Mum hisses in my ear. "Get back inside this minute."

"I won't."

It is really annoying that she has come out to look for me. I just want to be left alone. The panther slinks out of the bushes and lies down next to me. Turning his huge head, he begins to rasp his flank with his rough tongue.

"You are going to go back in there, sit at your table and behave like a normal person. Why do you want to upset me, Tanya? I do everything for you – I help you with your homework, I give you money, I buy you lovely clothes, I don't make you lift a finger to help me around the house. All I expect from you is for you to be pleasant and cheerful, and you can't even do that. When I was your age I had to look after my little brothers and sisters, pick them up from school, do all the housework…"

"Well poor you. I am sorry." Now is not the time for her martyr routine. I am not even going to tell her about my panther either.

"You used to be so sweet; we used to get on so well. What's happened to my little girl?" Mum pleads.

"Don't start that again. I'm doing my best. I am trying." I say, unable to even convince myself.

"What is it Tanya? Why can't you just be in there and talk to your family? I can't cope with this every time we go out of the house."

"Because they are so stupefyingly dull and there are no cute boys." I reply. She can hardly argue with that. "Anyway, I don't feel well."

"What's meant to be wrong with you now then?"

"I've got a headache. It could be meningitis, or maybe a sub-arachnoid haemorrhage." I'm not quite sure what that is but it sounds good.

Mum reaches out and presses her hand against my forehead, and her other hand on her own forehead, furrows her brow, thinks. "Well you haven't got a temperature, you're probably just worried about going back to school, aren't you, and seeing Lily?"

She is trying, I think. She is doing her best. We are both doing our best but I can't behave any other way at the moment. It's the panther's fault, I think.

I nod. I am worried about these things certainly, a bit.

"Go and sit with your brother, he wants to spend some time with you. He's going back to Oxford tomorrow. Come back in for an hour and then we can go, I promise?"

I know Mum loves me. It's just hard for her now.

"If I have to," I say, and follow Mum back inside.

Chapter 13

THE DOOR OF BEN'S HOUSE OPENS. It is 2 weeks since my uncle's wedding. Seb is standing there wearing glow in the dark fangs, pointed furry ears and a long striped tail. He's got diagonal black and orange tiger stripes painted on his cheeks. He is reflected in the hallway mirror and so his long furry tail is visible to us.

"Why are you dressed like that?" Emily asks him, nudging me and pointing at the reflection of the tail.

"I'm a Smilodon. It's a sabre-toothed cat." Seb says.

Looking at his real mane of thick blond hair and the actual gold fur on his tanned forearms, my stomach flips over. I feel very nervous suddenly and squeeze Emily's hand for reassurance. I wasn't expecting Seb to be the first person we'd see when we got here. However much I think I want to see him beforehand, once we're actually in the same room I feel out of my depth.

"I know what a Smilodon is. My mum did a degree in palaeontology." I say with a proud smile, and immediately kick myself for it coming out so smugly.

"The theme is 'Ice Age.'" He explains, ignoring my comment.

"No-one told us." I say. "We could have dressed up." I smooth my purple tie-dyed mini skirt down self-consciously. It is very short and I feel awkward with Seb's gaze on me.

"No, just for us boys. Ben is a woolly rhino and Lee is a mammoth. Anyway, you look nice." He smiles at me in an approving way, looking me up and down.

I'm not sure whether 'Ice Age' is really a good theme for a party or just ridiculous and I hate it when that happens, when I don't know whether something's hot or not. Seb leads us through the hall into a room which is brown and is obviously meant to be a cave. There is a log fire burning in the grate and rocks scattered around on the floor, presumably from Ben's parents' rockery.

Ben's house is massive and the décor is fab: William Morris 'peony garden' wallpaper which I recognise from History of Art classes, Art Nouveau tiles around the fireplace, Arts and Crafts style furniture. I can't believe his parents would be happy about Ben having a party here, especially as there's now mud from the garden all over the Persian rug.

"I'll leave you two to it then." Emily whispers to me and scurries off in the direction of the kitchen. Don't go, I think. Don't leave me. I miss Lily, I find myself thinking. Since we're still not speaking I don't know why she's not here tonight.

"Nice shoes. Your feet must hurt though." Seb says as we stand in the living room. I am wearing my open-toed silver wedge sandals.

"No, no they're fine. Wedges are much more comfortable than stilettos because there's less pressure on the ball of your foot and…"

"Let's sit down here anyway." He says, sitting down on the sofa at the edge of the dance-floor, putting his arm round my waist, guiding me down onto his lap.

It is comfortable, and I feel a glow of pride that I am sitting on Seb's lap, in public, where everyone can see that we are together.

"It never really mattered too much to me
That you were just too damn dull to see."

The music blares, fades out, and then it's Madonna's 'Frozen'.

"Frozen, where your heart's not open." Madonna sings. She is probably not at an Ice Age party though.

"Did you know this song was written for an ice-cream ad?" I say. "Ben and Jerry's and Haagen-Dazs both turned it down for being too dark."

This is meant to lighten the mood but it doesn't; it seems deadly serious with Seb. I feel nervous.

Seb doesn't reply and shoots me a strange look. I kick myself for never having anything interesting or witty to say to him. I need to start making lists of things-to-say-to-boys-that-make-me-sound-normal. His fangs glow in the dark. They are not really long enough, not sabre-length. His eyes are very convincing though, as ever.

I look into them and he holds my gaze, challenging it and then puts his hand behind my head, stroking my hair and guiding my lips down to meet his. I relax into him and just enjoy the moment with his arms round me and his lips are really soft and he slides his strong pierced tongue into my mouth and we just sit there, kissing for a while. It feels nice to be kissed and he tastes good: the same minty taste that I remember from the times before. I try to block out all the noise and just concentrate on Seb. My mind empties. I put my arms round his neck pulling him closer to me.

"Have you got any pills?" I blurt out.

"Yeah, of course, here. Open wide."

He puts one into my mouth and I swallow it, washing the bitter taste down with a sip of water, looking over his shoulder at the party going on around us. Ben is DJing, about twenty people are dancing: throwing shapes against the dry ice and smoke that pumps into the room. As the beams of the strobe lights hit the smoke they fragment and the smoke glows with green stripes. A slide projector throws swirling multi-coloured images on the walls and the wallpaper distorts them.

"Come with me a minute, I want to show you something" He says after a while.

"Yeah, OK."

I want to be on my own with him. I've never been alone with him apart from those few minutes in the garden at Lee's party. We get up from the sofa and fight our way through the crowd, into the hall and up the stairs. He leans against the first door on the left and it swings open. The room's empty so we go in and he shuts the door behind us and moves towards the bed and sits down on it, kicking his trainers off.

"Come and sit here."

He pats the duvet beside him and I walk over and perch on the edge of the bed. Here I am, on my own with Seb, in a bedroom. It's dark, but the curtains are open and a shaft of moonlight illuminates his face. We just sit there, looking at each other. He is still wearing his furry cat ears and his fangs. I am very still, waiting to see what he's going to do. I try to bat my eyelashes in a seductive way but they are too heavy with mascara and stick together a bit. He strokes my cheek, smoothing a tendril of hair behind my ear. I breathe in his familiar smell – Hugo Boss aftershave – and lick my lips, excited and nervous at the same time.

He lifts my foot onto his knee and slides off my shoe, stroking the arch of my foot, running his hand up my leg to the middle of my thigh and then he stops but I want him to keep going. Instead, he picks up my other foot and removes the other shoe. Without my shoes on I feel naked. I want to lean towards him but with my feet on his lap it would look like some edgy ballerina stretch, so I just wait. Suddenly he pulls me towards him, closing the space between us and I'm excited now and the nerves are dissipating because we are in the dark and because I dropped that pill earlier.

He stretches out on the bed and I stretch out next to him and this huge excitement bubbles up inside me that I might be about to have sex with Seb. As he slides his hand up my skirt I'm thinking that in a few minutes I'm going to have had sex, which is such a weird thought, and then I'll be able to tell all my friends that I've done it.

"Um, Seb, I've got to tell you something." I blurt out, feeling a sudden urge to confess my terrible secret.

"Go on." His voice is gentle. He rests his hand on the inside of my thigh and strokes it.

"Well, um, I haven't done it before, so, you know, if I'm not very good then that's why."

As soon as the words are out I wish I hadn't said them. He is going to think I have never done anything with a boy before, which is not totally true. I did do some things with Robbie. Also, we have not actually done anything yet or taken any clothes off so it's a bit ridiculous to be having this conversation already.

He laughs. "Don't worry, Tanya. It's going to be OK, I promise. Just relax." He says, sounding like a doctor who is about to perform a particularly nasty procedure – taking your tonsils out perhaps.

He hooks his fingers round the sides of my knickers and pulls them down my thighs and flings them across the room as if he has done this a hundred times before. The air feels cold on my bare skin and I remember Ben telling me that Seb has had a much older girlfriend and has been with lots of girls. The thought of his experience calms me. He knows what he is doing.

As he strokes my bum I am starting to come up on the pill, and I am warming to his touch and my muscles are relaxing and my skin tingles as he touches me. I grip Seb's hand, he's grinding his teeth, and the music pumps through us. I look down at Seb dropping a line of kisses down my stomach and I tangle my fingers in his thick gold hair. It feels weird to think that Seb wants to do these things to me and I can't quite believe that this is actually happening.

I close my eyes and I can feel his tongue lapping at me and it feels nice and I try to relax into it. I feel glad that all I have to do is lie here and show that I am enjoying it. I hear myself making moaning noises like women do in films. The part of me that is moaning is enjoying it but another part of me is not here, is dissociated from my body and floating above it looking at this inert girl lying on the bed. I attempt to pull the two strands back together. If I can go through with this then it will make things better, it will cure me. If I can throw myself into this then all my problems will vanish. I open my eyes and look over to the corner of the room. The panther is standing watching me and swishing his tail in an angry way and baring his teeth. I need him to leave me alone here with Seb. Go away, I think. Let me get on with this on my own.

You're not meant to be here, I think, shocked that he has just appeared, but then I begin to accept that the panther is now part of me and he comes and goes as he pleases. I try to relax into the experience with Seb but now that the panther is watching us I just can't. I want to go back to the party.

"Right," Seb says, lifting his head up. "Your turn." He pushes my head down, unzipping his jeans, pulling down his Calvin Klein boxers. His furry tail has fallen off the back of his jeans and lies on the bed between us. I concentrate on stroking the tail.

But I don't know what to do. I have never done anything like this before.

"I can't." I say. "I've got a problem with my jaw."

"No you haven't. Come on."

Then, surprising myself with my bravery, I take it in my mouth and sort of lick up and down in a perfunctory way. He groans a bit and digs his fingers into my back. After a while he pulls out of my mouth.

"That's not so bad, now, is it?"

I think he is pleased that I have had a go and made an effort. I am very pleased with myself anyway for being so brave.

"No." It actually wasn't that bad but I do want to have sex now. Feeling very grown-up I steel myself for the pain and the blood and…

…The door swings open, the light comes on. Seb pulls away from me.

"Shit, I thought I'd locked the door." He whispers.

A mixture of relief and disappointment floods over me in huge waves that rock my whole body. I sit up, brushing down my skirt so that it falls over where my knickers should be and grope around the bed for them.

Now that the light is on I can see the My Little Pony wallpaper, the doll's house, the model farm with plastic sheep and a border collie and cows and pigs and tractors – this must be Ben's sister's room. It looks just like my room used to look before Mum let me redecorate it. I feel a bit icky about what almost happened, but, thank God didn't happen.

Emily is standing in the doorway looking shocked. I have been rescued but I have also missed my chance of having sex. I am relieved though.

"Tanya, there you are." Emily says.

She sounds relieved, happy to have found me. Our eyes lock. Emily pushes a sweaty tendril of dark brown curly hair away from her face, where it has become entangled in her silver false eyelashes.

"Em," I say.

"Hi Seb," She says, giving him a disapproving dirty look. "You were gone for ages, Tanya." She says, turning her attention back to me. "We were worried that… I don't know, something had happened to you. Are you coming back downstairs now?"

"Hello Emily." Seb says, completely unruffled, smiling at Em as he pulls his jeans on.

I don't know why he is not embarrassed but apparently he is not.

I am so glad you're here, Em, I think, but I am also cross that she has disturbed this pivotal moment, or what would have been a pivotal moment anyway. I rummage around the floor for my knickers, locate them, and pull them on swiftly while Seb is occupied with his shoes.

"See you later, Seb." I say as I run out of the room, suddenly too embarrassed to look at him.

As soon as we are nearly at the bottom of the stairs Em hisses: "What have you been doing for all this time though…oh my g-d…. did you…"

"No, shhhh,'" I squeeze her arm, losing my balance as I trip over a can of lager, stumbling over a boy who has fallen asleep in his own vomit. "Shhhhh."

"He's really hot." She muses. "If I wasn't with Ian…"

"Stoppit."

The idea of her going after him is horrible. I push her comment aside as the enormity of what almost just happened sinks in.

"Are you going to…"

"Shhh." I hold her hand. "Thank you for coming to find me." I whisper.

"It's OK. I was a bit worried." She says.

"Can we go?"

I ask, looking at the scene of carnage: people passed out everywhere; beer and wine spills all over the floor; broken glass; feathers. The house is completely trashed. I don't know how Ben's going to sort it out for when his parents get home.

"What, now?"

"Yeah."

"But it's only 1.30?"

"I just want to go home." I insist.

There doesn't seem to be any point in staying at the party now that I am not going to have sex with Seb. I would rather go home and mull the experience over on my own. I feel like a coward for letting Emily rescue me, for not going through with it. I am a complete failure: I can't even manage to lose my virginity when about 80% of seventeen year old girls in this country have had sex.

"But why though? What happened?" She asks, gripping my arm, making me look at her.

I can't explain. I do not really know what happened myself. I just know that I cannot be here, that this is another place I can't be in, another test I've failed at, another mistake that I've made, that I'm making, that is going to get worse, that is getting worse even now as I stand here rooted to the spot.

"We have to go." I repeat. "We have to go home now. Tell Ben that we are going."

"OK, OK, if it's that important." She says, shaking her head and running off to get our coats and say goodbye to everyone while I stand by the door, itching to get out, stepping from foot to foot because my shoes are beginning to hurt my feet after all.

Chapter 14

"So, yesterday, we're at Rick's and you'll never guess who walks in." Emily says, as we sit on her windowsill with our legs dangling out of the window, kicking our heels against the outside of the house.

"Who?"

"Guess, guess, guess."

"Can you just tell me? Come on. You're so annoying."

"You have to guess."

"Who were you with?"

"Lily, Caitlin, Wendy…"

"Thanks for inviting me."

I feel a sharp stab of envy. I would have loved to have gone to Rick's yesterday rather than watching a programme about polar bears with Mum which is all I was doing instead.

"I did. If you remember, you said you'd rather drink Mrs Jones' period blood than go anywhere if Lily was there. Anyway, we're at Rick's and your Seb comes in…"

"He's not my Seb." I point out, whilst feeling a stab of envy that Em's seen him and I haven't.

"So, they're chatting and all flirty and he keeps touching her back and pushing her hair behind her ear."

"Eugh." It must be the older ex-girlfriend who is trying to get back into his pants, the scheming evil bitch.

"I know."

"What did she look like?"

"Older than us, properly ancient, at least twenty-one I guess. Pretty…"

It must be the ex, it must be. I wonder if he's got back together with her and that's why he hasn't called me.

"Thinner?'

"No, more, um, delicate, like a fairy: great cheekbones, green eyes, long curly hair like yours tied up in a ponytail but hers is red, it's gorgeous: she has pale milky translucent skin, petite…"

"OK, get on with the story." I can't take any more. That is just way too much competition.

"So, Lily walks over to them. Seb turns to say hello to her and without saying anything she just throws her glass of red wine over him. You should have seen the expression on his face with the wine dripping down his chin onto his T-shirt, and the orange seeping into his clothes and streaking…"

"Orange? Does he wear fake tan?"

I don't know why I haven't realised this before.

"Unless his skin has a top layer that is both orange and dissolvable."

"Soluble. Anyway, what did she say to him?"

"So, after she throws the wine over him she just stays there chatting with him and the girl for what seems like ages. When she finally pitches up back at our table she looks so pleased with herself, like she's just climbed Everest in a ball-gown and heels and won the Guinness World Record for the Highest Altitude Formal Dinner

And then she collapses in hysterics and I go 'What happened.' And she goes 'I went up to him and I said "Seb you're such a twat, Tanya really likes you."'

"No way! She didn't." Shit, Lily is so embarrassing.

"Shhh. So, the girl apparently said to Seb: 'What have you got yourself into now, Squibs? You're such a naughty boy.'"

"Squibs!"

"Heh, I know. And he said, 'Imogen – meet Lily – Lily – my cousin Imogen.'"

"And then?"

"Well, then we all went and sat with them and had a drink with them. She's really nice, you'd like her."

So Seb has a pretty cousin, someone who calls him Squibs and teases him. I think about my brother. It's weird, I've never thought about Seb having a cousin before – a pretty, cool, older cousin.

"These are nice aren't they?" Em licks her fingers, smearing chocolate round her mouth. Em's tucking into a bucket of mini chocolate swiss rolls. No matter how much junk she eats she never puts any weight on.

"You've got chocolate round your mouth, yeah, up a bit, no, there, yeah, that's right, it's gone now." I tell her.

It's a Wednesday evening after school two weeks into the Spring term. It really doesn't feel like spring yet though: it's freezing cold, sleeting, windy and we shiver in the January air. It's still dark at 5pm as well.

As I think about the story Em's just told me, the Antarctic iceberg of my anger with Lily begins to thaw. She did that for me, I think. She stood up for me. Of course it's going to be even more awkward for me than usual the next time that I see Seb, but she defended me, because she cares that I am upset about Seb, and she cares how he's treating me. She is not wandering around slagging me off to everyone, as I am doing about her. On the contrary, she is thinking about how to make me feel better. I feel suddenly like I've been a bitch to her for no reason and that I must make amends.

"You've got to sort things out with Lily. It's getting ridiculous now." Emily says, reading my mind.

"Yeah, I know but…" I don't want to, I think.

"No, you do. You have to. It's ridiculous. Call her now. The situation is just pathetic and you're both being really stupid and annoying about it and…."

"But you know how irritating she is though."

"Yeah, but…oh I don't know, T, I think you shouldn't be so hard on her. Shall I call her now and get her to come round so you two can make up?"

"No, I don't want to" I say, cringing, shrinking from the awkwardness that I anticipate.

"It's better if you two sort things out before we go back to school." Em points out.

She may well be right, but I'm just not going to tonight.

"Why do I have to call her though? Why can't she call me?"

"Because you're the more grown-up one? Because she's a bit scared of you?"

"No she's not!"

"She's scared of you being stressy with her. Can't you see how stupid you're both being? The longer you leave it the more awkward it's going to be, the more difficult it's…"

"You sound like my Mum. Alright, I'll talk to her at school tomorrow."

"Good. Chocolate Swiss roll?"

"Oh, go on then." I peel the purple foil off it and savour it.

I'm walking to our form room the next day when I spot Lily tottering down the corridor in metallic wedges, blue fishnets and a tiny fuchsia acetate dress. I think about ducking into the loos to avoid her then take a deep breath and stride towards her with a confidence I don't feel.

"Lily," I say. She starts at hearing my voice and turns round. A strand of pink hair falls over her right eye. She tries to push it away behind her ear and loses her balance, dropping the pile of books she's carrying. Her skirt flies up and I catch a glimpse of leopard-print knickers: she's a jewel-coloured beetle unbalanced on her back, her legs flail in the air. I pick the books up for her but don't attempt to help her up. Her roots are growing back dark and she must have slept in her make-up – the ring of cobalt eyeliner on one eye is a bit larger and darker than the other. Eventually she struggles to her feet.

"Here," I hand the books back to her, first removing my own biology notes that for some reason are in her pile of papers. I don't remember her asking if she could borrow my essay which is due in today. I've been looking for it for weeks: I was sure I'd done it and couldn't understand where it'd gone.

"Thanks." She says, hugging the notes to her.

We stare at each other for a few seconds. She bites her lip. I feel the distance between us – a chasm – the iceberg splits and the two sheets of ice floating away from each other. We are two polar bear cubs stranded on different ice sheets which float off in different directions gathering pace.

"I'm sorry." She says and puts her little paw out – reaching across the gash in the ice to pull me back to her.

I take her hand with its short chipped nails, the nails she's never been able to grow; the nails she's always said she wishes were more like mine. We entwine our fingers round each others' and put our arms round each others' waists and rub our cheeks together. Her cheek's a bit damp: she's crying and I start crying a bit, and I'm just so relieved that things are going to be OK between us again.

"I missed you T."

"I missed you too." And I realise that I have, although I've been pretending this is not the case to everyone and even to myself.

"Em told me, about Seb. Thank you, I really appreciate it you know."

"You should have seen the look on his face, T." Lily says, smiling. "It was hilarious, and the fake tan running down his cheeks and smudging his T-shirt. The T-shirt will be totally ruined, that stuff like stains for ever."

Our ice sheets slide back together, we climb onto the same one and it's not so cold once we're huddled together.

"Anyway, I chatted to Imogen, she's cool: she's a singer in a band. She says we should come down and see them at the Furnace on Saturday." She smiles. "We should go. It will be fun. You can wear your…"

"Carl's home though, we'll all be going out to dinner and…"

"That's even better – then you can both come to the Furnace after. Carl knows her anyway – she's at Uni too studying music, she's really pretty and…"

"How do you know Carl knows her?"

"Coz she said so. She asked me if I was Tanya and…"

This is getting weirder and weirder. My brother is seeing Seb's cousin. I remember Carl ditching my phone call for Immi in Oxford. Immi who is Imogen. I'm not sure if this is good or obscenely bad. On one hand, it means I can get close to, or closer to Seb, but it could be really embarrassing and…

"Maybe." I say. "I'll ask him."

I don't really want to go to Seb's cousin's gig though and have to see him after what Lily said to him, but I suppose it will be nice to spend some time together. I agree that I'll run it past Carl – who is probably going anyway if he's going out with Immi – to get Lily to shut up, and then we walk into Biology, hand in hand, united once again against the world.

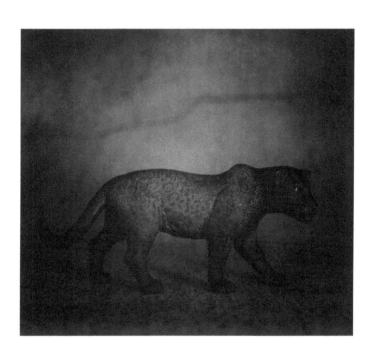

Chapter 15

"**WILL YOU TURN THAT AWFUL NOISE OFF?**" Mum screams at me from another room.

"Can't hear you." I yell back.

I can hear her but her voice is muffled and very far away. I don't see why I can't listen to Portishead's 'Dummy' in my room with the door closed; it's not even loud in here.

The panther is lying along my body with one paw pressing down on my chest and one over my mouth, arching his back and waving his tail. He is angry with me for sending him away and now he is punishing me by refusing to let me get up, even to turn the music down or to do a wee. He's roaring in my ear, but I can't understand what he's trying to say, it's just black noise. He licks my face, and although the idea of being licked by a panther is nice, his tongue is very rough and his breath smells of rotting meat. I can't believe I thought he was an escaped zoo animal when, of course, he is mine.

"I didn't send you anywhere." I tell him. "I can't control it. It's not suitable accommodation for you here anyway: you need open space and live prey to catch and other panthers to talk to who understand you and a warm climate."

He purrs. He is happy just to be with me, as long as I don't go anywhere, speak to anyone else, do anything or leave him alone at all. He rubs his velvety cheek against mine. His fur is sleek and shiny and close-up I can see the spots – a darker blue-black under his fur.

The door swings open and Mum appears. She ignores the huge feline who is lying on top of my duvet. Maybe she can't see him; like when Gertrude can't see the ghost in *Hamlet*.

"It's no wonder you're always miserable listening to that awful whining noise." She says. "When we were young we listened to Beethoven and the Beatles and you didn't hear teenagers moaning about how unhappy they were all the time and we…"

"Shut up! I shrill, as the panther nibbles sharply on my ear. That's because you were teenagers in the '60s and it was fun and you didn't have exams all the time.

"Well we didn't know how wonderful it was at the time. We had boyfriend troubles too, we never had any money, we didn't have all these new clothes and all these things you have, but we used to enjoy ourselves. In a lot of ways our lives were hard, but we used to look on the bright side and…"

"Look, Mum, just stop preaching at me, OK? I bet you can't remember what it felt like to be seventeen."

"That's simply not true Tanya, I…"

"You don't know anything about my problems." There is a panther right in front of you and you're so blind you don't even notice him.

Mum takes the inadvisable step of walking over the threshold of my sacred space, entering the hallowed ground of my room, and perching on the end of my bed; her bum is only inches away from the panther's claws.

"Would you like to talk to me about anything, Tanya?"

I shake my head.

"So what's wrong?"

Mum's question hangs in the darkness of my room. The black threads of my discontent and the red threads of my sadness also hang across the room and weave themselves into a spider's web that envelopes me and constricts my breathing, the silken ropes strong, pulling taut around me. I don't know where to begin so I say nothing.

"Look Tanya, I'm not as out of touch as you might imagine." Mum says. "And despite what you think, I was a teenager once too."

"I used to sit at home for days waiting for the phone to ring too."

"Did you?" I can't imagine this. Mum was so beautiful when she was young. I wish I looked like her.

"Of course I did. And the boys I liked never called me, and the boys I couldn't stand used to come round with flowers."

"Why don't we go out for lunch and I'll tell you about this boy who used to be sweet on me who we called 'Just Passing'?"

"OK," I say, even though I can't imagine ever having the strength to drag myself out of bed, wash my face, clean my teeth and get dressed.

"Here," Mum throws me a pair of knickers and a pair of socks with Tigger bouncing across them.

Mum used to call me Tigger because of my natural exuberance and bounce. This makes me laugh now, or cry. I'm not sure which. How can I have lost my whole personality? How can I have become a different person? I push the panther away.

He takes the hint, leaps off my bed and bounds to the corner of my room where he curls up on a pile of clothes, his chin resting on his front paws, eyes closed. His whiskers quivering, he pricks his ears: still but alert to the smallest movement. I pull the underwear Mum found on under my duvet and smear some roll-on deodorant over the crusty white coating that yesterday's and the day before's has formed under my arms.

"Why don't you put some bright make-up on and brush your hair?" Mum says, pacing around my room, as always, unable to keep still, unable to waste a moment when she could be doing something: tidying up, organising things, achieving something.

"You'll feel better if you make an effort to look less of a fright." Mum says; folding up the T-shirts that are lying on my floor and putting them back in their drawer.

"I won't."

Sometimes I want to hit my Mum. She always knows exactly the wrong thing to say, the perfect worst thing that will make me feel the most awful about everything.

"Well can't you just try it for once? Have you never considered that maybe I know more than you do about some things?"

I say nothing but I pull on my black flares and a brightly coloured top as a concession to Mum.

"You look lovely, darling." Mum says. "Where would you like to go for lunch?"

Somewhere where no-one will see me, somewhere where I can fade into the background and all Mum's friends from the tennis club won't be lurking with their hair-extensions, nail-extensions and lap-dogs. I hate Chihuahuas and terriers and all small hairy dogs. I hate those ones that are basically little sofas with legs – Scotties is it? The weight of living in this village presses down on me: this place where I can't avoid bumping into friends or acquaintances, at every turn – where I can't go to the pharmacy without the chemist telling Lily's Mum the Doctor that I've bought some thrush pessaries.

We end up in a restaurant in Primrose Hill which is far enough away from our usual stomping ground for there to be no one we know there. I'm still feeling sick with worry and terror but at least not paranoid that all my friends' mums and Mum's friends are watching me.

The panther has materialised in the corner of the restaurant, his amber eyes reproachful. He lies on his belly, his head resting on his front paws. The waiters bend round him as they bustle in and out of the kitchen, balancing plates of steaming food all the way up their arms in a manner that should be impossible: just as bumblebees should be too heavy to fly on their tiny, delicate wings and no-one knows how they do it.

"What do you want to eat, sweetie?"

I stare at the menu, the letters jumble, dance in meaningless sequences, wobble.

"I'm not sure."

"I'm going to have the Salad Nicoise. What about the Imam Bayaldi? You like aubergines. Or some falafel and hummus? Or some stuffed vine leaves?" The plethora of options makes me feel sick. Just choose me something, Mum. Just make the decision for me. I am incapable of making the choice myself.

"Could I just have a Greek Salad and some pitta bread?"

"No, you're going to have some proper food. You're wasting away. Have the aubergine and the Greek Salad."

Mum orders and eventually our lunch arrives. I pick at my food, eating the bits of cucumber and the red onions.

"I'm not cross with you." Mum says. "I just want to know what's going on."

"Nothing."

"That's not true, sweetie. I'm worried. Something's happened to you. Has something happened at school?" She gazes at me with a concerned expression.

"No."

"Are you being bullied?"

"Of course not."

"Is it to do with that boy?"

"No."

"If you won't talk to me about it, would you like to talk to someone else?"

"No."

"Well, you're going to, because we can't go on like this. It might help, talking to someone about it. And why aren't you eating?"

"Not hungry."

"Have a glass of wine. It's lovely."

I sip the wine; it tastes of metal to me though. Mum reaches her hand out and strokes the back of my hand and we sit there, sipping the wine, staring into the restaurant. I gaze at the other customers: laughing, talking, out for their normal Sunday lunches. I bet they have not got severe hallucination problems and feel so miserable they are unable to...

"Arabella, you're not having any tiramisu until you have finished your fettuccini," the mother at the next table says to her small child, a pretty blonde tot with waist-length curls and tomato sauce smeared all over her face.

"When you were little, sweetie," Mum says. "You would fall over and I would pick you up and cuddle you and kiss it better. I wish it was that easy now, and I feel so powerless sometimes that Mummy can't just make the pain go away. But if you talk to me I might be able to help."

I look at Mum. She does seem to want to help me, but I can't find the words to explain to her what's wrong.

"I'm scared."' I say. "I think I've got something wrong with my brain." A tear rolls down my cheek.

"I'm taking you to the Doctor." Mum says. "Don't worry sweetie, we'll get to the bottom of this."

"So who was 'Just Passing'?" I ask, not because I'm interested but just to change the subject from my imminent death from a degenerative brain disease.

"Well, when I was sixteen, before I met your Dad, there was a boy called Alvin who went to your Uncle's school and lived down our road...."

Chapter 16

"GOOD MORNING TANYA, good morning Mrs Marshall," the psychiatrist says.

"Good morning Dr Stein." We reply at the same time.

I think Mum is at my appointment with me so she can tell Dr Stein her observations on my behaviour. He is sitting on one side of a coffee table in an armchair, and we are next to each other on a sofa on its other side. My GP doesn't sit in an armchair, he sits behind a desk. This is the first difference. Also the office is plusher, larger, lighter and better situated. The walls are lined with books about different mental disorders: *Understanding Schizophrenia* jostles with *Overcoming Borderline Personality Disorder*, *An Unquiet Mind* rests next to *The Flight Of the Mind: Virginia Woolf's Art and Manic Depressive Illness*. I hope I haven't got schizophrenia, I think. I must not under any circumstances mention the panther who is sitting next to me, on the floor, nuzzling my hand. I don't want to be locked up for being mental.

"How are you, Tanya?" he asks.

"OK." I say.

"Pleased to meet you," he says, and smiles at me. "Don't be frightened. I'm going to help you. So, Graham referred you to me?" He says.

I'm confused for a minute, then I realise he means my GP, Dr Graham Porter, and nod. He glances at the letter. I try to read it upside down, something I'm good at, but he catches my eye and angles the letter away from me. It's taken a month to get an appointment with the eminent Dr Stein – we saw our GP in January and it's now nearly the end of February.

I watch him as he reads. He's an attractive man, Dr Joshua Stein, with his luxuriant chocolate brown wavy hair and large blue eyes fringed with dark lashes. He looks more like an aftershave advert than a psychiatrist. He's a lot younger than I expected as well: I assumed he'd be prehistoric with a white beard, and while he's obviously ancient (about 35 at a guess), he's younger than Dad.

I'm glad he's not a woman. It'd be too weird talking to a woman. All middle-aged women remind me of my mother, and if I wanted to talk to Mum I'd talk to her. I peek at Mum now to see what she thinks of him, and see her gazing at him and – eugh I don't believe it – she's flirting with him. Stop it mother! He's mine. Get your own you raddled old tart! She is so embarrassing. I watch her smoothing down her skirt that is unsuitably short for one of her advanced years and stroking her thigh and…. no, this is disgusting.

He turns his gaze on me and he's got a twinkle in his eye and I get a strong sense then that it's going to be OK, that he's going to save me, that he's on my side.

"Mrs Marshall," He says to Mum.

"Yes?" Mum replies, widening her eyes and looking at him whilst batting her eyelashes.

"I would like to talk to Tanya alone please."

"Oh." She says, disappointed.

"Would it be possible for you to wait next door?"

"Of course." Mum replies, shooting a warning gaze at me as she flounces out.

"So, Tanya," he says once we are alone. "How are you?"

"Miserable," I reply.

"I am sorry."

"It's not your fault."

"I'm sorry I couldn't fit you in earlier."

"I'm sure you've got lots of other patients."

"Yes. There's a lot of unhappiness around. When did you first start experiencing these periods of low mood?" He asks.

"About six months ago."

"And how many times since?" He says, his pen hovering above the paper.

"Five, about one a month. They seem to be quite regular."

"Has something happened? Have you broken up with a boyfriend?"

"About nine months ago," I say.

He scribbles something down in his notebook with his fountain pen.

"Are you having problems at school?"

"No. School is OK."

"Are you being bullied?"

"No."

"How are you sleeping, Tanya?"

"About 7 hours a night unless I'm miserable, when I wake up about 3 or 4 and get back to sleep about 5 and sleep for another few hours."

"And how do you feel when you wake up?"

"I wake up exhausted and think 'I can't believe I'm still alive', I dread the day ahead and have this terrible sense of foreboding."

It's embarrassing to formulate my darkest thoughts into words like this and to bare my soul to a stranger.

"How is your appetite in these periods?"

"I'm not hungry and everything tastes of metal."

"Are you socialising, still keeping up with your friends?"

"A bit. Not as much as I used to. I had a big argument with my best friend. We've made up now though."

"I'm glad to hear it."

"I thought that making up with my best friend would make me feel better, but it hasn't, not really." I say.

"I'm sorry about that." He says. "Are you exercising? Exercise can do a lot to lift a low mood."

"No. Not really, apart from dancing and a bit of walking."

"Do you have suicidal thoughts?"

"No," I reply after a pause.

I look out of the window at the bare branches of the trees slashing the sky. It is snowing. Snow falls and settles on the trees: icing on the cake of the world. There is a robin on the windowsill, head cocked, looking in, its chest a gash against the snow.

"How long do these periods of low mood last?" Dr Stein calls me back from the window.

"About ten days, well, between seven and ten days."

"Do you feel that everything is hopeless, that things will never get any better?"

"Yes."

"Are you able to get pleasure from activities you normally enjoy?"

"No."

"How is your concentration?"

"Um, not as good as it was, shot to pieces, I can't stick at anything for more than a few minutes."

"And how good is your memory?"

"I used to have a photographic memory but I can't remember very much at all any more."

"Do you ever feel anxious, frightened or panicky?"

"Yes, um, a bit, sometimes."

"Do you cut yourself?"

"No." I leave out the ruthless plucking of every hair on my underarms and bikini line and the peeling of the skin round my fingers, it doesn't count. He doesn't need to know about this. That stuff is private.

"Do you keep yourself clean when you're low?"

"Well, I clean my teeth but I find it hard to wash my hair. It seems too much effort to go in the bath and I get scared of the shower."

He sucks the end of his pen.

"Have you ever taken drugs?" He says.

I fidget, ripping the tissue into strips and winding the strips round my bleeding thumb.

"No, definitely not."

"Do you smoke?"

"No, I've never smoked."

He looks at me, raising an eyebrow, but doesn't say anything.

"Drink alcohol?"

"Yes."

"How many units per week?"

"Ten." I say, halving the number and then halving it again.

I am trying to tell him the truth, as much as I can; obviously leaving out the pills and the panther because the last thing I want is for him to think I'm a schizophrenic junkie and he listens, really listens, in a way that none of my friends have. And he's not patronising.

My attention wanders around the room – to the photos of two gorgeous children, presumably his sons and a woman with fluffy hair and too much lipstick and blue eye-shadow – presumably Mrs Stein.

"Well, we seem to have run out of time," he says, looking at the clock. "I'd like you to keep a mood diary for me, Tanya, and let's see what your mood patterns are over the next few weeks. I'll see you next week."

"What do you think is wrong with me?" I ask.

"I can't diagnose you immediately," he says. "I will need to observe your behaviour over a period of time."

I walk back into the waiting room where Mum is sitting doing the Times crossword. She looks up.

"So?" She asks. "How was it?"

"He's nice." I reply.

We get into the car to drive home.

"He's lovely, Dr Josh, isn't he?" I say to Mum.

"Lovely. Such an intelligent man. And gorgeous looking."

"He's a bit young for you" I point out. "He's young enough to be your son."

"No he is not, Tanya. He is at most five years younger than me which is perfectly… How dare you…"

Yeah, right. That would make Mum about 40, which she is not. She is 47.

"Anyway, I think he's going to help us." She says.

"So, sweetie pie," Mum says, as we sit in the kitchen chopping cauliflower and sweeping it off the chopping board into a casserole dish about 3 months after my first appointment with Dr Josh. "What would you like for lunch? We are having lamb."

"Bread and cheese?"

"Let's go to the farmer's market after your appointment with Dr Josh then."

"How many more appointments is it going to take before he gives me some drugs? I've been seeing him for 3 months." I burst out in frustration.

"You've only seen him five times. Putting drugs into the teenage brain is risky because it's still forming." She wipes her hands on her apron and takes it off.

I cringe inside.

"Let's go. We mustn't be late."

"Well, Tanya, your symptoms would indicate that you're suffering from depression." Dr. Stein says as we sit in his office.

"So why aren't I depressed all the time then?"

"Most people aren't. It's normal to have periods of depression interspersed with periods of normal mood. You seem to me to be exhibiting the symptoms of atypical depression."

"What's that?"

"It's a form of major depression that differs from melancholic depression in that patients react positively to external events and experience recurrent episodes of depressed mood, rather than being depressed all the time."

This is what it sounds like he says, anyway. Or maybe this is just what I read somewhere afterwards. All the words jumble up, fall over each other, it's too much to take in.

"So, I'm going to start you on an antidepressant and we'll see if that levels your mood out. Let's try Prozac."

My head is reeling with all this. Surely I don't need to go on antidepressants. Surely I'm just growing up, it's just a phase, and it'll sort itself out. But at the same time, I'm relieved: that there is something wrong with me and I'm not imagining it, that Dr Stein is going to fix it, he believes me and takes me seriously.

And it's cool anyway; to be on Prozac is seriously hardcore. And I like taking drugs. I'm a proper nutter now though, and I smile at this. My friends are going to think I'm so cool now I've got a psychiatrist. I don't think that Mum sees it like this though. She grips my hand and looks anxious and distressed.

"So, Dr Stein,"

"Call me Joshua." He says, smiling at Mum.

"So, Joshua," Mum smirks. "How common is it, atypical depression?"

"Oh, very common."

"Why don't I know anyone with it?" She says.

"You probably do."

"Right, we're going to start you on 30mg of Prozac a day and I'll see you in two weeks and see how you're doing. Then we'll probably put your dose up to 60mg a day." He writes out the prescription with his fountain pen. "If you hand this into the surgery Graham will sort you out with an NHS prescription."

"How long will it take, before it starts working?" Mum asks. "We really can't go on like this."

"Well, it varies. I'm starting Tanya on a sub-therapeutic dose in case she has a reaction to it. If she doesn't find any problems with the drug we'll put the dose up after two weeks, when you next come to see me. After that it will take between 4 to 6 weeks for the drug to kick in, but it could be anything up to three months before you see a significant improvement in her mood."

"But I can't wait three months." I blurt out.

"These things take time, Tanya, I'm sorry."

Three months. That's three more stretches of depression, three more weeks, possibly even thirty more days of feeling desperately unhappy.

"It's OK sweetie, we're going to get through this." Mum puts her arm round my shoulders and I lean into her.

"Thank you, Dr Stein. We look forward to seeing you in two weeks time." Mum says. "Come on sweetie."

Dr Josh squeezes my hand.

"Thank you, Dr Stein." Mum says again and for a minute I think she's going to burst into tears.

In the car on the way home I feel so much relief that I'm getting some medicine that will sort me out. I know it will.

"It's going to be alright now though, Mum, isn't it?"

"Yes, of course it is sweetie. I'm sure the worst is behind us now."

She doesn't sound sure though, she sounds terrified, but I pretend I don't notice this and we both smile forced smiles and stare straight ahead. I think about how I'm going to have some terrible accident and fall into a coma and Dr Stein is going to sit at my hospital bed and hold my hand and bring me back to life and realise that he is meant to be with me.

Chapter 17

"How much of a nightmare was that paper?" Emily says, screwing her eyes up. "Didn't you think the general Shakespeare question was impossible and…"

"No way! Seriously? The general one was really easy." I splutter as a few drops of Cava slide down my chin.

It's June and we've just finished our AS exams. I hope champagne won't stop the Prozac working. I've been taking my medication for 6 weeks now and so far I haven't had any side-effects.

"You're joking, right, T? It was way harder than any of the practice papers. I didn't know which question to do at all." She shakes her head and peers into her Buck's fizz. "There's an animal in my drink as well. Come on little chap."

She slides her propelling pencil down inside the glass. The fly grasps the pencil and starts to make his way up it, shaking the liquid out of his wings.

"We've pretty much done 'pathetic fallacy and wind on the moors' before really though." I point out, watching the fly – who is now sitting on the rim of Emily's polystyrene cup, rubbing his front feet together to dry them: a Bond Street jeweller on Valentine's Day.

"Is that what it was asking? Shit, I thought it was something about Gloucester and Kent and…" She shakes her head and strokes a loose tendril of pink hair behind her ear.

"Well it's English Literature isn't it? That's the whole point of it. You can write whatever you want really, as long as you make a proper argument and back it up with lots of quotes…"

"Yeah, but it was still ridiculously hard and…"

"Why didn't you do the open book question then?" I ask her. I don't know what she's talking about – this was by far the easiest of all our exams.

"Are you joking? Did you even look at that piece of prac crit and… oh whatever, Tanya. You're so annoying. You've totally rinsed it. You always do this. You always get As and best-marks-in-the-year and…"

I gaze beyond her: out over the lacrosse pitches, past the flock of Canada geese pecking round the hurdles, and up at the white Georgian façade of school.

Blocking out Emily's moans about the exam, I smile to myself. As well as my solid *King Lear* question I've written an inspired essay about *The Wife of Bath*, and a pretty watertight answer for the question on Fleur Adcock's house martin poem.

'House Martins' was Robbie's and my poem. Well, we didn't read it together or anything, and in fact he never knew that it was our special poem, but I did. Every time I read it I think of Robbie and his house martins and us and I feel that sentimental sniffly nostalgia, which is the sort of sadness that I like. Anyway, there is nothing to be miserable about now. I'm going to get an A in English. In fact, judging by the way all the exams have gone, I'm going to get straight As.

As I look up at the candyfloss wisps of cloud whipping the sky, I notice that I feel, well, normal actually: my old self, the me that I was before anything happened. The summer fans out: a peacock's tail, iridescent. As I down my drink I realize that -all of a sudden – I'm looking forward to everything: the summer; our final year of school next year; not being depressed any more. I just feel so alive. I feel like me again at last.

"You coming to Magic later, Lily?" Emily demands.

"Yeah, course." Lily says. She's tucking into a chocolate mini-roll.

"So am I." I can't wait to get back to Magic and see everyone and celebrate.

"Wow, that's cool, T. You haven't come to Magic for months. It'll be so fab for us all to go together again." Emily says.

It's a sunny day, and the leaves and flowers glow more intensely than I've ever seen them. The colours all look so bright. They throb and pulse in the sunlight with the coruscating brilliance of acid visuals. This must be a 'natural high', I think. Twinges of excitement rush up my legs and into my thighs, like I'm on a pill.

I look around for my panther but he's not here, and that's weird because this is just the sort of event he likes – a garden party on a sunny day where he can sunbathe and watch the Canada geese waddling and honking over the lacrosse pitches and stalk them a bit.

"Hey, T, look what I've got," Lily whispers as we lock our cubicle door in the loo at Magic. The club's busy tonight with the end-of-exams, and the air hums with the excitement of being-about-to-take-drugs. I nod; I'm already restless and anticipating getting mashed. In fact, I already feel mashed.

"What sort are they?" I ask Lily. "Let me see."

I wonder for a fleeting second whether I should mix pills with Prozac and then push that thought to the back of the enchanted wardrobe of my mind and shut the door, turn the key and walk out of the room.

"Dolphins," she whispers; uncurling her fingers so I can make out the tiny dolphins imprinted on the white background.

Dolphins are some of my favourite ones but I wish the manu-facturers coated them in gelatine or sugar so they'd taste a bit better.

It's horrible when they start crumbling and the bitter taste overwhelms your whole mouth. In fact, sugar-coated pills would be perfect.

"Wow, dolphins are fab aren't they? The last time we did dolphins we were really fucked." I whisper back.

There are no security guards around the loo at the moment but one could pop out of the woodwork at any moment, by which time we really need to have necked everything we've got.

"I reckon they're nearly as good as swans."

"But swans are a nightmare to get hold of these days." Lily says, as if we've been dropping pills for about forty years rather than eighteen months or so.

She digs her heels into the wall and slides her bum down it so she's sitting on her heels. Her metallic silver skirt scrapes against the steel cubicle and produces a loud squeak which makes us giggle, and then put our hands over our mouths because we're not meant to be in the same cubicle as each other.

In my diary I always note down which pills we've done each night, so I can work out which are the strongest, which ones we have the best experiences on, which are the most uplifting, which are the ones that leave us paralysed and dribbling in the corner of the room, that kind of thing. This pill tastes horrible but so strong that it's great and I shouldn't be doing it but this is it, isn't it. I've got to make up for this whole year of not going out, not doing anything, being too scared to go anywhere.

We leave the loo and walk over to the second dance floor upstairs.

Lily waves something in front of her: slicing the smoky air.

"What is it though? Keep it still and…" I swipe it from her.

"It's mine." She says. "I found it and…" She tries to grab it back but she's too late. I stare at it. It's the most perfect feather I've ever seen: a fake ostrich one that's fluorescent pink. I stare at the feather. The feather is pink and bright and it is meant for me: it is a sign of something.

"I can fly, look." I jump off the platform, feather in my mouth, and I really can fly. I am Dumbo fluttering down from the branch: feather in his trunk, sailing on his huge ears.

"I want a go." Lily clamours. She tries to reclaim the feather. "It's so not fair. I found it."

"Get off." I push her away and stroke the magic feather against my arm.

I gaze at myself in the mirror behind the stage. I look gorgeous: I have that glowing dishevelled Magic look. I've missed feeling beautiful.

All the energy that I've been suppressing for months is bubbling up. I'm wearing my violet Spank dress – the one with the silver eye across the chest – and my silver open-toed Ravel wedge heels. Lily's found Emily and they're snorting poppers together on the dance floor. I stroke my arm with the feather and I know I'm properly up now because the muscles in my arm rear up to meet the feather and my skin starts to tingle.

I'd like to find Seb and Ben and that lot, and I can't see them, but then I spot my old flame James walking towards me with a fluffy duck on a string round his neck. This is brilliant.

"Hi, Tanya. You look cute. Say hello to Mr Duck." He says, pushing his shiny dark dead straight hair away from his eyes and putting the duck up to my cheek. He always looks yummy.

"Hello, Mr Duck." I say.

"Hello, Tanya." Mr Duck says, his bill opening showing me a big pink tongue. I always forget that birds have tongues.

"Wow, he can actually talk." I say.

James gives me a funny look. His huge green eyes widen and even though his pupils take over much of his eyes I can still see bright green around the edges of them.

"No he can't. You must be absolutely battered." James says.

"Yeah, I am."

"You still look hot though." He says.

He leans down to put his hand on my waist – he's about 6 foot 3 – and guides me towards the side of the room. It's so nice to see him; I haven't seen him for ages. We squeeze into one of the cages. There is a pause. Then he moves his face towards mine and nuzzles my lips and his stubble is scratchy and his tongue is quite nice and firm and I close my eyes. I relax into the snog and…

"Tanya, come on we've got to go." A voice hisses in my ear.

I start and open my eyes. Lily. Damn. She shoots James one of her most evil stares and grabs my arm.

"What are you doing?" She hisses as she pulls me towards the cloakroom. "He's like a million years old and….oh, never mind."

She looks pissed off that James prefers me – even though she has no interest in him – that Greg's passed out on a beanbag with dribble trickling from the corner of his mouth and he looks like the goofy fool that he is. We emerge into the morning. Well, it's not morning, it's about 4am.

I stand with Lily waiting for the others. Outside the back entrance of the club the cobbles are slimy – it's been raining – and there is pigeon poo down the walls of the tunnels and tramps lying in the gutter. The club's closing and we have to go somewhere.

"D'you wanna go to Paul's cafe?" Lily says.

"Maybe." I'm not sure. It might be nice to just go and hang out at Lily's – her parents are away so we'll have the house to ourselves.

"Hey." Em tumbles out of the club.

"Do you want to go to Paul's then?" Lily asks her.

Emily bites her lip, thinking.

"Nah. Let's go back to Lily's." She says.

So we catch a cab to hers: the three of us and it's so fab to be together, and to watch the city whiz past us as we speed towards Lily's house and bed and the rest of our lives.

Chapter 18

"TEA?" LILY SAYS AS WE SIT at her house, smoking and watching the TV with the sound off so we can listen to the Magic Realms album at the same time.

"Coffee please." I reply, and turn back to the TV.

Emily and Lily look at me with don't-you-want-to-go-to-sleep-in-a-minute faces.

"Aren't you sleepy?" Lily says. "I'm sooooooooo shattered."

"Me too." Says Em. "Why've you got so much energy, T? And why are you walking in zoo-tiger-with-a-disorder circles around the room?"

"I'm not." I say, my jaw grinding.

"And why are you shaking?"

"Am I?"

"Look at your hand."

I look at my hand and there's a severe tremor going on.

"Maybe I've got St Vitus dance? Or Parkinson's?" I suggest.

"Yeah, maybe." Emily says, looking at me with an odd level of intensity, even for her.

Her gaze travels from my face down to my hands, down my legs and then up again, as if she's a boy checking me out. Weird.

"But that wouldn't explain why you're talking so fast." She says after a pause.

"Am I?"

"Yeah, and your speech is slurred, and…. Shit, what if you're about to die like that girl in the paper last year and…"

"Stoppit. Maybe I just did more pills than you two and…"

"How many'd you do?" Emily asks.

I count on my fingers. "One with Lily, then one with James, then… actually that's it. How many'd you two do then?"

"One with you," Lily says. "One with Neil. Yeah, that's it. Em?"

"One with Ian. One with Wendy," Emily says. "So, we necked two each then. So, maybe your one you did with James was a better one than our second ones, T." She looks irritated.

"Heh, well done me for snogging the better dealer." I say, turning back to the TV.

The TV is showing children at a zoo. They are outside the glass of a tiger's enclosure. He comes right up to the glass and stares at the children with his huge amber eyes.

"Lunch," he says. "If there wasn't this screen protecting you from me then you would be toast."

That is a strange expression for him to use, I think. He is a tiger, he doesn't eat toast. He wouldn't know what toast was, and even if he did he wouldn't eat it. And then I realise that it's strange that I can understand what he's saying. And then I realise that I have special powers. I am Dr Doolittle or Francis of Assisi. The tiger opens his mouth, showing his huge teeth and an enormous slab of pink tongue. His whiskers quiver with the effort of his yawn. He turns away and walks along the line of the enclosure, rubbing the glass with one side of his body and holding his tail up in the air.

"Yeah, OK. Milk 'n' two sugars." Emily says. "And is there any chocolate?"

"How can you be hungry when we've been doing pills all night?" Lily asks in her you-are-so-annoying-with-your-I-eat-lard-and-don't-exercise-but-remain-a-size-six voice. No one else I know has sugar in their tea, apart from our builders.

"I'm gonna crash." Lily says – and for a second I see Lily in some crazy sports car smashing into a tree even though she's sitting on the floor of her living room – but she drags herself up and off to bed. I sit there sipping my tea and staring at Emily who is staring at the TV with her mouth open and a glazed expression.

"OK, I'm gonna hit the sack." Emily says, picking up her sweater and her trainers and moving towards the stairs.

"I'm so not tired though." I say.

"I'm knackered." She says. "See you in the morning."

I can't sleep, I'm too excited about, well, everything I suppose. As I'm sitting on the loo I realise that Lily's bathroom needs tidying so I start to arrange the bottles of bubble bath in colour and height order and pour half-empty ones into each other and throw out the empty ones. Then I wash up everything in the kitchen, load and run the dishwasher and rearrange everything in the fridge. I have a bath, wash my hair, tidy the bathroom again and tidy Lily's brother Mike's room.

Eventually, the sun rises and it's a gorgeous hot sunny day. I just want the others to wake up so I can have some company. I drag some sofa cushions out into the garden and lie there in my underwear soaking up the rays and watching the ants carry leaves and going about their business. I need to move though. There's so much to do, so much to organise. I don't understand how the others can still be sleeping

At last Lily wanders into the garden, wearing an old Smashing Pumpkins T-shirt and knickers and rubbing her eyes.

"T, what are you doing up so early? It's like 8 o'clock. And why aren't you wearing any clothes? It's not even hot."

"Aren't you excited?" The sun throbs and the leaves and flowers pulse, breathing.

"About what?"

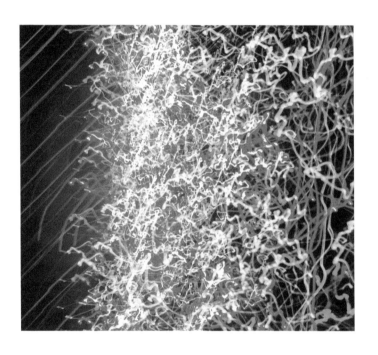

"Everything." A ray of sunlight lights up her hair from the back – a halo. She stands there with the hem of her oversize T-shirt grazing the top of her thighs and a ring of light pulsing out of her head and she's an angel. She thinks, furrowing her forehead.

"Um, no, not really. I've definitely screwed up my exams; I've got no money to do anything. What are you so excited about then?" She looks at me.

"It's the end of term, it's the summer holiday, it's…" I break off because there's so much that I'm excited about.

I look around the garden – at the writhing flowers and branches and singing blades of grass which sway under the weight of the insects. I rest my chin on my hands so the tips of the blades are at eye level and I can stare through a grass curtain. At the back, by the fence, there might be a rhino or a lion or…

"I'm going back to bed." Lily says. "It's too early." She wanders back inside, her T-shirt riding up so I can see her black g-string poking out.

I know Lily's kitchen almost as well as my own. I run inside to put the kettle on, and peer into the fridge, looking for something to cook. There isn't much in there. I reckon that Lily's spent the money that her parentals gave her for food on drugs instead. There are a few eggs squatting in there though. I pull them out and start cracking them into a bowl and whisking them with a fork because omelettes are going to be the best thing to cook. Some of the egg gets out and sprays over the hob and sizzles as it hits the blue flame that I've already switched on which crackles and roars.

Wake up, wake up, wake up everyone. It's so irritating that no-one wants to play. It's unbelievable that they can be so boring.

"What's that smell, T?" Lily stands at the door. "What's going on?" She stares at the bubbling pan.

"Omelettes, breakfast, ummmm….?"

"It's a bit messy though. What's all that…" She points at the egg white puddle.

"Some of the egg got out." I say.

The egg oozes.

I walk around the kitchen, cleaning plates, loading the dishwasher. I just want everything in the world to be ordered and perfect like my thoughts.

"Hey girls." Em says as she stumbles into the kitchen, mascara smudged on her cheeks and last night's silver glitter hanging around her eyebrows.

"What's with the breakfast?"

"Tanya cooked."

"Seriously?"

"You're on good form, T." Emily says. "It's great, you just seem so much happier. Why don't you sit down though? We can wash up and stuff later."

"So, what happened with James last night then?" She asks me, buttering her toast.

"Well, he introduced me to his duck, and then suddenly we're snogging!" I say.

"Wow!" Emily sounds impressed, despite herself. James is amazingly gorgeous after all.

"But then, just as things are getting interesting, Lily demands that we leave."

"Bet she's just jealous."

"That is so not fair! I'm just worried that T's going to get herself in trouble. He's like ancient, and he's such a sleazebag. He's got at least two girlfriends, and they're both pregnant."

"You're so annoying

"Stop attacking me you bitches! Enough already."

I exchange conspiratorial glances with Emily. The trouble with

Lily is that she's just so easy to gang up on, and her motives are so transparent. She really is her own worst enemy. And her feathers have been ruffled by my remarkable successes of last night. She's meant to be the irresistible one, but I seem to be taking over from her at the moment.

"Doorbell!" screeches Emily running to the door.

It's Lee and Ben.

"Hello boys. Do you want some breakfast? Lily, we seem to have run out of eggs…one minute while I send Emily to the corner shop for some supplies." I tell the boys.

"You're very chirpy this morning, Tanya." Ben observes.

He's not, of course. He gets terrible insomnia when he's stressed and consequently hasn't slept all the way through study leave and exams. There are huge dark patches under his eyes and his hands are shaking, he looks like a panda with Parkinson's.

"How was last night?" Lee asks. He is wearing his 'Masturbation Makes You Blind' T-shirt with the faint fuzzy letters.

"Fab," Lily exclaims.

"Amazing. What'd you lot get up to?" I ask, although I can guess the answer.

"Well, we just went to the pub for a quiet one and had a smoke at Lee's and watched TV."

"So, we thought we might go down to Apocalypse tonight. You lot up for it?"

"Yeah, definitely!' I haven't been to Apocalypse for about 9 months, but I want to go out dancing every night now our exams are finished.

"Why are you twitching?" Ben asks me.

"I'm not."

"Yeah, you are. Look at your leg."

I look down at my leg. I suppose it is wobbling a bit. Must be an involuntary muscle spasm, I think.

"Lily? You coming to Apocalypse later?" Ben asks in a faux-casual way, gazing at her Smashing Pumpkins T-shirt, which hovers just below her pubic bone.

Lily shakes her head.

"Honeys, I'm home." Emily says as she walks into the kitchen with a box of eggs.

"I've just got to phone Mum." I say.

"The phone's in the hall." Lily replies.

It's an old Bakelite rotary dial one and it takes about six weeks to dial the number. I keep needing to start again when I don't turn the dial round enough, or don't push it hard enough and it swings back or whatever. Finally I get through and it rings for one ring and then…

"Hello?" Mum answers. She sounds worried.

"Mum, it's me."

"Tanya, where are you?" Her words come out, breathless.

"At Lily's. You know I'm here, I told you we were staying here and…"

"Come home immediately." She says in her you're-grounded-till-you're-93 voice."

"Her parents are away, I don't want to leave her…"

"Why don't you ask her if she wants to come to lunch then?" Mum asks. Somehow, she still hasn't noticed that there's link between me going clubbing, and me not being on top form at family lunch the next day, if it's a post-clubbing day when I can force any food down that is…

"I can't. We're going swimming and then we're going to the theatre this afternoon."

This is not entirely true, but it will be more appealing to Mum than: 'We're sunbathing and then we're going clubbing and taking pills again.'

Chapter 19

"WHY DIDN'T WE BOOK TICKETS?" I ask Ben as we turn the corner into the street where Apocalypse is, and catch our first glimpse of the queue.

It snakes round the corner and out onto the main road behind the club, and is about 4 or 5 people deep. We join it at the back. We are not in the guest list queue, or the ticket queue. I feel suddenly wrongly dressed in my long violet tie-dyed dress with the hole in the middle.

All the other girls are wearing khaki combats and black vest-tops and trainers, with their hair dreaded or scraped back into high ponytails. They're drinking Smirnoff Ices and WKDs and smoking. I touch my moussed and glittery curls and feel both young and conspicuous.

"Is Seb coming?" I ask Ben, trying to sound casual and not too hopeful.

"Nah, he's gone on holiday."

Ben is wearing a black Lacoste polo shirt with his Moschino logo trousers. The trousers are properly disgusting, especially when they are worn with his Levis belt.

"Already? Exams have only just finished."

Bugger, I won't be seeing him. I'd just assumed that he'd be here tonight.

"Where's he gone?"

"To his house in San Diego."

"How come he's got…"

"His parentals are loaded." Ben says, with satisfaction.

I don't know why he sounds so pleased – it's not as if he's going to marry Seb or anything.

"ID?" The bouncer asks me when we make it to the front of the queue after what seems like six weeks.

He is a properly big, scary Incredible Hulk of a bouncer with holes in his ears the size of loo rolls and a pierced nasal septum and that bit at the top of his nose pierced as well. I hand him my ISIC card with a shaking hand – I look way younger than most people in the queue.

He raises a pierced eyebrow at me, but says: "Go through and over to the female security guard, over there." He points to the right hand side of the club entrance, his jowls wobbling.

I hobble over there on my silver Ravel wedges and lift my arms up so the security guard can feel in my sleeves, around my waist and the sides of my pants and up my thighs. I experience an unexpected rush to feel someone's hand so close to my crotch. I haven't got any pockets in my dress obviously.

"Open your bag please." She demands, scowling.

I unzip the main pocket of my bag, and all the side pockets. My plastic baggie of pills is stashed in my knickers where no one will find it.

"That's fine, you can go in. Cloakroom is to your left"

She looks bored and pissed off, as I'm sure I would if I was doing her job – watching rich kids waltz into her club to get wasted. Clasping the banister, I step down the UV lit stairs into the bowels of the club. It opens its jaws to swallow me and I'm sucked down its throat to its stomach. I stand at the bottom of the stairs waiting for the boys, tapping my foot, jiggling my leg. I'm not sure where all this energy is coming from but it throbs through me as the beats thump from the banging sound system. It's not the warm orange fluffy lift I felt at magic yesterday – it's a dark cloud edged with navy blue.

It's far darker and gloomier at Apocalypse than it is at Magic Realms, and smaller, hotter and more intense. The crowd are older and moodier; the music's harder and less uplifting. It feels like a much more serious, cerebral clubbing experience. I guess that's why the music's called 'intelligent' drum 'n' bass. There's nothing intelligent about the trance they flood us with at Magic. It's the mind versus the heart. The sound system is fantastic, really kicking, and we're in the cramped second room, the Lounge. The bass line thuds up through the floor and almost knocks us out, our ears throb, my brain thuds.

"Poppers?" Lee says, handing me the tiny glass bottle. I cover one nostril and snort the fumes with the other one, and then change nostrils and repeat. The amyl nitrate hits my brain and my head buzzes and pounds: it's about to explode – but then the effect wears off and I have to do it again. The lines of the club are black and metallic silver – there are no fluoro drapes or paintings of unicorns, forests or fairies. I slide a hand down the gap between the top of my dress and its skirt and into my knickers, fish out a pill and swallow it.

Ben's off pawing random girls on the other side of the Lounge; he's concentrating his attentions on one particular chick and bribing her with pills. I realise that none of my girls are here, it's just me and the boys, which is fine, but I miss Lily and Emily. It's alright hanging out with the boys but I really need to be able to dissect the night afterwards with my girls: who snogged whom, who wore what, who was there and so on. I stare up at the ceiling where the metal pipes are exposed and lean against the concrete wall, watching people dance with the jerky marionette movements that you have to do to stay with the four to the floor beats. Then I walk over to the queue for the bar.

"Vodka and Red Bull please." I ask the barman when I reach the front of the queue. "Oh, and a bottle of Volvic please."

He gives me a supercilious look. He's a scowly probably East European specimen – Hungarian maybe, or Serbian or even Romanian – with jaundiced skin and messed up black hair. His arms are scrawny. He's a far cry from the oily-limbed-tight-white-vest-clad hotties that man the bar at Magic, which is to be expected at a club which is gay every night except on our Magic Realms Thursdays. This bloke doesn't look as if he takes it up the bum, listens to ABBA, or wears a pink feather boa, I think. A spasm travels up my legs and into my bum and then my crotch.

He pours the Red Bull into my drink. It hits the ice and runs down it in a tangerine waterfall – a chemically-infused mountain stream.

"That'll be £6.20," he says, slamming the plastic bottle of water down on the bar.

"Seriously?" The Red Bull spreads through the vodka, clouding it briefly and then dissolving in the alcohol.

"All the drinks are doubles and the water's £2.00."

"But I only asked for a single."

I hand over a £10 note, and stuff the change back into my tiny purse which hangs round my neck on a ribbon. It slices diagonally across my body, through my cleavage. I sip my drink and look around the club.

"Put your hands in the air, for the one, the only…. ANDY C." The announcement rings out through the club over the sound system.

The crowd goes mental – whooping and raising their hands in the air as one. But I notice that everyone is dancing in slow motion – frame by frame. The trademark Andy C bouncy beats kick in and I tap my foot and think about joining the heaving throng around the stage. The club is constructed in the round, with the stage in the middle of the dance floor which makes for a more intimate involving club experience.

I haven't seen my boys for most of the time that I've been here but I'm not feeling lonely or anything like that. On the contrary, I'm feeling totally connected to everyone in the club and everyone in the world.

Men with blank stares stand around the edges of the dance floor with their hands in the pockets of their puffa jackets, looking moody and obviously stoned out of their heads. Some of them are dealers – I can tell by the fact that they're drinking beer rather than water.

I don't know how they're not hot in here though – the hot lime green beams of the strobe lights fan out from behind the stage, blurring as they catch the smoke from the machine. Clouds of smoke envelope and hide the dancers on the floor. The low ceiling presses down on the crowd who are ants following the gods of drum 'n' bass.

There's a long queue for the girls' loo and a loo attendant, which means I'm gonna have to pay for doing a poo. This must be my coming-up poo: the one that slides out as the pill kicks in. I stare at the chessboard of tiles on the loo floor and their sides move in and out – breathing and they dance around each other. I wipe my bottom and drop a pound in the ashtray next to the sink, checking my make-up in the mirror. Everything has started to smudge in a sexy, smoky way. I dab some more glitter lip gloss on my lips and dust some silver moon dust over my eyelids.

"Hey, Tanya, there you are. I've been looking for you for absolutely yonks. Ben's gone off somewhere with this absolute minger." A posh voice says as I leave the loo to go back to the dance floor.

It's Lee, who looks quite cute tonight. He's already up: his jaw is grinding and his pupils are huge and black. After a while Lee drifts off and I'm on my own again and I just watch everyone in the club dancing and chatting and think this is amazing, I'm so happy just to be here, dancing and interacting normally with people.

"Hey, T, I'm going to go home with, um, er…" Ben says as he comes up behind me, holding the hand of a girl I don't recognise. He's smiling.

"Shelley." The girl says.

Blimey, it looks like he's actually succeeded for like the first time ever as well. I appraise her. She looks quite trashy, in her miniskirt, stacked Buffalos and one shoulder top. Whoever decided that one-shoulder tops are a good look must be blind.

She's not ugly, but definitely doesn't bear close inspection: bad skin, too much foundation, eyes like piss-holes in the sand, no bone structure to speak of. Anyway, I should be pleased for Ben that he may be about to get laid. More likely that she just wants him to give her some more free drugs though. Ben disappears with Shelley and her trashy mates.

The beams of the strobe lights cut the dry ice in front of me so that it shimmers green, red, gold and violet: a kaleidoscope of colours throb to the thud thud thud of the bass line. Rotating mirror balls hang from the ceiling and as they turn they throw intricate multicoloured patterns on the walls. There are letters in the shifting lights. They are spelling out a special message that only I can understand. I know the real reality. Now at last I understand what it all means. God is sending me messages in the strobe lights and everything is starting to become clear at last. Lee is going to be so excited when I explain the meaning of everything to him, I think, as I start to sway with my sinuous trance moves. I stand out against the drum 'n' bass automatons but this is how I like to express myself and I no longer care. The music rushes through me – I'm at one with it, and with everyone, and I'm shooting up above the clouds – a shooting star on my way to the sun.

Chapter 20

I WAKE UP, NAKED, in a large bed in a pokey room. There are no curtains, and light streams in through the slats of the blinds. My whole body itches. There don't seem to be any sheets either: I've been sleeping under an uncovered duvet, on a bare mattress. The room smells of stale beer and mouldy food. I can hear the sounds of traffic outside: horns hooting and engines revving and people shouting. Rubbing my sore eyes, I look around this room that I have never seen before. I'm still wearing last night's eye make-up. The mascara sticks my lashes together and as I rub my eyes the glitter comes off on my hand.

As I sit up I can feel that my thighs are bruised and sore. Images of a man with no face pushing me down on the bed flicker for a moment and then dissolve. I don't know whether this is something that has happened to me or if it's something that I've seen in a film. This is not a place where I want to be. There are jaws closing round my brain, crushing it. My brain pounds against my skull. Energy courses through me as if I'm coming up on a pill. I'm lying in this strange bed but I'm rushing and my jaw is going and my blood is pulsing. I chew the elastic of my star bead bracelet to calm myself down, but as my teeth grind against each other electricity shoots through my brain. Blue lightning flashes across the room.

My clothes are on the floor – tangled up with crushed beer cans, Chinese takeout cartons, overflowing ashtrays. Wrapping the duvet round me, I lean forward and pick up my clothes from the floor. My hands shake as I pull on my underwear and dress. There are stains all over my dress, like it's got mixed up with some soy sauce from one of the ageing takeaways. My hair smells of smoke, and so do my clothes, and this smell makes me feel sick.

Opening the blinds seems to take a very long time. At last, I stare out of the window over rooftops and inner-city streets. The buildings on the horizon wobble. My vision is blurred and the sides of the buildings pulse in and out and I don't know what to do. Mum is going to be so cross with me because I didn't call last night to tell her where I was staying. I haven't been home for days and days.

I focus on what I can remember. Last night I went to Apocalypse with Ben and Lee. Ben left us and went home with a random girl. Then I danced with Lee for a bit. There were messages for me in the lights. I must have gone home with someone but I don't know who. There doesn't seem to be anyone else here. I listen out for any sounds of another person, but there aren't any.

I have to get out. This man, whoever he is, could come back at any moment. I can't have consented to anything, or I don't remember consenting to anything, but I can feel that he has done things to me. This is not really happening. I have to get out as quickly and quietly as possible. I might be in danger and no-one knows where I am.

No-one knows where I am. No-one, apart from me and this man, knows what has happened to me. I don't have to tell anyone anything.

Carrying my shoes so as not to make a sound, I open the bedroom door and tiptoe down the stairs. As I open the door onto the street the sunlight sears my eyes. I don't recognize this neighbourhood. As I walk away from the house some memories start to push themselves forward. An image of driving back here with a man in a car and then… I want to forget what happened last night and never think about it ever again. I could say that I had a seizure at Apocalypse or a reaction to the pills which has wiped my memory. I can't tell Mum. Mum must not know what has happened.

If I go to the police then I don't have to go home yet. There must be a police station somewhere.

There is a phone box across the road. I pick up the receiver and punch 999. It is ringing.

"Police, fire or ambulance?" A voice says.

"Police." I say.

"Police." A voice says.

"I can't remember anything but I've just woken up in a strange place, naked. Could someone come and pick me up please?"

There. I have said it. This is sort-of true.

"Where are you calling from?"

"A phone box."

"Can you read me the number on the phone box?"

I read out the number.

"You wait there. A car will come and pick you up."

I walk in circles around my phone box to keep moving. Oh dear oh dear oh dear. The police car draws up next to my phone box. I wonder how they know exactly where I am.

"You OK?" The policeman who gets out of the car asks me.

He is young and cute with brown spiky hair.

"Yeah, thank you for coming, I don't know what happened, I woke up in this strange place on my own and…"

"Get in the car, sweetheart." He says. "We have to go to the station."

There is another policeman in the car too – an older one.

"It's exciting being in a police car." I say. "I've never been in a police car before. Do you like your job? What do you like about it? What else do you like? I like clubbing and…."

I look out of the window as the streets rush past. I am safe and it didn't really happen. The police will look after me. None of it is my fault.

"We are going to take some swabs and we are going to take your clothes away and we are going to ask you some questions." The policewoman says.

I am in a room at the police station just with her now. She is pretty. Her hair is tied back in a ponytail.

"Please sit still Tanya."

"Can we listen to some music?" I ask. "It would help me focus."

"No, not at the moment, we have to…"

"I want to dance. There was this great tune last night at Apocalypse – have you ever been to Apocalypse? It's a drum 'n' bass club. Oh I suppose you're too old aren't you? I like drum 'n' bass, well, actually I prefer techno and do you like my dress it's by Spank?"

"It looks lovely on you." She says.

"What dresses do you like? I think you'd look great in a knee-length wrap dress, you've got a great figure."

"Thanks. Come on, Tanya. Take your clothes off and then we will do these swabs."

She points to a bed – another bed: there seem to be beds everywhere today. All the beds throw their sheets and covers off to suck me inside them. I am not going to get to sleep though because the beds have other plans.

"Someone will be with you to take those swabs in the minute. Would you like a cup of tea?" She says.

"Yes please."

I stare at the ceiling and it ripples and bubbles. A glow in the dark rocket sticker floats onto the floor as I take my dress off.

The walls are white the ceiling is white the bed is white. I draw the curtain around the bed and it is a plastic curtain with orange and pink and yellow roses on it.

"Lie on your back, put your feet on the bed, put your knees up, open your knees. Yes, that's right. Now I'm going to put the clamp in. If you breathe in then it will go up there more easily. Have you had a smear test before?" The nurse says.

"No, because I haven't actually done it yet…I almost did with this boy I was sort of seeing but my friend turned up and so I didn't have to and…"

I don't want to tell her the rest of that story, or I do but…

I open my legs and something very cold slides up there. It is already sore up there, which is a bad sign that bad things happened to me last night.

"This might hurt a bit. The clamp is going to open now."

At first it doesn't hurt but as it opens wider it hurts a lot. It is going to keep opening wider until it rips my whole body open and this serves me right for what happened last night. Then the clamp stops opening.

"I'm just going to take the swabs now." She says.

I can feel the cotton buds scrape around up there, which tickles.

"All done. You can put your knickers back on now. You're a brave girl."

My paper knickers are scratchy, but they have taken my clothes away.

"Which clothes would you like, Tanya? You can choose some from this cupboard here." She says.

"Oh yes I'll have that one and that one and that one."

"You can't have all of them. You have to choose."

I have to answer questions where I say over and over again that I woke up in a stranger's bed and I don't know how I got there and I don't know I don't know I don't know. They take my clothes away for tests and they are lovely to me but everything jumbles in my mind.

They put me in a cab which takes me home.

Chapter 21

I FUMBLE IN MY BAG FOR THE KEY and lift it up with both shaking hands and press it with all my remaining strength in the direction of the lock. I miss. I make a few more attempts but the keyhole keeps moving away from me and round in circles. Eventually, I give up and ring the doorbell.

I hear the thump of approaching footsteps and I see Mum running towards me, but her steps are in slow motion: a sprinter as she's about to cross the finish line on the first-place-finish replay. She slides the door open and pulls me towards her and I can smell Safari and talcum powder and it hits my brain and makes it sting.

"Tanya. Where have you been anyway? I've been worried sick about you, we all have. I phoned all your friends…"

My vision is blurred and I can't focus and I can see her face in double: the two relieved, distraught and angry Mums overlapping.

"None of them had the faintest idea where you were. Where have you been?" She asks, after a minute. "Why didn't you phone me? I'm not cross with you, Tanya. I was just desperately worried. We all were. Careful, sweetie pie." She puts an arm out to break my fall as I just collapse on the floor.

I close my eyes and I can feel the room spinning around me. The waves of nausea rise up through my throat and beat against my teeth.

"You're not well, are you, sweetie pie?" Mum asks me, her face against my ear and her hand on my forehead, feeling for a temperature that I don't know whether I'm running or not. I'm shaking.

"I was with Lee and Ben." I say.

There is a sharp intake of breath from my mother.

"But you told me that you were with Lily and Emily." Mum says. "I wouldn't have let you go out on your own with those boys – it's not safe for you to…"

"Do you want me to tell you what happened or not?" I demand, hauling myself to my feet, grasping onto the wicker edge of the glass table that stands in the middle of the hall.

I stand up and walk in circles round the room. If I keep moving it calms me down. There's energy pulsing through me, up my legs, through my fingertips. My legs shake and buckle underneath me.

"We were in Apocalypse." I say. "I was with Lee and Ben. Then Ben went home and I was dancing with Lee. And then I swear I can't remember anything until I woke up this morning in a strange place. I don't know how I got there."

"Why are you shaking like that, darling. Do you have any idea what might have happened. Was there anyone else there when you woke up? Did a man do anything to you?" Mum asks.

"I don't know."

"You must know." She stares at me. "Come on, Tanya. I don't believe that you can't remember anything."

"Yes, I think that the man did do something to me. I went to the police." I say. I can't bear to tell her this, it is too embarrassing.

"Why didn't you call me? Why didn't anyone at the police station call me?"

"I thought you'd be cross. I'm going up to my room." I say.

As I walk out of the room I can hear Mum pick up the phone and dial a number.

"Hello, can you put me through to Dr Joshua Stein immediately… yes, it is an emergency…" Mum's voice is quivering. "Oh, hello Dr Stein, this is Mrs Marshall. Is there any way you could fit Tanya in today?… yes, that's fine, see you then…. Something's happened…no, I don't quite know what's happened, you'd better see what you think when you see her…thank you ever so much Dr Stein, see you later…"

I run up to my room, slamming the door and cranking the volume on my stereo up so loud that the floor starts to shake. My fantail goldfish, Richard and Judy, are swimming around their Biorb, oblivious. I watch them discovering their world anew, like mine, their little memories are wiped clean.

"Hi, Tanya," Richard says. "Where've you been? We miss you when you're not here." He looks at me, waving his long feathery tail and goggling his eyes at me.

"I miss you both too, whenever I'm not here. How did you learn to talk though? And how come I can hear you, through the water and glass?"

"Because we have special powers. And so do you. You have special powers like St Francis, or Dr Doolittle." He smiles.

I didn't know that fish could smile, but he does.

Wow, this is amazing. I can communicate with the animals. This is unreal. I want to see if I can understand any other animals, but then we have to go to Dr Stein for my appointment.

"Now, Tanya, you are going to tell Dr Stein the truth." Mum says as we sit in the car on the way to my appointment. "I am not cross with you, I am just worried about what has happened, and that you say that you can't remember it. You are not going to be punished. If you don't tell us what happened then we won't be able to help you. And stop doing that thing with your leg." She puts her hand on my thigh.

"Stop what?" I look out of the car window where the trees are waving their branches in spiral patterns and the sky swirls blue, pink and yellow: we're in a Van Gogh painting.

"Stop doing that with your leg."

"I'm not even doing anything. Watch out. There's a castle in the road."

I point to an island in the middle of the road where a castle is sitting. It is a mediaeval Motte and Bailey one, Norman probably. The walls are crumbling and the turrets rise into the sky. I've never noticed it on this route before and…

"No there isn't. What on earth are you talking about? If you don't stop jiggling your leg and grinding your teeth like that, I'll, I'll…well I don't know what I'll do." Mum is biting her lip.

"I'm not doing it on purpose to piss you off you know."

The castle in the middle of the road wobbles and then we pass it, and when I look back, it's gone.

"Before we get there, can you tell me what actually happened, Tanya?"

"There isn't anything else to tell. I can't remember anything. I don't know."

"Slow down, I can't understand what you're saying."

"Dolphins! Dolphins! Look!" I squeal, pointing to where a school of dolphins dive into the road and bounce back up, arcing in front of us, rippling the tarmac.

"Tanya, I don't know what you're talking about. Just be quiet."

At last, after what seems like about three weeks, we turn into a gravel drive. The sign says 'Honeysuckle House'. This isn't where I normally see Dr Stein. There are rhododendrons lining the long drive which are flowering. Cerise, violet and scarlet blooms erupt all over the sides of the road which closes over us: a multicoloured flume

pressing in on us. I want to hurtle down it but Mum is insisting on driving at about three miles an hour.

"Can't we speed up a bit?" I ask Mum.

"We're going at thirty miles an hour, look."

I look at the speedometer and I can't tell what it says because it shimmers and the lines spin round and bleed into each other: a tiny Catherine wheel. And then the house comes into view, careering towards us: a stately home, Manderley perhaps or even Pemberley. It's a far glammer, posher place than my usual hospital. Mum screeches to a halt outside the front of the house and hustles me out of the car and up the porticoed marble steps lined with Doric columns to the door.

"Tanya Marshall, for Dr Stein." Mum says to the receptionist. "Tanya, come back here. Stop pacing around."

I walk in a circle, anti-clockwise round the room back to my mother.

"Hello," I say to the receptionist. "Have you been working here long?"

"About three months." She replies.

Her hair is streaked white-blonde and chilli red.

"Great hair." I say. "Where'd you get it done?"

"At my local hairdresser."

"How much was it?"

"Tanya, stop being so rude. Sorry," Mum says to the girl. "She's not well."

"Mum! I'm not… I've just…"

"Come on Tanya. Let's go and sit in the waiting room." Mum says, dragging me towards the stairs.

We start to climb the stairs but I trip over my own foot and collapse in a heap on the landing. I stare up at the ceiling where there is a pastel-coloured painting of cherubs blowing trumpets on a cloud and God in the middle, flanked by angels. I can fly; I can fly down the stairs. I spread my wings and take off but the stairs jump up to meet me.

"Tanya, behave yourself." My mother hisses, picking me up, digging her nails into my arm. "We'll be late for Dr Stein."

The waiting room is light and airy. Sunlight streams in and warms me as I sit on the gold brocade sofa. There are pots of fresh coffee bubbling on the carved mahogany cabinets. I run over to the windowsill and gaze over the grounds of the hospital. The cedar trees wave in the breeze and the sun dazzles me as it hits the glass of the huge bay windows. The enormously long draped gold and red curtains are held together with gold tassels.

"Tanya, Mrs Marshall." Dr Stein says, poking his head round the door of the waiting room. "Do come into my office."

He looks so gorgeous today with his luscious brown hair falling over one of his blue eyes. He ushers us into his office, placing a hand on the small of my back, and that one small touch sends waves of lust all over my body.

"So, Tanya, how are you today?" He says.

"Oh, Dr Stein, I don't know what to do." Mum says.

I get up. I can't sit still.

"Tanya, sit down." Mum says.

"I can't." I say.

"Tanya, what seems to be the problem?" Dr Josh says, his fountain pen poised over my notes.

"Nothing. Well, I mean…."

"Tanya hasn't been home for several days." My mother says. "She says she woke up this morning in a stranger's bed, and she tells me that she has no memory of the night before. She has just been at the police station. But I don't know if…"

"Really, Tanya?" What happened?"

"Well last night I was out clubbing with my friends Lee and Ben. Then I woke up in a strange place this morning." I say.

"Did you go home with a stranger?" He asks.

"I don't remember going home with anyone." I say.

"But you must have gone home with someone." He says. "You must remember something."

"I don't remember anything else. If I did I would tell you." I can't tell him. I can't bring myself to tell him.

"Tanya's mood is dangerously elevated." Dr Stein says to Mum. "I could tell that as soon as she walked in the door. She is pacing around the room, her speech is rambling and disconnected, she got herself into a dangerous situation with a stranger. These are symptoms of mania." Dr Stein says to Mum. "Tanya is suffering from bipolar disorder and not unipolar depression as I had previously thought."

"What's mania?" Mum asks.

"Mania is an elevated mood characterised by rapid thoughts and speech and dangerous impulsive behaviours as well as grandiosity, hypersexuality, self-delusion and often psychosis. We need to bring her mood down." He says.

"But I'm fine, I feel brilliant." I say. "I've just had a bad experience last night, that's all. After months and months I've just started to feel normal and happy again and now, as soon as I'm starting to feel better, you're telling me that…"

"Your mood is very high. I think it might be the effect of the Prozac. It's called the 'manic switch'. If you add in an anti-depressant when your mood is already stable it sends your mood further up. This is what seems to have happened, I'm afraid."

"But you told us that Tanya was suffering from depression." Mum says.

"Yes. She was. In bipolar disorder the periods of depression alternate with periods of mania."

"So what are you going to do about this?" Mum says to Dr Stein. "Why have you let this happen to my little girl?"

"I'm very sorry that this has happened, Mrs Marshall. It's a common but unfortunate result of giving anti-depressants to people who suffer from bipolar disorder. We're going to give Tanya some tranquillisers and anti-psychotics to bring her mood down back to normal, and she is going to have to stay in hospital until her mood has stabilised."

"Why did you give her those anti-depressants if this was going to happen?" Mum says.

"There was no way of knowing that this was going to happen, Mrs Marshall. Tanya, would you like to stay in my hospital for a few days?"

"Yeah, that sounds fab." I say.

I can stay here. I can stay here with Dr Josh in this gorgeous place. It will be fun. I will be away from Mum and I will be able to do whatever I want.

"Mrs Marshall?" He says.

"Yes?" Mum says.

"Why don't you go home and pick up some clothes for Tanya and everything she might need for a few days. She's going to stay here for a while. Oh, and Mrs Marshall, nothing like that." He gestures to my dress. "Nothing revealing." "Will she be safe?" Mum asks. "I'm not leaving my child in here if she's going to be assaulted again."

"We will provide her with a one-on-one nurse to be with her all the time, Mrs Marshall, don't worry. I won't let anything happen to her. Would you like to have a look around here, Tanya?"

"Oooh yes please, Dr Stein."

"A nurse will give you a tour of the hospital." He says, pressing a buzzer on his desk. "Yes, Marjorie, yes, you can come up now."

I skip off with the nurse through the beautiful grounds of the hospital. Wow this is so exciting! What an adventure. The sun beats down; it's hot and very bright.

"Hi, I'm Tanya,' I announce to a young man sitting at one of the tables outside.

"Mick." He tells me. "Pleased to meet you."

He holds out his big paw. He is tall with ginger hair and freckles: he's also built like a wrestler.

"What are you in here for?" I pull up a chair and fix him with an I-am-interested-tell-me-about-yourself expression.

"I'm an addict." He doesn't elaborate.

"What are you addicted to?"

"Heroin."

I appraise him. He doesn't look like a heroin addict. I mean, he doesn't look like Ewan McGregor in *Trainspotting*. He's got toned arms and he looks healthy, glossy hair, quite built. I'm going to have so much fun here, it'll be like being on holiday with loads of gorgeous young people: I can already see them sunbathing and playing badminton and drinking coffee…

Chapter 22

"HAVE YOU GOT A LIGHT?" I ask a girl who's sitting on a bench by the path that leads from the garden to the door of the dorms.

"Yeah, here, let me light it for you." Her voice is slow and measured.

She lights my cigarette, bending her head down so that her hair falls over her face and encloses it in a tepee. It's cut in a bob and is a mousy-brown. When she looks up and hands me the lit cigarette I see that her eyes are hazel flecked with amber.

"Hi, I'm Tanya." I say.

"Gemma," She mutters without meeting my eye. "You're new, aren't you?" She asks me.

"Yeah. Just came in today."

I sit down next to her on the bench and she shuffles further away from me so she's pressed up against one arm of the bench with her body turned away from me.

"What're you in for.?" She asks me, still looking away from me.

"Manic depression." I love saying it. It sounds so hardcore.

"You?"

"Depression. Self-harm. They put me on Seroxat and I think the cutting is a side-effect of that."

"Really? That's weird."

"Yeah, well, I've never done it before. Look."

She rolls up the sleeve of her grey sweater to show me a lattice of cuts, and then pulls her sleeve down again with a quick glance around, presumably to check that the nurses aren't looking or something.

"Can I sit with you at lunch?" I ask.

"I don't go to lunch. I can't eat in front of people. I just get them to send my food up to my room." She says.

This girl is obviously a complete freak. There is a pause while I'm literally lost for words.

"So, who do you know around here? How long have you been in?" I ask her eventually.

"You've met Mick? There's Violet – she's in for depression. Then there's the alkies – Anya and Pauline. That old tramp on the bench over there:"

She points to an old man slumped on the floor, leaning against a bench. I nod.

"That's Noxious Niall. He's an addict – booze, meths, whatever he can get his hands on. There's Oliver – he's a coke addict, so's David. I don't know what's wrong with Roxanne – she's just mental." She breaks off. Oh, and there's Ewan."

Her voice changes, becoming a mixture of despairing and irritated.

"Who's Ewan?"

"Ewan has decided that he's in love with me," screwing up her face in disgust. "He keeps asking me to be his girlfriend. He's sweet but…"

"But what?"

"He's mental, isn't it? Another fag? I just chain it in here." She holds one out that she's already lit.

"Thanks." I say. I think I've made a friend already.

'Oh tell me why

   Do we build castles in the sky

Oh tell me why

Do we build castles way up high'

The voice sings.

'Do you ever question your life

Do you ever wonder why

Do you ever see in your dreams

All the castles in the sky'

Ewan plays this song on repeat on the CD player in the smoking room where all we smokers congregate, chain-smoking. Right now the volume's cranked up so we can hear it outside where we are sitting on the tree stump at dusk. He is...well I don't know exactly what's wrong with him but he paints and he shows me his pictures and tells me stuff.

"I'm in love with Gemma." He says as the midges buzz in a cloud above us.

I scratch my shoulder where the bites are starting to itch. We are smoking Marlboro Lights.

"Does she know this?"

Of course I know that she knows because she's already told me, but I'm pretending not to know to get him to tell me everything without him worrying that I'm going to run straight back to Gemma and tell her what he told me.

"Well yeah, I told her and...well...she says that she doesn't want to get together and it would be a bad idea and...well...she's got a boyfriend anyway."

The rhododendrons are in bloom. There are pink ones and red ones. They are huge mutant flowers: they swarm over the hospital's grounds, billowing, expanding almost before our eyes. As I stare at them the leaves move and swirl in spirals. I do not think I know what psychosis is – which is what Dr Josh says I've got – but it seems like an acid trip. This must be 'doing a natural'.

"What are you laughing about? It's not funny." Ewan says, hurt, peeved that I am not acknowledging his pain in an appropriate way or something.

"No, nothing, sorry…" I hadn't even realised that I was laughing.

"But how am I going to get Gemma to fall in love with me?"

"Just get to know her and she will get to like you and maybe she will change her mind."

It's not a very good answer but then Ewan has no chance with Gemma. I know this because she has already told me that she is not up for it with him and wishes he would stop following her around.

"Here," He says, handing me a rolled-up piece of paper. "It's for you." I unroll it and it's a picture all done in wax crayon all in reds and yellows and oranges with flames and black shadows and it's really good but it scares me.

"Thanks. It's really nice." I say, and I know I'm going to put it in a cupboard when I get home and never look at it because already it's got bad vibes pouring out of it, creeping out to engulf me and suffocate me with noxious fumes.

At lunch time I find myself sitting with Patricia, one of the anorexics, and she takes about an hour to eat a baked potato, cutting it into tiny pieces, chewing each mouthful twenty times. Her fingers are white Twiglets. It almost puts me off my food, but not quite; my appetite's enormous at the moment. She chews from side to side, very slowly and deliberately, like a tortoise. She looks like a tortoise as well with her long neck and shrivelled skin.

With a lot of my fellow patients it's hard to work out exactly what's wrong with them. The depressives are easy to spot. They just stare into space and don't communicate, or eat. You can't miss the anorexics; they're all stick thin, they look horrible.

But apart from these easily identifiable mental types, there are lots of others. I just don't know exactly what some of them are in here for. Some people have been here for weeks, or even months – Roxy's quite a long-termer, she's been here about 6 weeks already. Others, like old Niall, are regulars and have had several previous visits. The addicts tend to be out for a bit, then relapse and are back in here. It's Mick's third time and Oliver's second. I sort of have to wait for people to volunteer the reason for their incarceration; it's not the done thing to ask. I'm having the best time though, I love it. It's just amazing in here. The addicts are the best fun, and I generally hang out with them, although they spend a lot of time in Addiction Group. I don't know what they do in there, but I think it's really tough for them not being able to drink, take drugs, sniff glue or whatever.

"Can I come to your group, Dr Stein?" I beg him when I spot him striding through the grounds of the hospital a few days later.

I'm sunbathing with Gemma, and of course Ewan – who's always a few feet away from Gemma – and Roxy, and Mick, and Oliver the coke addict who I quite fancy.

"No, Tanya, not at the moment."

"Why not?"

"Your mood is too high, you'll be disruptive."

"But I really want to come into the group and…"

"I daresay you do, but you can't. And there's no point in you sunbathing either. Your anti-psychotic has an anti-tanning agent in it. You won't get brown."

"Never mind." I say as I turn over on to my front. "I'm not going to sit on my own in the shade am I?"

Out of the corner of my eye I can see Roxy propped up on her elbow, her head thrown back, laughing, showing off her tanned chest in Oliver's direction.

The sun shines all the time. It's quiet and peaceful. There are squirrels everywhere, chatting away to each other. Unfortunately I can't understand what they're saying, and they ignore me. It might just be fish that I can communicate with, and I can't speak to my fish as I'm not allowed home and they don't seem to be able to use the phone. It wouldn't work in the water would it?

"Tanya, there's something I need to talk to you about. Can you come with me a minute." Dr Josh says.

"Do we have to talk about it now though?"

"Yes, we do."

"Oh, OK then."

I glance over at Oliver and Roxy. She is smearing tanning oil on her long brown legs, stretching them out, flashing her pants at him. She is such a tart. She must be about thirty as well. I tear my eyes away from him and trot off after Dr Josh.

"So, do you want to press charges?" He asks me as we sit on the bench across the grass from the others.

I scrunch up my eyes and I can see the silhouettes of Oliver and Roxy and the others if I stare hard.

"No."

"Why not?"

"No point. I can't remember what happened and I don't want to have to go through it all again." I don't know if I'm imagining it or if Roxy has moved closer to Oliver.

"Are you absolutely sure?"

"Yes, I'm sure."

"Well, if you're sure, we'll say no more about it at the moment. Think about it, and we can always talk about it in a while."

I don't want to think about it. I want to get back to the others and sunbathe and empty the thoughts that have started crowding into my mind.

"I'm looking forward to going home and going back to school in the Autumn." I tell Dr Josh, changing the subject.

"Well let's hope you'll be well enough, Tanya."

"I will be, won't I?"

I haven't really thought about not going back to school in 2 months' time.

"If we can stabilise your mood, yes."

"But I want to go back to school and be with my friends."

"I know you do. We want you to have the best chance of coping with…"

"I'm going to Australia to see Robbie at Christmas."

"I'm afraid you're not."

"Why not?"

"Because, oh never mind. You're just not. We don't need to discuss this now."

"Why can't I?"

"Tanya, do you have any idea of how ill you are?" He asks.

"No. No-one's told me anything about it."

"You're going to be on medication for years. Possibly for life."

"Life? Are you serious?"

"A lot of my patients go on to lead perfectly normal lives."

I totally can't think about this now.

"Can I go back to the others now?"

"Yes, OK. See you later."

He winks at me in what he imagines is a conspiratorial manner but I'm cross now and I scowl back at him and hurtle across the grass and plonk myself down between Oliver and Roxy. That'll teach her.

When I go up to my room to change for dinner I run a bath. I'm having about five baths a day at the moment. It's an outlet for the manic energy, and my skin is so soft from all the moisturiser that it's well worth it. I wash away everything: the dirt, the sun cream, the mud, the grass stains.

Chapter 23

"ISN'T IT NICE IN HERE?" Emily asks.

We're sitting on the grass in the shade of a purple rhododendron in the beautiful grounds of my hospital. I look away from the flowers which are still moving. Emily and Ben have come to see me at last. They're the first of my friends to make the trek here and I've been in here for ages, I don't know how long exactly, but as I'm not really sleeping it could be any amount of time. The days stretch out to be filled with all manner of glittering pursuits: art therapy, badminton, sunbathing, discos, anxiety management. I'm still not allowed into the classes though apart from art therapy.

"Lily says she's really sorry but she had to help her Mum get ready for Mike's birthday party." Ben says.

"Don't apologise for her Benjamin." I snap. "She should be here. Tell her she'd better bloody come and see me."

It's just typical of her not to bother. She just doesn't want to be infected with mental illness, or feel awkward around me and the other nutters. It's cowardice really, and I'm not impressed. And it pisses me off that Ben always covers for her, always excuses her inexcusable behaviour. When Lily was in hospital with a boil on her bum and had to have it removed, Mum dragged me there to see her and we were there before she'd even come round from the anaesthetic, at her bedside, handing her magazines and grapes.

"Why shouldn't she be expected to behave properly anyway?" I say. "You two know you should come and see me, why doesn't…"

"Shhhhhh sweetie, you're getting upset."' Emily says, placing a hand on my arm which I shrug off. "Please sit down. Why are you pacing around?"

"Because I've got to go places, do things, anyway I'm not upset. It's just that… why can't she behave properly? I mean, I bet you two don't want to be here when you could be out drinking or…"

"Don't be silly, T, of course we want to be here with you. We miss you. Don't we, Ben?" Emily prods Ben in the ribs.

"Yeah." Ben rubs a blade of grass between his fingers, avoiding my gaze, and avoiding the view of a couple of the oldest addicts who are leering at him.

"Alright lad."

Noxious Niall yells over in Ben's direction, raising his can of Dr Pepper as if he's toasting Ben. Niall is about a million years old and smells of wee. Alcoholism is so not glamorous in the old.

"You new, love? Haven't seen you here before?" Niall calls to Ben, leering at him.

"Um, no I'm just visiting Tanya." Ben blushes and looks away.

He is a bit pathetic, to be scared of the Noxious One's advances when Noxious is so obviously harmless.

"He won't bite." I tell Ben. "Don't be such a pussy."

"So, um, how are you?" Ben asks after a pause, looking embarrassed.

"Yeah, great, I love it here." I reply.

"Really?"

"Look how gorgeous it is here."

I gesture to the sunny grounds, the badminton net, the picnic tables,

"Don't you want to be at home?" Em asks.

"No," I answer, truthfully, because I don't really.

I've made lots of cool mates here, it's sunny, the food is nice, it's just like being on holiday, I can see Dr Stein every day.

"Is there a loo?" Ben asks.

"Yeah, over there, but keep your back to the wall, Noxious might follow you in there and…"

"Stop it, Tanya." Emily says. "Don't make Ben anxious."

I look at Ben, jittering and shaking, no doubt from too many pills and too much coke at the weekend, unable to cope with the basics of social interactions. He should be in here with these nutters, not me, I think. I'm absolutely fine. I don't believe I need to be in a mental hospital.

"T, please sit down, for one minute, I want to talk to you."

"We can talk while we're walking." I say, pacing.

"Where are we going?" Em sounds tired and irritated.

"Just want to keep moving. Let's walk round this tree stump."

"Why though?"

"I dunno. Tracking a woozle?"

Em looks confused.

"You know, that Winnie the Pooh story where they're tracking a woozle – Pooh and Piglet – and there are two sets of tracks, and it turns out to be…oh never mind."

"Right." Em is not impressed.

Pause.

"Miss you." she says, hugging me.

She is as gorgeous as ever in pale blue bell-bottomed denim flares and a tight orange T-shirt.

"I can't keep up with your thoughts, T, but listen: don't you dare mention that I told you but…" Em whispers, checking that Ben is still out of earshot.

"What?"

"Shhhhhhhhh," Em looks around nervously. "Ben snogged Lily."

"Seriously?"

I can't believe it. She's always sworn she never would.

"You mustn't let Ben or Lily know that you know or that I told you. She doesn't know I know, but he told me on the way here."

"That's unbelievable."

"Isn't it?"

"Does she like him, do you reckon?"

"Dunno." Em says, her brow furrowed, thinking.

" It's hard to say. He's in the most ridiculous state of excitement and hope and…"

"I can imagine."

"Poor Ben," we both say in unison.

I feel weird about it though. I sort of feel happy for Ben, but I'm used to having him as my best friend, it will be horrible if he goes off with Lily and they both prefer each other to me. I can't see it happening though. See what happens when I turn my back for one minute. I'm so out of touch with everything suddenly.

"What about Greg?"

"He's finally had enough I think, she's bored with him anyway. This split seems to be final."

It's so weird to have Em here, to be talking about normal everyday stuff, about our mates and their relationships. It's not that we don't talk about anything normal in here – we do talk about other stuff than meds and suicide attempts, illness, death, abuse, drugs, depression, mania, anxiety – but everyone's so screwed up. All these new words trip off my tongue now: 'borderline personality disorder', 'schizoaffective disorder', 'co-dependence', 'transference'.

"Come on, Emily, We'd better get going." Ben says when he returns, smoothing down a sticking-up patch of his hair where the gel has rubbed off.

"Why?" slips out before I can stop it.

I don't want them to leave me. I don't want to know why they have to go, and yet perversely I sort of do, sort of want to torture myself with the information.

"We've, er, got to get back." He says, as always not convincing me with the weak answer.

"Seeing Lily?" I ask, testing his reaction.

"No, um, got to see Seb and Immi…" Ben says, looking shifty.

"Who?" I pounce on the unfamiliar name. Seb, my Seb. I feel a pang of longing for him.

"Seb's cousin, you remember her don't you, T?" Em reminds me.

"Oh yeah." I vaguely remember this.

"Wasn't there some connection between her and my brother as well?" I ask, I'm not letting it go.

But why are they all getting on with everything without me? I feel a sudden wave of rage against all of them. It surges through me.

"Why don't you just all fuck off then?" I yell. "Go on then, leave, go off with each other and Lily and Seb and leave me to rot in here! I hate you both!"

I surprise myself with the vehemence of my reaction which seems to come from nowhere.

"Shhhhhhh T." Em says, putting her arm round me. "Look, I'm sorry you're here, but you'll be home soon."

I don't know why she's being so nice to me; I really don't, when I'm so horrible and poisonous to her. It's not her fault that Lily isn't there, that Seb doesn't want to be with me, that Ben and Lily are running off with each other hand in hand into the sunset like a couple of gay cowboys.

"I want to go home now." I say, shaking her arm off me, cross with her for the situation that I both know isn't her fault and yet here she is, the obvious and only available punch bag.

"I know."

"I want my Mum." I sniff as a sudden wave of tears comes.

"But your Mum was here earlier." Em says. "Don't you remember?"

"No she wasn't."

"She was. I saw her leaving as we came in. Do you really not remember seeing her?"

"No."

I don't. I have no recollection of seeing her today. I can't remember when I last saw her. I can't remember seeing any of my family.

"We'll be back next week if…" She says, her voice tailing off.

"I'll be home by then." I tell them.

"Hope so." Em squeezes my shoulder. "Have they given you any indication of when…?"

"When my mood comes down. I'm going to need constant supervision Dr Josh says."

"So about a month?"

"I guess."

"That's not that long. We'll still have about a month of summer hols left." Em says.

"Bye, T. See you next week then."

Ben pecks my cheek. I watch their forms recede into the distance. They climb into Ben's battered red Ford Capri, Em gets her shoe stuck between the seat and the door and has to wiggle it out. The car accelerates into the log in front of the space. There's a screech as Ben scrapes the side of Dr Stein's Bentley and pulls away and clatters down the drive of the hospital. I wave and wave at Em until I can't see the car anymore and then I sit on the grass, my legs buckling beneath me.

This is not what I wanted, I think. This is not the alternative reality I dreamt of where I would live in a community outside the private education system. This bundle of misfits, dribbling schizophrenics and violent addicts are not the glamorous trendy cool clubbers I was going to live with in my other world. I wipe away a tear.

"Supper?" Oliver asks, striding across the grass towards me… "What's the matter?"

He puts his head on one side, and gives me a concerned look. Oliver is giving me some attention. I pull myself together.

"It's tough, when your visitors go home, isn't it?"

I nod.

"You'll be out soon. Anyway, you'll be able to come to group soon."

He smiles at me. "Let's go to supper."

Yippee, Oliver wants to sit with me. I cheer up. He squeezes my hand. Oliver is hot. He is tanned with black spiky hair and big brown eyes. He looks Italian. I think he's Jewish which is good, but he's in his twenties, and a coke addict. I feel the warmth of his palm against mine and bury my head in his shoulder. He smells of Davidoff Cool Water.

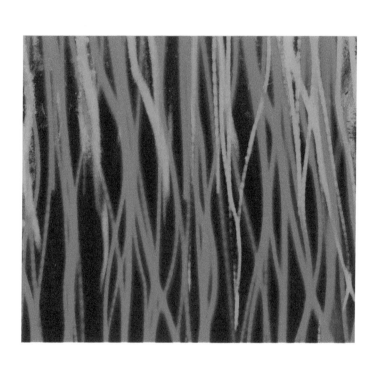

Chapter 24

"HURRY UP, TANYA, WE HAVEN'T GOT ALL DAY." the nurse leading our expedition says as I blow kisses and wolf-whistle at passing motorists.

They wave back, hoot and shout 'Hi gorgeous!' at me. Pedestrians speed up and pass us with traumatised glances, then look away or down at their feet. I wonder if they're worried they'll catch mental illness if they get too close to us. Our crocodile of inmates shambles along the road from the hospital into the village towards the newsagent where we are being taken on our daily walk to buy treats.

Tropical rain pours out of the warm summer sky. Now we are in the rainforest my panther has vanished. I run down the queue to join Gemma at the back, even though I want to go faster. She's dawdling. I want to run in the rain, feel it whip my face and stream off my hair.

"Come on, Gem." I coax her.

"God, T, I'm exhausted. Sorry, my feet are just so heavy," she whispers.

I hold her hand.

"You can lean on my shoulder." I tell her. "They'll wait for us anyway. They're not going to leave us here in the street are they?"

She forces a smile and we move, slowly. I suppress my need to run because I can sense she needs my support. I let her soak up some of my strength. She's pale and distracted today: her eyes deep dark wells in her pale face. She's so thin as well.

Sometimes I catch myself wishing I was as thin as her, but looking at her now I decide I don't really want to be quite so scrawny: she looks ill and her clothes droop off her shoulders as if they're still on their hangers. I can see a dusting of downy hairs around her jawline. Her hair's lank and dull unlike mine which shines with health since I've been washing it so often, apparently several times per day although I can never remember.

The road comes towards us frame by frame: like I'm on acid or driving a Formula 1 car.

"What fags do you want, T?" Gemma asks when we finally arrive at the newsagents.

It seems like hours have passed although when I check my watch it's only been ten minutes.

"Menthols – any menthols."

I'm smoking so much in hospital, it gives me something to do with my hands, and all the cool people are in the smoking room.

"These ones are nice." She points to a pack.

I look at all the cigarettes lined up against the back wall of the newsagent behind the till facing us: powder blue Camels, gold Benson and Hedges, white Marlboro, silver Superkings, white and purple Silk Cut, blue, green and red Mayfairs, white Lucky Strikes with black and red stripes: a rainbow of nicotine.

"OK, those ones." I say, pointing at the white and green Marlborough menthols.

The different cigarette brands arc over my head, branching into the distance, a tree with an infinite number of branches.

"Anything else?" Gemma says.

"Well we don't need any more food do we?" I'm still stuffed from lunch and it'll be teatime when we get back.

Gemma picks up a Kinder egg, turns it over in her palm, stroking the wrapper, and puts it back down, settling on some sugar free chewing gum. She doesn't like eating in front of people. She always takes her meals on her own in her room, I don't know why – I make a mental note to ask her when we're alone.

"Please can we go to the jewellery shop?" I ask the nurse.

"No we haven't got time, we've got to…"

"Please?"

There's a beautiful necklace made of red plastic beads that I want in there now, someone might have bought it by tomorrow – it has to be mine. It's calming to be in the jewellery shop with all the sparkly stones and metals, the necklaces displayed on velvet and glass. It reminds me of the Destiny New Age shop at the farm.

The nurse's voice jolts me back to the present. "Maybe your Mum can take you when she visits?"

"Don't worry Tanya, we'll go tomorrow." My one-to-one nurse Debby says.

"I want to go now."

"We're not going now, we'll go next time."

We begin our long walk back to the hospital. I trip over wobbly paving stones and Gemma flinches from the gazes of the members of the public we pass. She recoils as I grab her arm when I lose my footing.

"Sorry, did I…"

"It's OK; it's just a new batch of cuts there." I notice that despite the heat Gemma is wearing a long sleeved T-shirt which I now realise is to hide the cuts from the nurses.

We're not allowed knives in hospital. "How are you…?"

"Oh, I broke a vase and used it to cut myself." She whispers.

I put my arm round her. "I'm sorry, Gem, are you OK?"

She doesn't reply. Gemma's family don't come to see her that often. She's not as outgoing as me either so she hasn't made friends so easily in hospital.

"You're really lucky, Tanya." She says. "Your Mum and Dad and brother come to see you every day." It's as if she can read my thoughts.

"Yeah, well, your parents live further away."

"No they don't, they're just round the corner, they're way closer to here than your parents are. They don't care about me, and they're embarrassed that I'm ill, about what people will think."

"What do you mean?"

"The neighbours, I don't know."

"It's not your fault you're ill. If anything it's their fault."

"Come on, girls." The nurse's voice booms: chivvying everyone along.

"We could run away." I whisper to Gemma.

"No you can't, actually, Tanya. Debby will make sure of that." The nurse says. "I can hear you, girls."

The hems of my trousers drag in the puddles. They feel a bit tight. My feet are heavy, my steps wobbly: my balance is screwed. I slip in the rain but it's fun, like being in the rainforest. I giggle and start to run along the road and Debby runs after me, her bingo wings flapping in the rain, a blancmange wobbling along the pavement towards me. She's a laugh, Debby, but she's a bit fat.

When we pitch up at the hospital Mum's there waiting for me on the bench, doing a crossword in the paper, sucking the end of her pen. She looks up as I approach.

"Sweetie," Mum is here to see me at last.

"Mum," I launch myself at Mum, almost toppling her over. "I haven't seen you for ages."

"I was here yesterday." Mum says.

"When?"

"Yesterday lunchtime."

I attempt to think back over the vast swathes of action that have occurred since yesterday lunchtime but can't recall Mum visiting.

"What have you been doing today sweetie?" Mum asks, gently, slowly, as if she's talking to a five year old with learning difficulties.

"I had a baked potato for lunch with cottage cheese. I've been writing letters to everyone and some poems."

We go to my room. Mum has brought me some new trousers and vest tops.

"What's this?" Mum picks something which had been a red dress with white roses on it but is now ripped and fraying.

"Um, I thought I'd turn it into a skirt." It had seemed like a great idea at the time but then I'd abandoned the project and forgotten about it.

"By ripping it to pieces? I'll make it into a skirt for you, you leave it alone. I'll have to cut this bit off and, no, I'll sew some elastic in here, make a waistband, it will be fine. Why do you always have to ruin everything, Tanya?"

Mum scrunches it up and stuffs it into her handbag, then pulls it out again with a sigh of resignation.

"I'll make you a lovely skirt out of it over the weekend. It was never a very nice dress was it? Don't worry sweetie, I'll fix it."

"What have you been doing this afternoon?" She asks after a pause spent examining the dress.

"We went for a walk to the shops."

"That's nice. What did you buy?"

"Nothing." I can't remember buying anything.

"Shall we watch Wimbledon?"

"Yeah."

Mum turns the TV on. I lie on my front on the bed and Mum perches on the edge of my bed. They're hitting the ball so slowly though and the screen crackles and after a minute I get up and start pacing around the room.

"What are you doing, sweetie, watch the tennis. Look, Tim's 40 -o up. If he wins this point he's won the set."

"Can't we just put my clothes in colour order though?"

The strawberries and champagne of Wimbledon belong to another lifetime.

"Why?"

"Because it's neater." Because the certainty of a colour-coordinated and ordered wardrobe can solve everything and anchor me to this present that trickles through my fingers like flecks of gold in the silt of the Amazon.

"Please, please just sit down for a minute, Tanya. I really want to watch a bit of this match."

"But it's so slow."

"What do you mean?"

"It's…look how slowly they're hitting the ball."

"I don't understand. They're hitting the ball just how they always do."

So maybe I've only just realised that tennis players hit the ball too slowly, but I can't un-know this now I've discovered it, like I can't unlearn the smell of mouldy Chinese takeaways; the order Martine the anorexic eats the components of her dinner (lettuce, then carrot, then a tiny piece of potato skin and one mouthful of cottage cheese); or the patterns of the lines of silver healed scars on Gemma's arms. I know these things and now I will always know them, I see these patterns behind my eyes.

"Oh, I can't explain. It's just in slow motion."

"No it's not."

I walk over to the window and start lining my CDs up along the window-sill in alphabetical order. I pull *Screamadelica* out and put it in the CD player. The first song comes in, but after the intro I realise the moment requires something else and play Massive Attack's 'Protection.'

"Please sit down sweetie." Mum says.

"But we need a different song now."

After the first verse of 'Protection' I change to Orbital's *Insides* but it's still not right. Somewhere there is the perfect song for this moment and I'm going to find it if it takes all night. Somewhere in my music collection there's a song that could be subtitled 'Music for a daughter on her mother's visit to her mental hospital at the beginning of the second week of Wimbledon tennis tournament.' I put on 'The Lunatic is On the Grass' from Pink Floyd's *The Dark Side of the Moon* and it seems to do the trick of encapsulating the moment.

"Turn that thing off and watch the tennis, please sweetie?" Mum begs. "I can't bear that terrible noise."

Her face is drawn, she's got bags under her eyes, she looks like a corpse.

"Let's go to supper." I say.

She puts my shoes in front of me for me to step into them. I rest my hand on her arm for support because my balance is not very steady at the moment.

The dining room is empty, we're early. We sit at one of the large round tables: me, Mum and Debby my nurse. I order the baked potato again but with baked beans this time for a bit of variety.

Chapter 25

"So, um, how are you?" Seb asks me – his voice a mixture of concern, awkwardness and not-wanting-to-be-here.

He looks very big in my room with all its white walls and white ceiling and not much stuff anywhere. He is the only unsanitised thing. The only non-hospital-regulation thing.

"I'm OK. Thank you for coming." I say.

It is brave of him. He didn't have to. It must have taken a lot of courage for him to come here. It is strange to have him here, in my hospital bedroom, seeing me like this. He has never even been to my house.

"Well of course I'm here. I wanted to see you. I was worried."

It was obviously worth going completely mental to lure him here then, when he wouldn't even come round to have a drink in my garden. The last time I saw him was at Ben's party when we almost, but didn't quite…. It seems like a lifetime ago now though – or a scene in someone else's life that bears no relation to me at all.

My one-to-one nurse Debby is sitting on a chair in the doorway, pretending to read a magazine, but of course she is listening to our conversation and keeping an eye on us because I am not allowed to have a boy in my room in case he tries to do anything to me, or I try to do anything to him, whichever way round it is.

I'm not sure how to reply to his comment about being worried about me, so I don't. Instead I pick up my new pink glittery pen and begin to write.

"What's that?" He says, pointing to the book I'm writing in.

It's the one Lily gave me for my seventeenth birthday: covered in fuchsia silk and gold sequins.

"It's my diary. " I say, which isn't completely true.

In fact, I'm keeping a checklist in this notebook of which of my friends and relations have been, and how many times, for future reference. It's at time like this that you really learn who your friends are. My Mum has been every day, sometimes twice a day. My brother has been every day, so has Dad. My aunts and uncles have all visited – Mum's sister Aunty Olivia has visited every week, most of the other aunts, uncles and cousins have visited about 2 or 3 times each, except cousin Richard who is in Singapore.

Emily has been every week – she is my most attentive friend, Ben has been every other week. Lily has not even been yet, but this is hardly a surprise. Wendy has been once as has Lee. Some people haven't come to see me yet: Caitlin hasn't visited as she's in Ireland, Greg hasn't been but then since him and Lily split up he probably doesn't feel he has to see me in hospital.

Seb is sitting on the only comfortable chair in my room, legs splayed, affording me a close-up view of his indigo denim-clad crotch. I give it a cursory glance and then turn my gaze away. One of his blond curtains is a little bit longer than the other one: the one on the left grazes the top of his cheekbone and the other one hovers above his lip. It looks a bit silly but I don't mind because I like him how he is. His skin is not flawless close-up in the natural sunlight but it doesn't matter because he is here and even though I have no energy a pulse of love rushes through me, a weak signal.

I realise I have only ever seen him in the dark, UV light or when totally drunk or wasted on drugs before. Now I can see the tide line from his fake tan around his jaw and this makes him even more endearing: that he would try so hard and yet not get it quite right.

I am lying on the bed propped up on my elbow facing him because it's too much effort to sit and the muscles in my legs are spasming, and I don't want him to see this. I look around my room – at my books and CDs and the bare white walls. I look at the African violet wilting in the corner of the windowsill. I look at Debby sitting outside my room with the back of her chair to us, so that we can feel that we are in private, when of course we aren't. I can see the headline of the magazine article that she is reading: 'I lost five stone by eating more'.

I do not want Seb to be here, seeing me like this, but at the same time I am so glad that he has come. I do not want anyone to see me like this apart from my Mum. I would prefer Carl and Dad not to see me like this, but they are family. This is not one of those hospital scenes in the movies where the unconscious heroine is lying in bed with an artfully positioned bandage round her head but freshly washed blow-dried hair, full make-up and a just-see-through-enough sprigged cotton sleeveless nightdress with her pale but toned arms protruding from her shift and the boy she has loved hopelessly from afar at her bedside, clasping her hand, willing her back to consciousness. She opens her eyes and the first thing she sees is his eyes filled with tears.

This is not that scene. I am lying on my side on the bed wearing no make-up because what's the point. My unwashed hair is dry and is scraped back and tied up in an elastic band and I can see how many split ends I have from here because I haven't been allowed to get out of the hospital yet to get a haircut and there are no hairdressers that visit here.

"So, um, how are you?" He asks again. "I brought you this." He says, thrusting a parcel at me.

I take it from him and place it carefully on the floor, dropping it as my hand shakes too much for me to hold on to the parcel.

"Well aren't you going to open it?" He says. "I want you to open it now while I'm here. It's really nice."

He picks it up and places it on the bed next to me. I pick it up with both hands and shake it gently. It doesn't rattle. It is soft. It must be either an item of clothing or…

"Open it, open it," he says, looking at me as if he really wants me to open it.

"Later."

I decide. I am saying as few words as possible because the new antipsychotic drug olanzapine is slurring my speech, so I don't want him to hear this. I want to save opening the present for when he's gone so if I don't like it he won't know. I'm not sure I could hide my disappointment at the moment.

Anyway, this room is my world, this is my life now. This is my cell. I am the anchoress walled up here to have my visions and talk to God. I might never get out and nothing will come in here except food which will be passed through the metal grill at the top of the wall under the ceiling. I might have to spend the rest of my life here. At the moment Seb is too far away to reach me and I don't know how exactly we could do anything about this.

"Come on, I promise you'll like it."

He puts his hand over mine and my stomach clenches in a nice way.

"OK."

I turn the package over in my hand and unpick the sellotape from one corner and rip the paper gently. The paper is silver with purple stars. I pull the corner and a furry ear protrudes, and then I rip it across the whole length of the present and a pair of yellow-green eyes is staring into mine and I draw a sharp breath in because it is a smilodon. I look at the furry beast. He looks like a lion apart from the fangs: all whiskery and golden with a chestnut mane and a tail with a furry bobble on the end. He is squatting on his hind legs. He has a fluffy brown chest-mane as well, and black spots on his bottom.

"Thank you." I whisper.

Seb brushes my cheek with his hand.

He remembers. He is sending me a signal that he remembers and that it is something that means something to him; it is something we have together.

"When you come out of here," he says. "When you come home, can we…"

"I don't know."

Those three whole words come out fuzzy. It is weird for even my speech to have gone, not to be able to come back with something witty – not just because of my mood but because the words are unable to squeeze out through the anti-psychotic door.

"Well we can give it a go. I want to." He says, in what I think is probably a sincere voice.

I want to. But I am scared. I am scared he will hurt me.

"Do you? Will you try?"

"Yeah, OK." I say.

He brushes my cheek with his lips.

"OK babe." He says. "I'll come back soon."

And he gets up and lopes off towards the door and I sit on my bed stroking the smilodon and touching my cheek where his lips have been.

He leaves and as he leaves I turn back to the wall, get into bed and pull the covers up round my ears. I pull the little smilodon under my covers and the panther burrows under the covers and nuzzles the little smilodon with his nose.

This is what I wanted to happen. This is the result I wanted but it seems so empty now, because even if we are starting from here there's so much stuff to break down. I miss Robbie. I know that if it was Robbie who'd just been here then I wouldn't feel like this. But of course I don't know this either because Robbie has gone, Robbie has been gone for ages, and it doesn't even matter who the boy is because I'm still me and the problem isn't exactly which boy is saying that they do or don't want to be with me, the problem is inside me. There is a big M branded onto my forehead like murderers were given in the old days. 'M' for manic depressive and 'M' for 'Mad' and M for…oh, whatever. I can't finish the thought. I turn my face into my panther's flank and I feel his fur get wet as I cry onto him. He licks my tears, his tongue rasps my face and I like the pain, it tickles and he starts to purr, with his tail wrapped round the little smilodon. I close my eyes and I fall asleep, soothed by his low purr and his warmth and solidity in my shifting world.

Chapter 26

"It's London Fields weather." Ben comments when he visits a week later with Lily in tow. I've been in the hospital for a month now.

"Eh?"

I can't remember the weather in *London Fields*.

"The weather we're going to have at the end of the world. You've read *London Fields*"

"Oh yeah, I see what you mean, course I have, you're right, it is."

"Well this is *London Fields* weather. It's dark, oppressive, tense – a storm brewing without the relief of it breaking."

The sky is indeed an ominous grey with a close, muggy, apocalyptic sense in the air.

"What's *London Fields*, Benjy?" Lily says, her face upturned to his: a sunflower to the sun of knowledge.

She is so thick.

"It's a book by Martin Amis, darling." Ben explains.

Eughhh I'm going to puke, he called Lily darling.

"His best book." I say, knowing Ben is going to disagree with me and Lily won't say anything because she hasn't read anything by Martin Amis, or anything by either Amis in fact, or anything by anyone else, not since all the Trebizon books and the whole Sweet Valley High collection.

"Er, no, I think you will find that *Money* is his best book." Ben says, pulling himself up to his full height, which is considerably shorter than my full height.

He looks even more puny than usual next to my panther who is stretched out on the grass beside him sunbathing and watching my guests through wary eyes.

"Who cares, anyway." Lily says. "I don't know why you two spend so much time reading, it's a total waste of time."

Shut up you stupid tart, I think. Like you're so amazing anyway, lowering yourself to go out with Ben who you swore you'd never stoop to in a million years. The supply of boys must have dried up while I've been inside. Maybe there is now a worldwide boy drought like after the First World War and when I get out of here I'll spend the rest of my life as an old maid.

I look at Lily. She is wearing a crotch-length stonewashed denim mini-skirt with frayed edging and a tight scarlet T-shirt. Her hair is feathered at the front and shoulder length at the back: it's reverted to its natural mousey brown which I haven't seen for five years and it looks great, much stronger and healthier. She's not wearing much make-up and she looks gorgeous: natural and fresh and suffused with the glow of happiness which seeps out of all her pores.

"Oh, shit, T, I've got something for you," she says. "Ben where's the…"

"Don't look at me, I haven't touched it." Ben says.

Oh God, they're already sounding like a middle-aged married couple.

"I must have left it in the car then, I'll be back in a sec," she says.

We both watch her totter off across the lawn in her silver heels, Ben with love and lust and me with a sudden realization…

"Hey, Lily, those are my shoes." I shout after her.

"She asked your mum if she could borrow them and your Mum said yes." Ben explains sheepishly.

"How the fuck, she's such a nightmare, those are my favourite…"

It's a stab wound right to my heart. I'm Peter Pan, coming back to his home and seeing, through the window, another boy in his bed, his Mum having replaced him, and then flying off again broken-hearted back to Neverneverland. How could my Mum do such a terrible thing as give Lily my favourite shoes that she bought me last year as a birthday present. When I get home my whole wardrobe is going to be empty, there will be darker patches of purple on my walls where all my pictures have gone: given to my friends and…

"Well you're not using them in here are you?"

"It's so none of your business. Just keep your nose out of it and enjoy what short amount of time you're going to get trailing around after her Majesty before something better comes along for her and…"

"Tanya, that was totally uncalled for. Lily and I are…"

"For fuck's sake."

"Why are you being so horrible?" He asks, obviously upset, doing his wounded spaniel expression. "You know I've liked Lily for ages. Can't you just be pleased for me? Huh? Just this once, I've got something I want and…"

"She's my best friend. Why can't you go out with someone else? Why do the two of you have to rub my nose in it?"

"What the hell are you talking about? For fuck's sake, Tanya, this is ridiculous. This is nothing to do with you. It's between me and Lily and…"

"Oh, Ben, I'm sorry. I am sorry. I am pleased for you, for you and Lily." I lie in a completely unconvincing sarcastic tone.

"I know you are," he says, his triumphant smile irritating me even further.

Lily returns. "Here:" she thrusts the package in my face.

"Take my shoes off. You may not borrow them; I don't care what my mother told you, she didn't ask me." I tell her, ignoring the present.

"But I haven't got any others."

"Shut up."

She has a wardrobe full of shoes, a separate shoe closet.

With deliberate slowness and a pained expression she unbuckles the shoes, hands them to me.

"You shouldn't have worn them here you silly cow." I tell her.

"I know, I forgot. I've only worn them once," she lies.

I know this is a lie because they're all scuffed at the front and one of the straps is ripped and, well, I didn't do that damage. I've never even worn them, they're too uncomfortable.

"Open your present, open it, open it," she says.

I unwrap it, peeling the sellotape off so as not to rip the gorgeous silver hologram paper which somehow catches the sunlight that I haven't even realised has broken through the clouds. I have to peel off several layers of tissue paper, each containing a single Opal Fruit or whatever they're called these days, playing pass-the-parcel on my own: fuchsia, violet, lavender, white, the layers peel off, the rainbow of opal fruits scatter on the grass.

Finally, then, there it is: a framed photo of the three of us is staring up at me. I'm in the middle, flanked by Lily and Emily. We're all wearing our Spank dresses. Lily's wearing her cobalt blue one with the silver flower, I'm wearing my lilac one with the eye and Emily's wearing her green one with the moon. We look excited, flushed with anticipation. It was taken just before the last Magic Realms, the last Magic Realms I'll probably ever attend, just after our last AS exam, I remember, by Emily's Dad, outside the front of their house. We look pretty, happy, innocent of the horrors that are a mere 48 hours away. Our hair is all freshly washed and bouncy: adorned with silver sparkly butterflies; our make-up perfect, unsmudged, bright.

Emily's apple tree is visible in the background, the tent we've fixed up in the garden as practice for pitching our tent in the dark when we arrive at Glastonbury. I realise they must all have been to Glastonbury without me earlier in the summer. That's probably where Ben and Lily got together. We were all meant to be going there, a huge group of us.

"Well, do you like it?" She asks.

I nod, not trusting myself to speak without bursting into tears.

"You'll be home soon, T," she says. "We'll go out and have lots of fun when you're home. We'll have plenty of summer left."

We won't. I think. We won't go out and take drugs together ever again. We won't have plenty of summer left either, it's August already, back to school in 3 weeks and I'm still here, they're not showing any signs of letting me out.

"You seem much better," she says in an encouraging tone.

"Um, yeah, well, I suppose." I say, even though now I'm not high anymore I feel much, much worse.

I'm sure she doesn't really want to hear this though, and I don't have the energy to explain how I feel. This is how I feel: hospital no longer seems fun, in fact it has becomes unbearable. Whereas before I've been outside socialising the whole time, now I don't dare to leave my room in case someone tries to talk to me. The addicts whom I've so enjoyed hanging out with now seem vacuous, irritating and self-obsessed. Why don't they just pull themselves together, I catch myself thinking. I mean, how pathetic is it to throw your life away just to be drunk or wasted or stoned the whole time. I've always avoided the other depressives, for obvious reasons, they're just not a barrel of laughs. Now I find myself pushed into an uneasy alliance with them. We sit on the bench and stare into space for hours, not speaking to each other. I perfect my blank stare. I don't tell Lily this though.

"We'll be back soon," she says, squeezing my hand and patting my arm like a Grandma. "Won't we, Ben?"

"Yeah, bye T."

I watch them walk away across the grass, Lily barefoot, resting her hand on Ben's forearm for balance: Lily-and-Ben together. Go away then, I think. Go on, get out.

"Dad, I want to go home." I plead. 'Please take me home. When can I come home?"

We're sitting in the courtyard of a restaurant down the road from the hospital on the evening after Ben and Lily's visit. There are spider plants and ferns and yellow stone walls with moss growing on them and plants sticking out of gaps in between the stones. Obviously, I'm not allowed alcohol, and I won't be for weeks or maybe even months while Dr Josh sorts out my medication.

"When Dr Stein says you are well enough." Dad says, taking his thick glasses off, breathing on the lenses and wiping them with his sweater sleeve, holding them up close to his face so he can see them. As he bends his head I can see how grey his hair is, and that it's thinning on top.

"But I am. I'm not exactly a danger to myself or society in this state, am I?" I say, leaning my head against the pub wall because I'm just too tired to lift it up.

There are red terracotta urns propped up against the walls with orange geraniums growing out of them. My panther leans against the wall, rubbing his shoulder against the stones, scratching an itch. I hope he hasn't got fleas.

"You're not well enough to come home yet, Tanya." Dad says.

"How do you know?'

"Because Dr Stein says so."

"Why can't you and Mum look after me at home though?"

I look at Dad and he looks very old, grey stubble dotted around his jaw-line and hooded eyes like an iguana.

"Because I have to work to stop us from sliding into penury, and you're not well enough to come home yet, according to Dr Stein."

"We're not exactly on the breadline, Dad."

I look around us to make sure the other customers aren't listening to our conversation. No one seems to be. They are all enjoying an early evening pint after work.

"We have to tighten our belts, Tanya. The insurance company aren't going to keep coughing up forever you know. They stop paying once it's more treatment for a pre-existing condition."

"What's that?"

"Well, now you've been diagnosed with your illness, if you need to be hospitalised for it again the insurance company won't foot the bill."

"Oh."

"And it's not cheap, this hospital. They might stop paying for Dr Stein as well."

"I'm sorry Dad."

"I'm not cross with you. It's just the way it is. We're going to get through this, however much it costs."

Dad pats my hand. This is a rare display of emotion for my father. Maybe he does love me after all.

"Come on, drink up. I have to get back. I've got an early meeting tomorrow in town."

Dad pays the bill and we amble back to the hospital. Dad deposits me at the hospital and I wave goodbye to him and return to my room where I cry myself to sleep.

Chapter 27

THERE IS A KNOCK AT THE DOOR which jolts me out of my slumber. I have been up to get my morning meds but have returned to bed where I am dozing and listening to Portishead: wrung out, exhausted. The walls of my hospital room are white and now that I have been here for so long I have blu-tacked up some of my old Apocalypse and Magic Realms flyers which now seem to belong to another life, or maybe to someone else's life entirely. I ignore the knock, but it is persistent.

"Come in." I call.

The door swings open and Dr Josh strides into my room.

"Good morning Tanya," he says.

I raise my heavy head from the pillow and look at him. His blue eyes sparkle. He strides across the room and settles himself down in the brown chair next to my bed. He is energy, beauty, strength in this cold room. The panther is lying next to me and I can hear his loud purr and feel the warmth of his body and the tickling of his fur on my skin through my thin nightdress. My skin is so sensitive, now that my mood has dropped, that the combination of the panther's body heat and the cold air in the hospital room is almost too intense.

"Good morning Dr Stein."

I put on a face that says: look how much better I am. I'm back to normal and I don't need to be in a mental hospital anymore.

He pulls a pen out of his breast pocket.

"How is your mood, Tanya?" He asks; his pen poised above his notepad.

"It's a bit better." I reply.

"Good. Well, now that we have brought your mood down your parents will be able to manage you at home."

"Can I really go home?"

Despite my constant pleading I haven't dared to hope that I could be allowed home just yet. He smiles at me. I look at his lustrous brown wavy hair, his blue eyes. I'm going to miss seeing you every day, I think.

My mood is not really a bit better though. It is the same as it has been the last couple of weeks since I crashed out of the mania. The panther lies beside me on my bed, under the covers, along the length of my body: his tail laid out flat across my shins, his thigh against my thigh. He is keeping me as safe and warm as he can: his whiskers tickling my face: his right front leg across my chest, pinning me to the bed; his claws retracted because he doesn't want to hurt me.

"I want to go home." I say, even though I'm not sure that I do. A part of me is scared to go home and to be catapulted back into my life.

"I have spoken to your mother. She is coming to pick you up at 3 o'clock."

"OK."

My Mum is coming to take me home at last. I've been looking forward to this day for two whole weeks, but I don't feel the happiness I expected to feel – just flatness.

"You have been having a rotten time of it, haven't you?"

He looks at me, a gentle, paternal look, full of compassion. He reaches out and pats my hand. A big tear falls out of my eye and rolls down my face. I feel so sorry for myself at this moment.

I try to say something, anything, in response but there are more tears coming and I draw in a sharp breath, trying to stop them but then they tumble down my cheeks. My life has gone rotten. My life is that pot of cottage cheese with the green fungal spores in it that someone has forgotten about because it's at the back of the fridge, or a furry over-ripe peach. Actually, peaches are furry anyway, a furry over-ripe orange then. Dr Stein is talking and I thrust the rotten fruit back to the back of the fridge of my mind from whence it came. I swing my attention back to his words:

"…but now we've brought your mood down with the olanzapine, taken you off the anti-depressants and added in a mood stabiliser you're not going to become hypomanic again."

"What will happen, when my mood comes up next time then?"

"You'll experience a normal mood."

A normal mood, eh, Dr Josh, I think. It will be interesting to see what one of those looks like after a year of abnormal moods ranging from depression to elation and back and round in circles. I don't believe him anyway. I want to believe that somewhere out there there's a normal mood in a box with my name on it just waiting for the right spell to be uttered which will summon it up to appear and sit next to me and become my constant companion, but it just seems too fanciful.

"I'll leave you to get ready." he says, getting up and walking out of my room.

The door swings shut behind him.

After he's gone I pull some clothes on: my navy linen drawstring trousers, silver adidas shell-toe trainers, coral pink T-shirt and powder pink zip-up sweater. There's time to have a last walk around the hospital gardens while I wait for Mum.

It's raining and no-one is sitting outside around the wooden tables with their sun umbrellas today. Chairs glisten with raindrops:

tiny spines on lizard skin. The badminton net sags in the middle with the rain. The non-smoking lounge is empty. Only old Niall is in the smoking room: dozing, snoring, dribbling down his egg-stained cardigan. I pull the door of the smoking room shut behind me and leave him there sleeping.

Most of my friends have left hospital and returned to their real lives. Gemma was discharged a week ago, the various addicts have dispersed – some to stricter rehab facilities, others home to keep drinking. My hospital already has the feel of a bed-and-breakfast establishment in a dilapidated seaside town out of season. Our summer holiday from reality is over: time to go back to school. My private nurse Debby has moved to a different hospital.

As I walk around the grounds of the hospital I feel a new optimism, despite my mood. It is a feeling that breaks through my mood and buoys me up. I have been given a second chance. I have survived, I am fighting the illness. I am lucky to be alive. I look at the bright pink rhododendrons and I see them with fresh eyes. I'm going home, everything is going to be OK. I'm sure everything will be so much better once I'm home.

I can see my Mum walking towards me across the grass. She is wearing her long purple skirt which swishes around her ankles. As she approaches, her face breaks into a smile and then I'm running towards her and I throw my arms around her.

"Mum," I say. "You're here to take me home."

"Sweetie pie," she says. "Of course I'm here. Of course I'm taking you home. I'm going to look after you. I'm your mother. I love you."

She strokes my cheek.

"I'm going to look after you too." I say. "I love you, Mum."

I reach out for Mum's hand, and we walk towards the car, hand in hand, into the rest of my life.

At home, however, I sit in the garden and grind my teeth, and stare into space for hours. It's nearly the end of summer and the flowers are dying, the lawn is brown and scorched, the geraniums wilting and over, the petunias having a last gasp. The fennel in the middle of our herb garden has shot up – it's taller than me now. It's changed colour from russet to pale green and has yellow flowers like cow parsley.

The garden birds are light enough to rest on it. There are baby goldfinches, greenfinches, robins, great tits, blue tits. All our birds have chicks which look as if they've been in the washing machine: their feathers fluffed up, their colours washed out; their movements uncertain like mine on olanzapine.

"Stop staring vacantly into space like a mad person," Mum says.

"I am mad though, Mum."

She just twitches and looks uncomfortable. It's affecting Mum, my illness. She's terribly thin and I don't have the energy to encourage her to eat, or any appetite myself. Normally I'd say 'Right, Mum, I'm not eating my pizza unless you eat yours,' but now we both sit there with untouched plates of food in front of us on the table. I stare at the birds as they perch on their feeders in the garden.

Chapter 28

"Look, Robbie." I whisper, as I catch a glimpse of a striped leg and bottom through the trees. "It's an okapi."

We are in the rainforest.

"A what?"

He's obviously still thick, even though he went to Australia about a year ago and I'm surprised he hasn't learnt some more natural history while he's been in the outback and whatever. I don't understand how he can possibly not know what an okapi is.

"It's a relation of the giraffe." I explain, pulling my hair back into a ponytail because it's swelteringly hot here.

My hair feels really soft and not frizzy at all.

"Seriously?"

His big green eyes widen and I see his long eyelashes flutter. I hear the cogs of his brain turning. He bites his lip.

"So, if it's a giraffe…"

He fiddles with his dried seed pod necklace, and pulls his swimming trunks up – they've started to slide down a bit and they look as if they're made of ivy: they're all leafy and the leaves are thick and dark green and packed tightly together.

"It's not a giraffe. It's just related to them." I repeat, pushing the strap of my halter neck fern leaf bikini up my shoulder, which must be sunburned – it's starting to itch. "Europeans thought it was a mythical beast till the beginning of this century and…"

"Where do you read all this stuff, T? Why do you learn all these things? What's the point?"

He's much more toned and tanned since he went away, he looks quite buff and his hair is all platinum blond from the sun, longer and mussed-up.

We creep closer to the okapi, passing kookaburras croaking and koalas curled up in the trees. When we're right up near the velvety brown animal he reaches his head down and stares at us with huge liquid eyes, his lashes longer than Robbie's. I reach my hand up to stroke his velvety neck and he sticks out his blue-black tongue and licks my hand. I lock eyes with him and then…

…I wake up crying that I'm not in the jungle with Robbie and all those fabulous animals. I haven't heard from him at all since he left, I'm not sure whether anyone has. He's probably having a wonderful time having barbecues on the beach, surfing, drinking Fosters, playing lots of rugby, cricket and whatever they do there. It's a whole world away, the other side of the world, another life, somewhere I'll probably never go, certainly not while I'm on shed-loads of medication and unable to leave the house without my mother. Robbie is gone and I don't know if anything is happening with Seb and…

"Time to get up and get on with the day,' Mum announces, pulling my curtains open. "Look what a beautiful day it is."

"I'm sleeping. Go away." I mumble into my pillow.

"No you're not. It's time to get up."

"What time is it then?"

"It's nearly nine o'clock."

This could mean it's anything from about 7am onwards. I stretch a hand out to my bedside table and scrabble around for my watch, pulling it under my covers with me. It is not nearly nine o'clock. It is 8.03.

"Do you know what it is today sweetie?"

"No. And I don't care," I reply from under the covers.

"AS level results day."

"I'm not…" I refuse to go to school and see everyone and open the envelope. I'm bound to have screwed up – I was hypomanic when I sat those exams, probably wrote a load of rubbish.

"Yes we are. Come on."

Mum is dressed in her tennis outfit – a white Adidas mini-dress, white tennis shoes and those stupid socks which only come up to just below your ankles. She is too old to wear such a short dress, I think. It's a teenager's dress.

"Put on something pretty," Mum says. "And brush your hair and put some make-up on."

"Like that's going to make any difference."

"You don't have to make yourself look horrible, sweetie, just because you feel miserable."

"What's the point though?"

"If you look better you'll feel better. Well, you certainly won't feel any worse. Come on, put these on." She holds out a pair of tight flared indigo jeans and a turquoise vest-top with a flower in the centre of the chest.

"I need my halter-neck wonder-bra with that one, my black Freya one."

"Here it is sweetie."

She pulls a black strap that is sticking out from under a pile of exercise books on my chair: she's already found the bra in question with her mother's eye for detail, her mother's x-ray vision for homing in on something. Her nose is twitching: a shrew's long, mobile nose.

I pull on the outfit selected by my mother but being dressed doesn't make me feel any better. I'm terrified that I've screwed up my exams; my face still itches because I can't work up the energy even to run a cleansing wipe over it. I don't want to see any of my friends either – I really don't want to see any of my friends.

It's a hot, sunny day. The sky is blue and there are a few candyfloss wisps of cloud. We hurtle up the driveway of my school, or our speed only seems rapid because my mood is so low. Objects build their pace up as they come towards me. I remember how slow things seemed when I was high in hospital, and I can't imagine seeing the world in slow motion like that. Now it's the opposite: it's time lapse photography where flowers push up out of the soil, grow and change and blossom and die before my eyes. The cedar trees on the drive up to school leap towards me, the road jumps up towards me, the horizon tunnels, we're bombing down a flume to school. School looms towards us: huge, forbidding, white; framed with cedars. The cedars cut the sky into horizontal segments – bands on shale or sandstone – or any sedimentary rock where fossils live. The cedars have been here for 400 years. They have seen generations of girls pick up their exam results. They have experienced years of tears of disappointment and rage. They have born witness to screams of laughter at As that never seemed possible, and silent floods of pain at Cs that shattered dreams.

As we pull up at school – alongside all the Chelsea tractors and luxury sports cars – I spot Emily, Lily and Wendy: chatting, giggling, looking their usual gorgeous selves. I pretend I haven't seen them though. I avoid Clara and Helena as well, who are grinning, no doubt because they've got 4As.

I walk up to school and the groups of girls part – the Red Sea before Moses – to let me through. No one tries to talk to me: they probably don't know what to say. They probably think it's infectious. People are scared of mental illness apparently, according to something I read, and think it's contagious. Leprosy of the brain where you look normal only your brain falls out of your ears and puddles in a rainbow oil spill on the pavement.

I don't try to talk to them and just amble, wobbling, up to the desk where the envelopes are laid out in alphabetical order. The lady behind the desk smiles at me. She has got a frizzy perm which reaches her shoulders and half-moon glasses. Her lipstick is smeared on her teeth as she smiles a toothy smile. She probably didn't do A-levels. They must've had that exam the Romans did when she was at school – geometry, rhetoric, oratory and orgy studies.

"Don't worry, dear," she says. "It will be OK."

"How do you know?"

"Well, what depends on it?"

"My sanity."

She thinks for a moment, chewing the end of her biro. "You can always retake your modules."

"I might not be able to. I don't know whether…"

"What's the worst that can happen?"

"I might have to go back into hospital and…"

"So what? The thing about education is that it's never too late. I did my degree when I was sixty seven."

"Really? What subject?"

"History of Art. I specialised in Cold War sculpture."

"Wow."

She smiles again. "You see?"

I don't know what she means exactly. I can't really wait another five thousand years or whatever to go to university. I look at my envelope sitting there – between Amy Mankowitz's and Felicity Matterberg's – and touch it. Then I pick it up and carry it over behind a Doric column.

My hands shake. I luxuriate in this last moment of not knowing. And then I take a last deep breath and rip it open, just like pulling off a plaster. I stare in disbelief at the grades. 4 As in English, Biology and History and Maths. It's not possible. I'm stunned. How can I have achieved these marks: it just doesn't seem possible. I stumble back to the car on olanzapine stilts and stare into space.

"Well?" Mum asks, her face hopeful. She struggles for the indifference which stars strive to feign at the Oscars, as the results are read out.

"4 As." I say, keeping my own voice flat, maintaining a blank stare into the distance just above her left shoulder.

She lets out a yelp and throws her arms around me. As if anyone could doubt that a mother's love is conditional on results.

"But, sweetie, aren't you happy? That's wonderful."

She strokes my hair and she's actually crying. Pull yourself together, I think.

"Why? I'm still insane, I want to die anyway. What's the point? It's just totally meaningless."

I can't believe I ever cared, ever imagined it mattered whether I got As or Bs or whatever. My life has been ripped apart by the illness and reassembled upside-down, back to front with holes and tears and misshapen bits dangling in the wrong place, sewn up with a huge fat needle so the stitches show every wound and seam.

"You are going to go to back and finish school sweetie. You are. Don't worry."

Mum's sudden burst of confidence seems inadequate of course. The outlook is bleak. I may have to spend the rest of my life in mental institutions, or at least prolonged periods of the rest of my life, like Vivien Leigh and Zelda Fitzgerald who rotted away in asylums for years before their deaths. A lot of use 4 As at AS Level will be to me then.

A week after results day we all go to my Aunty Beatrice's house in West Hampstead for a lunch to celebrate…something – probably one of my cousins' birthdays. It is sunny. We sit on blankets on the grass – my cousins and I – while the adults sit at tables. Everyone else is drinking Pimms, I can't drink for the foreseeable future. I observe with mounting disbelief that no-one mentions the fact I've been in hospital for six weeks, no-one asks me how I'm feeling. This is ridiculous: I'm with my own family and not a single one of them has even acknowledged the situation, expressed any human impulse. The panther lies next to me on my blanket, resting his head in my lap. I stroke the soft back of his neck. He won't leave me, I think.

I lie on a blanket observing them all laughing, joking, interacting. If Carl was here he'd talk to me. Why can't someone make some effort? Why can't *I* make some effort to pretend to be normal? But a part of me is thinking: this is me. This depressed, uncommunicative, fat creature is me. This is the other side of the illness and I will not deny it. I will not pretend to…

"Tanya, a very good friend of mine has had manic depression for 25 years. Would you like to meet him?' one of my aunts says.

She's walked over to my patch. Well there's an acknowledgement if I wanted one!

"Yes, thank you Aunty Gloria I'd love to."

"OK. Here's his number. You call him when you feel up to it." She pushes a piece of paper into my sweaty hand, and sweeps off to be reabsorbed into the bosom of the family.

I look at the piece of paper with the number in it and put it in my purse. I'll call him when I feel a bit better than this. I stretch out my legs – now I'm off the Olanzapine at least I can try and get a tan. The panther's attention is caught by a squirrel. He stretches, bum up, then collects himself and stalks off.

The dahlias are flowering all around the borders of the garden. My grandpa used to plant dahlias. They grow round here as it's warm in Hampstead and the soil is right for them. I wish we could have them but the slugs eat them in our garden – Mum thinks pest control is cruel. I suppose it is, but then on the other hand no pesticides means that slugs eat certain plants and dahlias are a particular favourite of theirs. Aunty Beatrice has pink and yellow and purple and orange ones – pom-pom ones and lily ones, peony, anemone, cactus types, collarette, semi cactus, laciniated, novelty, ball. I know all these types because there is a dahlia show ground at our local garden centre, and every September I go with Mum and we walk along the rows of all the colours and types of dahlias deciding which ones we're going to buy and plant for our slugs to eat.

I think about our dahlia failures and start crying and it seems like the most upsetting thing in the world. As I look at my family spread out across the garden, I feel the force of my illness and the intensity of my difference from all of them. They can't reach me – the only one who can communicate with me is my panther. He's lying next to me on my blanket again with his head in my lap. His green eyes follow Aunty Beatrice's cat Snowball as Snowball chases a feather across the garden. Snack time, I know he is thinking.

"You can't," I tell him. "Snowball is not lunch, he is a pet, and he is a pedigree white Persian descended from Blofeld's cat in the James Bond films, he is not a snack. Stay here with me. I'll feed you something else.

Fortunately, I'm not really hungry so he eats my kebab and potato salad while I restrict myself to watermelon because I'm trying to lose some of the weight I put on in hospital.

Chapter 29

THERE ARE TWO BABY BLUE TITS in the house, lying on the table and quivering. They must have just hatched, they look as if they've come out of the washing machine with their colours faded and feathers sticking out in all directions.

"We have to keep them in here." I tell Mum.

"No, we're putting them out in the garden. There are nest boxes out there."

We carry the chicks out into the garden, which is filled with nest boxes. In each box there's a different bird family: bullfinches, goldfinches, greenfinches, collared doves, wood pigeons, green woodpeckers, lesser spotted woodpeckers. I notice that some of the birds are dead. The panther must have killed them, I think. No, it must be something else: the panther would not have been able to get inside the nest boxes, or even to get one paw inside one.

"We've got to keep these blue tits in the house. It's not safe for them out here."

"They are staying out here." Mum says.

I start screaming as I feel their bodies go limp and then cold in my hands, and wake up sweating and screaming. My relief that it was just a dream is subsumed by panic as the reality of my life sinks in. I check the clock: it's 3.30am. I always wake at this time when I'm low, it's the worst time. I'm desperate to get back to sleep but I must fall back into sleep naturally. I've already taken one sleeping pill tonight and I don't want to become resistant to them. I have endless nights of sleeping pills ahead of me: an unrelenting regime of mood stabilisers, anti-depressants, anti-psychotics. I measure out my life in medicine spoons.

"There's a rare fatal disease afflicting goldfinches, greenfinches and chaffinches throughout the country." Mum says as we sit at the breakfast table the next day.

She is spreading marmite on her toast and drinking her coffee and reading *The Times*. According to Dr Stein it is important for us all to sit down at the table and eat our meals together as a family so that I don't develop any more problems. Dad is not here though.

"No, there can't be."

The lifeless bodies of the birds in my dream float behind my eyes.

"Well that is what it says in the paper this morning. It's spread from bird to bird by their saliva, and as it's been such a hot summer people have been making bird baths for them and…"

"Stop it."

I don't want to know. I have made the garden birds die with the powers of my mind.

"We have to scrub all the bird baths and feeders regularly."

Their little throats bleed, their feathers fluff up. They fall out of the sky. It is a painful, slow death according to the article. Just like my dream. I have killed them as surely as if I've broken their little necks or slashed their tiny throats with a razor. Being able to predict the future is a gift I don't want. The spookiness of the bird dream entwines itself with the rest of my dark thoughts.

I look out of the window into the garden. There is a pigeon in the bird bath with its feathers all fluffed up just sitting there in that dopey pigeon way. Don't die, I think. Please don't die. The wood pigeons and collared doves sit on the trays of the bird feeding station, unbalancing it, rocking it under their weight. I love them. My world has contracted to them and my garden. I want to stop taking my medication and I want to be better. I want to forget everything that has happened in the last year. I want to rewind to just after GCSEs and live this whole year again differently without being ill.

"Do you want to come down to the tennis club with me and…?"

"No," I answer without letting Mum finish her sentence.

"Well you are coming whether you want to or not, come on. It'll do you good to get out of the house."

"I'll be ready in a bit."

"Five minutes."

"Oh OK. Stop hassling me."

I climb into the car over the boxes of tennis balls, rackets, bottles of orange squash and lemon barley water that are Mum's props as deputy captain of the veteran ladies' B team. Part of her job is to take refreshments to the matches.

The panther crouches and springs onto the back seat where he drapes himself over the tennis rackets and swishes the tip of his tail. He doesn't get on with the cat at the tennis club but he likes chasing the pigeons there and sunning himself on the astro-turf and sitting by the side of the net and jumping out to pat the balls as they fly over it. I'm used to his presence now. I imagine that he will be with me always. In a strange way he comforts me – he is big and warm and reassuring. He doesn't like me interacting with other people so I don't. That's easy enough most of the time, but now I will be forced to socialise with Mum's tennis friends.

"Thank God you're here." Lily's Mum says as we get out of the car. She looks distressed. Her Perfect hair is dishevelled, her mascara has run. Apart from a few extra lines and an increased leatheriness of skin she looks so much like Lily.

"What's happened?" Mum asks.

"There's an injured pigeon on the court. He's just sitting there."

She leads us outside the clubhouse to where a pigeon is nestling on the court. He looks very weak, his feathers fluffed up. He has a ring round his leg which I see as Mum picks him up.

"He's a racing pigeon." Mum says. She examines the ring. "Look, it's got his owner's telephone number on here. I'll phone him, and get him to come and pick his pigeon up."

She walks over to the phone that is by the bar of the clubhouse.

"Hello, Mrs Marshall from the tennis club in Radlett, Hertfordshire here." She says.

"I have your pigeon here, can you come and pick him up?" There is a pause.

"What do you mean just leave him to die?"

Another pause.

"What shall I do then if you're not coming to pick him up?"

She is visibly shaken. "Oh, OK, if you're sure?"

She turns back to me.

"The owner says that the pigeon has been lost for two weeks and he won't have eaten so I should just leave him to die." She sniffs. "He's not coming to collect him as he lives in Cheltenham, and he says it's not worth coming all that way to collect a pigeon who is going to die."

I lift the pigeon, he weighs hardly anything. He looks very tired. We put him in a cardboard box with some water and carry the box back into the clubhouse.

"You can't put that bird in here. I've got a bird phobia." The club manager says.

Pam the club manager looks like a fat turkey herself with her long nose and short grey hair and jowls and three chins. Mum rounds on her.

"So see someone about it. This pigeon needs to be here. Don't be so pathetic Pam."

"Well only…" Pam's jowls wobble with distress.

"Oh shut up." Mum says.

I snigger. Lily's Mum tries to look serious and snorts into her lemon squash.

"Here you go little fellow." Mum says to the pigeon.

He looks up at us from inside his new nest in the cardboard box. He cocks his head on one side. Lily's Mum puts her arm round me. It is what I think a Mum's arm should be like, a bit chubby and soft and rounded and scented with one of those Mum perfumes.

"How are you feeling Tanya?" She asks.

"Much better thank you."

"Lily's not very happy to be back at school," she says.

"No, I know."

She can't bear to be parted from Benjamin's thrusting member for more than a minute, I think, and then realise that Lily has not divulged whether or not they have done it yet. I must ask her as soon as I am not standing next to her Mum.

"She's spending a lot of time with young Benjamin. She's not a good girl like you Tanya, still not doing her homework. He seems alright though, for a boy. At least he's Jewish."

"True."

Lily's Mum does not have Ben at the top of her 'Husband List' unlike my Mum. I don't know why. She probably thinks Lily can do better. If so, I don't know why my Mum doesn't think I can do better, apart from the Severe Mental Illness Problem.

"She's with Benjamin now," she says, as if she needs to offer an explanation for Lily's absence from the Sunday Morning Veteran Ladies' Social. "I don't know why they have to spend so much time together. Benjamin…"

I giggle, imagining Ben and Lily in bed together.

"What is it?" Lily's Mum says.

"Nothing," I say.

"Well you look a lot better," she says.

I don't know whether this is or isn't a good thing, let alone whether she means it.

"Thank you." I say.

I do not feel better. I miss my Lily and my Ben separately and hate the new hideous Lily-and-Ben creature they have morphed into which spends all its time in bed together when it should be looking after me.

"You're a good girl Tanya." Lily's Mum says and pats my hand. "I wish she was more like you. More sensible, more grown up. I wish she wanted to spend time with me, like you do with your Mum. But then she never has, she's always been so independent, so....couldn't wait to get away from me."

"It's not your fault." I say. "She doesn't want to be with me either these days."

I see myself through Lily's Mum's eyes for a moment: Tanya, Lily's responsible, grown-up, academically gifted friend who is close to her Mum, who comes to the tennis club with her Mum, unlike her own feckless daughter who is off with her boyfriend doing her best to get pregnant. I see the regret Lily's Mum feels that she is not close to her daughter, that they don't do things together. They never have done though, it's not because of Ben.

"I'm sorry," she says again.

Please stop saying you're sorry, I think. It is really not helping. You are not... I mean you are just trying to make yourself feel better. It is not helping me, you.... Oh G-d I feel so much older, centuries older than these tennis club ladies. I have been to the abyss, I have looked into the abyss. I have come back up. I have come some of the way back but actually – although it was cold and windy and there were roaring waves – I would still rather be there than here, trapped in this village, taking tentative steps back to that mountain settlement they call normal.

The metaphors mix and I'm so so so tired, more tired all the time. The cars with their personalised number plates in the tennis club car park; the tennis club cat; the lemon squash: I hate it. I hate Lily for leaving me; and Ben; and Emily – where is Emily? And Caitlin, what the fuck happened to her? And Wendy, even dim Wendy with her owl eyes; and Robbie of course – if Robbie was here he would understand – he might not be here for me always but he would at least know what I mean. Know what though? And where is my brother and why is he not here and why am I at the end of my tether with only my ex –best-friend's mum trying to make me sympathise that she has a difficult relationship with her daughter?

If I could just have a haircut all this would be better. I will chop it out of my hair like Samson or, no, wait, it was his strength, his hair, wasn't it? His strength. And all these things I knew have gone or become mangled: slain on the rock of my illness, sacrificed at the stone table of my illness like Aslan before the White Witch.

Mum appears looking old, exhausted and drained. She doesn't say anything for a minute. I look at her. We share a moment.

"The pigeon is dead," my Mum says at last.

I look at Lily's Mum and back to my Mum who is crying over a pigeon who lost his way, who should never have been here and who has died – starved to death amongst strangers in a strange place – and they do not care. We care though: my Mum and I. I care with this deep anthropomorphic empathy that floats around in me waiting for any lost animal to latch on to.

"It's only a pigeon," the club secretary says to my Mum.

"They were all my sons." Mum says.

"What?" Pam says.

"It's from a play you wouldn't have seen." Mum says to her, almost conversationally. "Come on Tanya we're going home."

Chapter 30

MUM IS SITTING AT THE DINING ROOM TABLE when I get home from school. She is doing some marking – a pile of unmarked papers on her left, a pile of marked papers on her right and her register where she records each girl's scores in each test in front of her above the papers that she is working through with a red pen.

"Your clothes came back from the police," she says, without looking up. I do not know what she is talking about. My panther appears. He stands next to me and leans against me. I can feel the supportive pressure of his shoulder pushing against me, and the warmth of his body.

"The clothes you were wearing the night you…the night of the…." She cannot say it. "The night before you ended up in hospital," is what she settles on. Fragments of memory come back to me: handing my clothes over to the police so they could look for evidence; having to wear paper knickers and new clothes that they gave me.

"The policewoman said I should know that there was something inside the lining of your bra." She says. "Would you like to tell me what that was, Tanya?"

She stares at me, hard.

"I don't know." I say.

"A plastic bag of something?" She hints, staring into my eyes, challenging my gaze.

There is a sickening thud in my brain as I realise what she is getting at. No, she can't be – it can't be…

"No, I don't know." I say.

"A small plastic jewellery bag containing two round white tablets of… Ecstasy." She spits the word out as if she has never said it before, which maybe she hasn't.

I had some pills left that I didn't take, I think. That never happens. I always take everything I have on me. This is extremely bad luck. This is worse than bad luck. I thought that all this was behind me now that I've stopped taking drugs, but now it is coming back to mess things up.

"The police woman said: 'I think you should know, Mrs Marshall, that we found a bag containing two tablets of Ecstasy in your daughter's bra.'" Mum says, narrowing her eyes, pursing her lips.

Her voice is hard and cold.

"She said that they are not going to press charges because you were very unwell at the time." She pauses. "How could you do this to me, Tanya?"

I look down at the floor. This used to be the thing that I feared the most: Mum ever finding out that I took pills. Whilst everything else with the police and hospital was happening this all faded into the background, but now here it is again. I lean against my panther. I take refuge in his warmth.

"I'm sorry." I say.

"Well sorry isn't good enough." Mum replies. "You lied to me," she says. "I trusted you. How many times had you…"

"I only did it once, just to see what it was like." I say, in a tone of voice which couldn't possibly convince anyone that I'm telling the truth.

"Don't give me that rubbish. Do you think I was born yesterday? Do you? It all makes sense now – the clubbing, the not eating, the mood swings. I can't believe I've been so stupid. And I can't believe you've been so stupid, not to mention... Why didn't you tell Dr Josh the truth, even if you felt you had to lie to me?"

She looks so tired. She looks angry, of course, of course she is angry, but she has aged about 100 years since I've been ill.

"I didn't think it was..."

"How is he meant to help you if you don't tell him the truth? It could interact with your medication or stop it from working – it has already interacted with your medication – SSRI anti-depressant plus serotonin-releasing MDMA was what sent your mood so high. Don't you see that? Didn't you think of that?"

"It's nothing to do with it – all my friends take it and it hasn't done them any harm."

"That Robbie, it's him isn't it? He's made you do it. I'll kill him when I get my hands on him, he's..."

"It's not Robbie. I haven't even seen Robbie, he's gone away: it's all my nice Jewish friends who you like."

There. If you want the truth here's the truth.

"I refuse to believe that Benjamin and Lily..."

"Ben, Lily, Emily..."

"Not Emily, she's a nice girl, her mum is..."

"Nice girls do it too."

I sound like an advert for ecstasy: *'Ecstasy – the leisure drug of choice for middle-class private-school-educated teens. Nice girls do it too.'* This advert could be voiced by Cat Deeley for example, or a Blue Peter presenter.

"Well they didn't in my day." Mum says, her voice quavering, an inadequate dam against the raging tide of drug use swamping the seaside town of the middle classes.

"Well, they do now." It is better that she knows the truth now that we've started. "All my nice Jewish friends, the ones whose mums are teachers and doctors, whose dads are stockbrokers and barristers, the ones you encouraged me to be friends with, the pretty ones with the highlighted hair and…"

"I just don't believe Lily and Emily and Benjamin and Wendy and Sebastian would do such a thing." She says, scraping a hand through her hair, her scarlet nails flashing.

"Well they do."

If I'm going down they are all coming down with me. I have not, of course saved myself. I am not saved, and they are not punished, and they are all still out there, not mentally ill, still clubbing and taking pills and living a normal teenage life.

"But they're not mentally ill." Mum points out, reading my mind. "How on earth am I meant to trust you, how am I supposed to look after you, when you're so stupid and irresponsible? I'm just so disappointed in you, Tanya."

"I'm sorry," I say again because I don't know what else to say.

This whole conversation is excruciating, but at the same time a huge weight has been lifted. She knows, I think. The thing that I have always been terrified of happening has happened. The worst is over.

"How can I trust you to behave sensibly Tanya?' She looks straight into my eyes.

I think about this. "Well, I've been punished now, haven't I?"

"And what have you learnt from it?" She asks in her teacher voice.

"That I can't take drugs anymore. Ecstasy's very safe though."

I say. "No one I know who has taken it has had any kind of…"

"For G-d's sake, Tanya, I can't believe you're spouting this rubbish. I'm a scientist."

"It's true." I say. "You don't know anything about it apart from those scare-mongering articles you read in the papers…"

"Don't you dare patronise me!"

"You've always got to have the last word, you've always got to know more than me, be the expert, why do you have to treat me like a child?"

"You're seventeen years old, you're totally financially dependent on us, you're ill, you're vulnerable, you haven't got any common sense, you think you can control drugs, but you can't, they control you, you go out and get yourself into life-threatening situations, you could have been killed…"

"Yeah, but I wasn't."

"I do everything for you. I care for you as if you're a baby bird, all you have to do is sit here whilst your father and I rush around feeding you and keeping you warm and keeping you amused and…"

"Stop making such a fuss. I'm a teenager, I go out with my friends and I've taken drugs a few times. It's normal. You grew up in the sixties didn't you?"

"Nice girls didn't take drugs then. I would never have smoked cannabis, or taken LSD."

"So, now they do. Things have changed. Everyone takes them now. It's normal."

It is pointless trying to defend my whole generation to Mum, when she will never ever in a million years understand, or even try to understand. I am repeating myself now and so is she.

"I don't care what everyone does, and nor should you. Have I brought you up to follow the crowd blindly like an anaesthetised sheep? Have I?" she stares at me.

"I make my own decisions. I chose to take it. I wanted to."

"So if you hate your middle class life so much, go and live in a squat with the drug addicts and tramps who you identify so strongly with. Go and dig a tunnel under the motorway and live in it. Go and live up a tree…"

"What are you talking about?" She is just so predictable and well, so prejudiced.

"Go and live with those people. Go and…"

"Which people? I'm trying to explain to you that it's not a 'those people' thing. It's us, it's our people, and it's my friends who you like and…"

"Why do you have to reject everything your father and I believe in? Everything we have brought you up to respect?"

"I don't. I just…"

"Go and get away from your riding lessons and waxing appointments and all the trapping of this middle class life that you so despise and then you can tell us how uncool we are, how closed our minds are because we don't take psychedelic drugs."

"It's not LSD." I say. "It's Ecstasy."

"Acid house." She states triumphantly, so proud of herself that she knows what it is, that she's down with the kids.

Only of course she doesn't.

"That's just… that's just what the press call it, but they're wrong. It's nothing to do with Acid."

"It's drugs, isn't it? It's all the same. I bet you're taking heroin as well."

"This is ridiculous Mum, you're being ridiculous. You sound like an article in the Sun 'Ecstasy is destroying our society and sending our young people insane.'"

"Well it is. It has. You are taking a mood stabiliser to treat your mental disorder, and I've just discovered that you've done this to yourself by pumping that rubbish into your body. You don't have any idea how Ecstasy could react with your medication. There could be a fatal interaction, or you could lose a leg, or… "

"Well obviously I'm not doing it anymore."

"How am I meant to believe you when you lied to me? Anyway," she pauses for effect. "If all your friends did it too, why are you the only one who's got a severe mental illness? Now. After taking all

those drugs. A severe mental illness that you did not have before entering upon this regime of Ecstasy and repetitive beats. Huh?"

She looks pleased with her powers of detection, or what she thinks are her powers of detection.

"Um, I was unlucky? Our family history of depression and anorexia?" I hazard a guess.

She looks a bit shocked.

"My anorexia, which I am better from anyway, has nothing whatsoever to do with your desire to screw up your life by…"

"Why do you always have to over-dramatise everything?"

"What, exactly, am I over-dramatising? You were a normal child, good at your schoolwork, well-behaved, and then you thought it would be a good idea to give yourself a severe mental illness and ruin all our lives."

"I didn't think this was going to happen." I say.

"And you expect me to look after you," she says eventually, more to herself than to me. "Well, I'm not going to look after you any more. You did this to yourself. I told you not to take drugs, and you did and look what you've done.'

"It's not my fault though, it's not it's…"

"Well, you can make as many of your own decisions as you want to from now on. You can be an adult if you want. You can look after your father. I'm going away."

Mum pushes her chair back. The metal legs screech against the floor. She gets up and stares at me, and then picks up her handbag.

"You're doing what?" I stutter.

"You can think about what you've done, and about how you're going to make amends, while I'm away."

She takes a step away from the table, looks at me one last time with a look full of disappointment and then turns and walks out of the house without looking back.

"You can't leave me. I'm ill. You can't do this." I shout after her retreating form.

Mum doesn't answer me, or even turn round. She just keeps walking, slamming the door behind her. I'm shaking with shock. I don't know what I'm going to tell Dad when he comes home. I sit down at the table and start to sip Mum's abandoned glass of wine. The panther rests his head on my knees. I stroke the top of his head and he starts to purr.

Chapter 31

"WE'RE LEAVING IN FIVE MINUTES." Dad shouts. I force my feet into my boots. I haven't unlaced them properly but they're black suede knee-high ones which lace all the way up and it's too much hassle to unlace them or pull them loose enough. I push my foot in and get it about half way down the leg of the boot.

I hobble into the dining room where Dad has spread lots of bank statements and stuff out on the table which he is going through.

"Here.' Dad passes me a polythene bag of sandwiches which have disintegrated, without looking up from his calculations.

I can see the dandruff in his hair.

"Those are…"

"I put them in a plastic bag."

"Mum puts them in foil to make them stick together." I point out. The sandwiches are fallen apart already and the cheese has fallen out.

"It doesn't matter does it? They'll still taste OK. Come along or we'll be late for Dr. Stein." Dad says.

He is wearing a crumpled blue shirt with a stain down the front and a purple tie that doesn't match it. A red silk handkerchief pokes out of the breast pocket of his grey suit. The brown shoes don't go. He looks a mess. His hair is going grey, which I have never noticed before, he looks old and careworn.

"Where's my…"

"I don't know. We're leaving. We'll be late. It's not cheap seeing Dr Stein you know. I'm going to get my money's worth. Where are my sunglasses?"

"Where you put them?"

"I always put them down here." Dad gropes around for his sunglasses in the manner of an ageing mole fumbling for a worm.

"Here." I pick them up from the dining room table, where they are squatting right in the centre.

"Let's go then." Dad says. "Tanya, have you seen my car keys?"

"They're in the biscuit tin in the hall, where they always are."

"I can't see them." Dad scrabbles around the empty shortbread tin where all the keys live.

"These ones?" I pass him some keys.

"Ah yes, how did you…"

He holds the keys right up to his eyes and then looks at me, struggling to refocus for a longer distance. He hasn't got bifocals yet, but it can't be long before he moves onto glasses-for-the-very-old. I feel a rush of love and warmth for him. I love my Dad. He is always nice to me. He does his best. If I had to choose one out of him and Mum it would be him. He never shouts at me.

"Never mind. Come on Dad." I take his arm and guide him out of the front door, towards the car.

"So, Tanya, how has your mood been?" Dr Josh asks me, fountain pen poised above my notes. His dark brown hair is as thick and glossy and healthy as ever. His shirt is clean and he is not going grey and his skin is perfect and his eyes are cornflower blue.

"Low. I've been miserable since 2 weeks before I came out of hospital which is…" I count on my fingers. "Eight whole weeks. That's too long." The panther rubs his head against my leg. I want to stroke his head but I can't, not with my psychiatrist watching.

"It's natural that after a period of mania you will…"

"Can I try something else?" I say. "Please can I try another mood stabiliser?"

Out of the window the trees are in their autumn coats which are about to be ripped off them by the wind. The leaves are flaming with colour. An Autumn melancholy hangs in the air.

"The lithium is going to work. It just might take time. You have to be patient."

"I haven't got time. I'm seventeen. I don't like it. I feel exhausted, drained, fat, not me. Please can I try something else?"

The panther settles down by the side of my chair with his head resting on his front paws. He loves me. He will not leave me.

He furrows his brow. "Well, carbamazepine is often used as an alternative to lithium, especially for patients who rapid cycle."

"Can I try it?" I say, grasping at the slim straw of hope.

"Will I lose some weight if I switch from lithium to…"

"It is weight neutral, yes."

"I want to get back to my old weight."

"That could well happen, yes. Because it's a new drug it has fewer side effects than lithium. Now you're off the olanzapine you should just lose the weight anyway, I would imagine."

"When can I…"

"You can try carbamazepine if that's what you really want, Tanya. We'll have to take you completely off the lithium first though. There's a rare but possibly fatal interaction between the two drugs."

"Please. I want to stop taking lithium. It's horrible. I'm thirsty and hungry all the time."

He lifts a heavy paperback down from the shelf. It's as thick as a dictionary or the Bible.

"Let's have a look in the manual."

"What's that?"

"It's a directory of the dosages and side effects and contrain-dications of all the drugs."

He starts leafing through it. I look out of the window at the squirrels scampering about with acorns and conkers in their mouths which they are about to bury for the winter.

"Aha, here we are. Carbamazepine." He runs a finger down the page, his lips pursed, his expression thoughtful. "Side effects – here we are. Rash, ankle oedema…"

"What's ankle oedema?"

"A swelling of the ankles. Hyponatraemia, that's low sodium levels in the blood; agranulocytosis is the only worrying one."

"And that is?"

"Low white blood cell count. It means you become more susceptible to infections. It's quite rare. We'll have to keep on with the blood tests."

"OK." I don't care if the side effects are leprosy, coma and death. I just want to get off lithium.

"Are you taking the pill?"

"Obviously not. Why would I…"

"Well, if you are, carbamazepine breaks it down and makes it less effective. So you'll need to change to a higher dose pill. Anyway, you could be sexually active. Girls of your age often…"

"I'm not."

I think about Seb. I wonder what he is doing. I wonder if he has met someone else.

"We have to cut down your lithium slowly, if you halve the dose this week, then half that dose next week, and so on, until you're not taking any. Here's a private prescription for your first packet and I'll write to Graham so you can get the next lot on the NHS."

"Oh, thank you Dr Stein."

I beam at him. New drug, new hope.

"I'll see you next week anyway to see how you're going with it. How's everything else?" He says, looking at me.

I am not going to say anything about my mother. I am not. I am not, even though I miss her dreadfully and I am worried that she will never come back.

"Your father tells me your mother has gone to stay with your aunt." He pauses, waiting for me to tell him something.

It is quiet in the room. I don't say anything. The clock ticks.

"Oh really? He hasn't told me anything. Which aunt?" I ask, eventually.

Dad has not mentioned Mum's disappearance and has not told me where she is. She has not been referred to. In some ways, it's nice being on my own with Dad who leaves me to my own devices, although his sandwich-making and other domestic skills are not up to scratch. It's good not to feel Mum watching me like a hawk the whole time to check I'm taking my medication and stuff. I am taking my medication but this depression seems impregnable anyway. I think I might be depressed forever.

"Your father told me about what happened with the police." Dr Josh says, in his you-are-a-naughty-girl-who-deserves-to-abandoned-by-your-mother-and-left-to-fend-for-yourself voice. "He told me that they found Ecstasy pills secreted in your clothes that they took away for tests."

I look down. I am going to be sick.

"I'm sorry."

"I am so disappointed in you, Tanya. You haven't given your drugs much of a chance to…"

"Are you cross with me?" I cannot bear it if he is cross with me.

"It's not about being cross with you. There's little point in me trying to treat your condition if you are deliberately sabotaging my efforts by self-medicating with street drugs. Do you…"

"I think I've been punished enough."

"We're not living in Biblical times, Tanya. It's not about punishment and confession – not that you confessed of course. It's about you taking some responsibility for your actions, and resolving not to do it again. Do you understand?"

"Anyway, it's my parents' fault for being so over-protective." I say.

"I daresay it is, to some extent. You really have to stop behaving in such an irresponsible, not to mention illegal, manner though. I hope you've learned your lesson."

"Yes, I have."

"Good. Your father is very distressed about what happened Tanya."

"Are you cross with me?" I repeat.

"Yes."

I burst into tears. I cannot bear it that he is cross with me. I am desperately upset that I have let him down. He passes me the box of tissues which are cheap scratchy ones and not up to the purpose. I cry into one and throw it towards the dustbin behind his desk in the far right hand corner of the room and I miss.

"Nearly," he says.

I try another one and miss by much further, the rolled-up tissue bounces off the wall and dribbles onto the floor.

"I want my Mum." I say, and start sniffling again. "I miss her. I need her to be with me. I'm ill…" I can't go on because the tears are pouring out now.

"She'll be home soon," he says. "She needs a break from everything, it's very stressful for her Tanya: she needs to look after herself so she's well enough to look after you."

Can I come and live with you? I think.

"Your Dad is looking after you isn't he?"

"His sandwiches are rubbish. He doesn't wrap them in foil. He just puts them in polythene bags and they fall apart. I want my Mum." I say.

"You could try making your own sandwiches?"

"But then I'd know what was in them and it wouldn't be a surprise." I explain.

"I see. Well when would you like to see me next Saturday? I've got 9, 11 and 12."

"11 please."

"I'll see you next week at 11 o'clock then, look after yourself. Call me if your mood goes any lower."

"When can I start on the carbamazepine though?'

"In about a month."

"I can't wait a month."

"Yes you can."

"When is my Mum coming back?"

"Soon." he says.

The sun has come out. It is still raining and a rainbow arcs across the sky. I notice the colours as if it's the first time but they don't help. I see the colours but am unmoved: I cannot feel anything for the rainbow. The colours are fluorescent fimo beads at Magic Realms where I will never go again.

My Mum is never coming back and my clothes will never be properly clean again and I will have to eat my Dad's sandwiches until I leave home and I will always feel like this: flat and grey and there is no hope that it will ever change and I'll never lose any weight and the sounds inside my head roar and the panther watches me from across the room. He doesn't even come near enough for me to stroke his head because even he cannot bear to be near me but he can't leave me either – we can't leave each other ever.

Chapter 32

THE GARDEN BREATHES after the rain, and shines.

"Look, here come our little goldfinches. Do you know what the collective noun for goldfinches is, sweetie?" Mum asks me, pointing at the first couple of feathered arrows shooting past us on their way to the feeders.

She has returned from exile. It is a relief to have her back – the sandwiches are better – but she is still watching me.

I don't answer. Mum sips her white wine which has melting ice in it, despite the cold weather. Her fingers clasp the stem of the goblet: her fuchsia talons clash with the lurid urine of the drink.

"It's a charm: a charm of goldfinches. Isn't that perfect?"

Her voice is soft as she looks out of the glass back door at the prettiest birds in the whole world. The first pair of birds perch either side of the Perspex column of thistle seed, now that the rain has stopped.

"Yeah."

The word is perfect. The rest of our charm of goldfinches swoops in. No-one else flies like them, with that air-filled bounce of joy.

"We are so lucky that they have chosen to charm our garden." Mum says in her we-must-count-our-blessings voice. "In Christianity they represent the foreknowledge Jesus and Mary had of the Crucifixion and…"

"Why?"

I need to get out of the house and do something in my life that isn't listening to my Mum talking about rubbish like this.

"Because they eat thistle seeds – in Christian art they foreshadow the Crown of thorns that Jesus wore. They are also symbols of endurance, fruitfulness, and persistence because…"

"That is so cheesy." I exclaim.

But despite myself I feel their feathers around my heart, stroking and squeezing me. They are the birds of recovery. My Mum has come back to me and the goldfinches are carrying me to recovery.

Their little heads bob up and down as they tweeze the tiny black thistle seeds out, one by one, with their beaks which are longer than the greenfinches' beaks.

"How can you tell that they're finches?" Mum asks me, in her I-know-you-have-been-diagnosed-with-a-mental-disorder-but-you're-still-my-gifted-child voice.

"By their multi-syllabic calls and their short, fat legs." I recite, by rote, because it is still in my mind somehow, despite everything.

"Come on. There's another one."

"Their…I can't remember." I grope around for it but this information that I have always known has been ripped out of me by the illness.

"Their triangular bills that can split and roll seed husks. You know that."

Mum must be even more disappointed in me than usual because she turns back to her crossword.

Raindrops rest on the window, frozen into polka dots on the glass. The copper beech at the bottom of the garden glows. I am the girl in the copper beeches paid to sit in my own window as a decoy in a blue dress. All I am doing is sitting at the window watching the goldfinches and letting the twittering honey of their melodies slide into my brain.

I gaze at Mum's glass of wine with a deep, profound longing. It's the only drink I want now, the perfect drink for this moment.

"Mum, please can I…"

"No you can't. You're not allowed to until Dr Stein has sorted your medication, you know that. I know it's tough sweetie." Mum says, sipping her wine.

"Well you shouldn't be drinking in front of me then. It's no wonder that I've developed a severe mental disorder being brought up by you and…"

"Don't you think I've got enough to cope with, with you being ill? I don't see why I can't…"

"Don't you think I've got enough to cope with? I'm the one with the severe mental disorder. I can't believe you're drinking in front of me. How can you be so…"

"There, then," she says, pouring the elixir of life and eternal youth away onto the already-drenched purple heather and variegated ivy. "Happy now?"

"Happier," I say, as she walks off into the bowels of the house.

I started on carbamazepine a week ago. It is the Christmas holidays. My brother is home. He seems to be seeing a lot of Immi. She is here now, and the energy in the house is calm and restful whilst she is here. They are in his bedroom.

This time is the time where my mood never comes up. This is the time I stay depressed forever. I think of Nick Hornby in *Fever Pitch* being depressed for ten whole years. I am going to be depressed till I'm 27, by which time I will be ravaged by age, wrinkled, everything will have started to sag.

I will be an old maid still living with my parents while all my friends will have left home and married billionaires. I will be here with my doddering, infirm, incontinent, blind, deaf parents who will smell of wee and boiled cabbage. The garden will be overgrown: choked with weeds because no-one will have the energy to tend it. We will all lie in our separate areas of the house – them coughing in their bedrooms with their catheters and knitting and NHS glasses; me in my bedroom with the peeling walls and old flyers for Magic Realms and Apocalypse to remind me of my misspent youth when I was normal before I was a dried-up husk. The panther will be lying there, arthritic, his coat dull, his teeth worn down and rotten, his flanks thin with that scragginess old cats have, his belly slack, no shine on his coat and rubbed away bits where his skin pokes through, his fur coming out, his claws blunt, his eyes dull.

I press two carbamazepine tablets out of the dimpled pack and into my hand and wash them down with water: they're not coated so if they sit on my tongue, even for a few seconds, they start to dissolve into bitter chalky powder. I listen to the engine of my mood roaring inside my head, the cogs turning and clattering – could that be a twinge of something that isn't suicidal depression? I wait. No, it isn't. It can't last for ten years really though – nothing can.

The rapid cycling seems to have been broken, but then I've had a far deeper pit to climb out of this time and it's a long way up to that village called normal which might be different when I get there on this expedition. If I get there this time. If I get there ever. If I don't freeze on the way up and am found like Edmund Hillary or whoever it was frozen solid on the side of the mountain by climbers a hundred years later.

"Tanya, stop sitting there looking like that. Go and tidy your bedroom." Mum says, coming back into the room to check on me, no doubt.

"Why?"

"Because it's a terrible mess. And why are you doing that to your fingers?"

"Because I've got a disorder."

"I daresay. But if you don't stop doing that you'll get your fingers infected and you'll have to have them amputated and then you'll really have something to be miserable about."

"Oh, shut up."

"And what have you done to your underarms that I saw earlier? You'll get them infected as well."

"No I won't. It will look fine when the swelling goes down."

"But it looks disgusting now. Look at yourself Tanya."

I examine my underarms which apart from a bit of redness like a shaving rash look fine to me. Certainly they look better than if they were covered in long fur like my panther. Anyway, it relaxes me; it makes me feel as if I can still achieve something when I've plucked every single hair from my underarms.

And I like the pain – it's nice pain, it takes my mind away from the mental pain, I prefer it. The second when I'm teasing the hair out from under the skin and pulling it away and making it clean and perfect is wonderful. I look at my underarms and know that in a few days they will look good and I am calm from the adrenalin. I am sure that my fingers will heal up too. They will. Obviously I am not going to have to have them amputated.

Mum sits next to me.

"It's going to be alright sweetie," she says.

Why did you leave me? I think.

"It isn't." I say.

"The carbamazepine is going to work. Your mood is going to have to come up soon anyway."

"What if it doesn't? What if this is the time I stay depressed for ever?"

"It isn't. It's just taking longer because you were so high in hospital. Anyway, I think you seem a bit better. You look a bit brighter. I can tell. It's going to be OK sweetie. We're going to get through this."

"Are you cross with me?"

"No."

"You are."

"I'm sorry you are going through this. I want to be able to kiss it better like when you were little."

I hold out my hand and Mum kisses it and then I start crying. I am not normal. This is not normal. My life is completely fucked up. I want to die quickly and painlessly in my sleep. I want my panther to put his paw over my mouth so I suffocate.

He would have to put his other paw over my nose I suppose, and maybe tie me to the bed with his tail and slash my wrists with his claws. I feel a slight stirring of something which might be a weird lust at the prospect of being sexually assaulted by the panther. If it is, then the carbamazepine is starting to work, because loss of libido is the most noticeable side effect of depression and here it is: coming back, flowing back into my body, and my mood is starting to lift. I think of the panther pinning me down on my front, pressing my shoulders down with his paw and scratching down my back with his unsheathed claws and mmmmmmmmmmmm that is nice.

It is raining again. It is raining so loudly that the house rattles. Rain beats on the roof and puddles everywhere inside and out. It bangs on the ground, bounces and fountains back up into the sky. This must be the apocalyptic flood, which is comforting to know. I must find another panther from somewhere though, a girl one, as they will not let me bring just one of him on the ark. I can't see where the ark is though? We must not be invited, in which case we are going to drown, which will not be a bad death. I sit in the house and wait for death, watching the water running down the windows.

It will cover us, cover the house, and there we will be: fish in a bowl. Soon it will all be over.

"It's raining a lot, isn't it?" Immi says.

She has come into the room and sat down next to me at the window. I look at her under my lashes so she can't see. I wish I looked like her. She is beautiful and also cool – she is perfect. Her long chestnut hair frames her face in Regency ringlets and isn't frizzy, her skin is flawless and porcelain pale, her eyes are huge and grey, her cheekbones are high and her face is a perfect heart shape. She's tall and has a wide mouth. She's wearing a violet velvet dress – which should clash with her hair but doesn't – and clumpy brown boots.

I remember about purple and orange being complementary colours from that picture of Monet's garden at Giverny with all the purple and orange flowers next to each other in the foreground and recognise what she's doing.

She has black eyeliner on her upper lids, in long streaks with flicky corners and violet eye-shadow at the outer corner of her eyes. There is a dusting of periwinkle glitter over her top lids.

"Yeah I think it might be The Flood mark II." I say. The rain forms huge lakes on the tops of the white plastic garden tables which Dad hasn't put away in the garage for the winter yet. The plastic sags. So does the drowning table tennis table. The net sways in the wind and droops in the middle. I really want my mood to come up so I can say something witty to Immi so she will think I'm normal and diverting company. I want her to like me, and whilst I am sitting here doing my Cassandra act – prophesying doom – she is not going to, but I can't think of anything to say that is not depressing.

"I like your hair." I say.

She smiles. "Thanks. It's a nightmare a lot of the time."

239

"Yeah, mine too." Somehow her curls are soft and shiny ringlets, unlike my wiry pipe cleaners.

"Well, at least you can wear whatever colours you want. Hardly anything matches my hair, or doesn't clash. I used to wear pink but…"

"The fashion police have changed the rules now though. Pink and orange now match." I point out.

"Yeah, true. When I was little my Mum said that pink clashed with my hair though. Shall we go out for a bit?"

"In this? It's pouring."

"I mean let's get in the car and go somewhere. You'll like my car."

I can't go out on my own with her. What will I say. She'll find me so dull.

"Carl's sleeping. He's got work to do when he wakes up anyway. He'd prefer us to get out of his way."

"Do you really want to take me out somewhere?" I say.

"Yeah, we've hardly spent any time together really have we?"

"Not really. Not on our own." You are going to find me so boring though.

Imogen's car is amazing: it's an old lilac Beetle. It matches her dress. It's exactly what I would drive if I could choose any car in the world.

"Your car is fab." I say.

"Isn't he?" she says with a wide smile that lights up her beautiful face. "I saw him in the street with a 'For Sale' sign, he chose me really."

She strokes the dashboard. I want to be exactly like her when I grow up, I think.

"Where are we going?"

"Wherever you want. Where do you want to go?"

I think. I don't know. I can't think of anywhere I want to go. Everywhere has so many layers of anxiety attached to it: what will I do, what if someone looks at me, what if I freak out, what if Immi realises how weird I am and stops feeling sorry for me because I am insane and decides that I am horrible, which I am and she tells Carl I am horrible and he decides he doesn't like me any more. If I was Immi I wouldn't like me.

"The cinema?" We could watch a cartoon – something with bright colours and talking animals and a happy ending that is slow enough for me to follow.

"Sure. What do you want to see? I thought about that new Disney film with…"

"Yeah, that would be nice." I say. She likes the same stuff as me. This is a very good sign that is cheering me up already as I settle into the soft seat of the Beetle and watch the rain lashing the windscreen.

Chapter 33

"FOR THE SIN WE HAVE COMMITTED by misusing sex." The Rabbi says.

Well, I'm not guilty of that one. I can't find anyone to misuse sex with: Robbie wouldn't, Seb wouldn't, I haven't had any offers since I left hospital. I thought boys were meant to be up for it all the time. They're not. Well, they're not with me anyway. We are in synagogue, on Yom Kippur, and I'm meant to be asking God for forgiveness for all the bad things I've done during the year, and apologise to all the people I've upset. All I can think about is how horrible everyone has been to me, including God, during the year.

"For the sin we have committed by lying and deceiving each other." The Rabbi continues.

There's no way I could have told Mum those things. She would never have let me out again. I'm not apologising for that one.

"Stop that." Mum says. "Stop sniffing."

She is wearing a purple top with a grey cardigan and a grey flared mid-calf skirt, and turquoise, magenta and violet open-toed stiletto sandals. They do not go with the rest of the outfit. Her new caramel highlights are not nice either.

"I've got a cold." I say, looking into the middle distance at what everyone in shul is wearing and who is here.

"Well blow your nose then." She replies in her I've-had-enough-of-your-attention-seeking-behaviour voice.

"I haven't…"

"Here," She produces a tissue from her sleeve. "Stop drawing attention to yourself. Just try to behave normally."

"For the sin we have committed by our worship of material status." The Rabbi drones on.

Oh for God's sake, this is ridiculous. I flip to the back of the prayer book to the study anthology and it falls open on the page of my Batmitzvah passage. I stare at my 13-year-old pencil scrawls: 'Ladies and gentlemen please be upstanding. My study passage is about how we must not be cruel to animals'. I think of how I have lost my 13 year old crusading fervour for animal rights and feel sad. I used to spend days and weeks trying to persuade my friends to convert to vegetarianism with me, thrust leaflets about factory farming under their noses.

"But don't you see how cruel it is, keeping animals in those conditions?" I used to ask Clara and Helena.

"Yeah, but maybe I just don't really care." Clara replied.

The thirteen year old girl wearing the horrendous purple trouser suit with the velvet Alice-band and frizzy hair… I can't believe that was me, but that was me, and I was happy, and sure of myself, and knew what was important to me – abolishing factory farming, and vivisection, and halting trade in endangered species and…

"The children's service for age seven to nine will take place in the shul hall." The Rabbi announces.

I jump up from my seat, as do all the teenagers who are blatantly not aged 7 to 9, as we always have done. I scan the marquee for any of my friends and see that there are so many families I don't recognise here. Fake-tanned Mums wearing hats crowned with ostrich feathers and short tweed skirts with knee-high, stiletto boots sit next to balding dads who look as if they'd rather be at the office while their kids run around, playing with toys, eating biscuits.

At last I spot Emily over on the right side of the bimah at the front and Lily and Ben together over at the back near the door. It's an exciting treat to have Ben here. He's come up from South London to stay with Lily for the High Holydays. Lily winks at me and points at the door as she gets up, losing her balance. Ben puts out an arm to break her fall but I see her blush. I get up to follow her and Emily gets up to follow me.

"Where are you going?' Mum hisses, grabbing my arm. I shake her claws off.

"Out," I say. "Outside. It's too hot in here. Anyway, I need to see my friends, Lily and Ben and Emily are here…"

"Well make sure you're not too long." Mum says.

She looks haggard. She hates all this, I know she does. She does it to keep up appearances, to do the right thing. Well, it's a bit late now, now that the whole community know I've just come out of the mental hospital.

I find my friends sitting on the steps on the other side of the fields, smoking. The safest act of rebellion we can manage here.

"Hey, Tanya." Ben says. "How are you?"

"Well, you know, it's Yom Kippur. What do you think of our shul?" I ask him.

"He loves it, don't you darling?" Lily says, putting her arm around him and patting his head as if he's a puppy. "Marlboro light, T?"

She holds the packet out and I take one.

"Thanks.

I wonder where Seb is today. I don't know whether Seb even goes to shul with his Mum. I wonder whether I like Seb more than I liked Robbie. It seems very different. He's nothing like Robbie, which is probably a good thing – or it would be a good thing if I saw him.

"What are some of those Mums wearing?" Lily exclaims with horror.

"I know," Em says. "Do you think they believe that their tans look natural?"

"They can't do? If they stood next to a tangerine then they would blend in with it." Lily says, and giggles.

Then we're all laughing, and I feel a sudden flash of love for all of them. Here I am with my friends who haven't abandoned me and don't treat me differently from before-my-diagnosis.

I go to the loo in the portaloos which are the smart ones with wooden bits at the back, mahogany, shelves to put handbags on etc. I look at my face in the mirror and I look the same. My eyeliner is wonky, smudged under my eyes, running into the creases. The lighting is harsh in here and makes me look worse than I do, well; I hope I do not look as bad as this. I look exhausted, drained…I shouldn't be thinking about how I look anyway, I should be atoning for the sins I have committed but I don't care and it seems that I've had ample punishment already from God for my surely minimal transgressions.

"Thought you might be here." Someone coming through the door says to me.

It is Immi, wearing another purple dress, damson this time, with her lilac sparkly eye shadow and violet liner. It doesn't look garish and over the top as it would on me, but just right.

"Are you OK?" she asks. "You've been gone for ages."

"Yeah." I say. "I've just been talking to my friends. Do you want to come and sit with us?"

"Sure." She puts her arm through mine.

We walk outside.

"Hi," she says to Lily.

"Hey, Immi, how are you?" Lily says.

I watch Ben's eyes bulge as he looks at Immi.

"Hi, I'm Imogen, Carl's girlfriend."

"Ben," he says. "Seb's mate, Lily's boyfriend." He flushes with pride.

"Oh, Squibs has told me about you," Immi says.

With Immi here with me I feel safe and secure, and that my stock has risen in the eyes of the others. I don't know if she knows this. I hope she does.

"Do you want to go home?" she turns to me. "I'll go and tell your mum that we'll go home and…I don't know, get dinner ready for when we break the fast this evening."

She smiles, that big smile, her wide mouth spreading even further across her face, showing her gleaming teeth. I wonder if she has them whitened.

"We'd like to come," Ben says, "Wouldn't we, babe?" He squeezes Lily's hand.

"Yeah, we're coming," Lily says.

"Me too," Emily agrees.

"Wait here then everyone, I'll tell Tanya's mum that we're going."

Immi disappears inside and I stare after her with a surge of love: marvelling that she knows exactly what to do to make me feel better, and the thought niggles at the back of my mind: why is she doing this, why does she want to hang out with me? She must just be a really nice person, well, my brother wouldn't like her if she wasn't, but how does she know exactly how to be with me, what to do all the time? She returns to us, smiling.

"Ok, done, let's go." Immi says.

She is carrying my cardigan which I must've left on my chair without realising. I rub my foot where my shoes have been digging into the skin. I know I mustn't pick my blister but I know that as soon as I get home I'm going to start worrying it so I can feel the pain properly.

We walk through the grounds of the shul, our heels sinking into the mud, out on the street and back through the village. The kids are out on the streets, flitting between the reform shul (our one) and the united (the more religious one where men and women sit separately and where my brother goes when he doesn't have to be with us). The young teenagers are in mini-skirts and knee high boots and tight cardigans, the boys in baggy chinos and even baggy jeans. They are all smoking. I look at my village, trying to see it how Ben and Immi must see it.

"You're lucky to live here", she says.

"No I'm not."

"But it's so pretty," Ben says.

I look at WH Smith, Boots, the deli, the hairdressers and estate agents as we pass them, the kosher butcher, the little supermarket.

"It's rubbish. I wish we lived further into town in a less Jewish area."

"But it's nice to…"

"No it isn't. It's like living in a ghetto." The claustrophobia of living in this place closes in on me. "I can't wait to get out of here."

"Where are you going to go?" Ben asks, a bit petulantly.

"I don't know. I want to go to uni far far far away from here."

"It gets easier." Immi says, her voice soft.

"What does?"

"Dealing with life, dealing with yourself."

"What do you mean though?"

"I think as you get older you just learn how to cope with things better. I don't know how to explain it, but it just gets less intense, your emotions, the way you view things."

We're walking towards Robbie's house now and I can see the wires fan across the sky and the flatness of the sky stretching down the road with the electricity wires fanning across it, radii that lead out. I must turn a bit as I pass Robbie's lilac house because she feels me flinch I think.

"Whose house is that?"

"Oh, you know, someone I used to…"

"Her twat of an ex-boyfriend," Ben clarifies for Immi's benefit.

She puts her arm round me and squeezes me tight.

"It's going to get better, I promise."

"How do you know though?"

"Because now you know what it is, and you're tackling it."

And because you're here, I think.

We turn into my road. It is good to be nearly home. My feet hurt. I stop to rub my foot and rest for a bit. I look at the leaves and notice the weakening light and stand still for a moment just to feel the autumn.

As I approach the house I can see that someone is sitting on the low wall in front of the house, kicking the pebbles with the toe of his shoe, and I know who it is before he lifts his head up.

"Hi," he says, looking up at me from under his thick gold mane.

"Hi Seb," I say, my heart hammering.

It is so good to see him, at last. We look at each other. I'm not quite sure what to say. I feel a profound peace and calm that he is here, as if I always knew we would turn round the corner and he'd be here.

"How are you feeling?" he asks, looking at me in a concerned way.

His eyes are very green.

"Fine," I say. "Good actually."

He smiles. "You look good," he says.

I sit down on the wall to rest my feet.

"You always wear such uncomfortable shoes," he says, looking at my feet. I remember the night of Ben's party when he took my shoes off. I wonder whether he is thinking about this too.

"I didn't want to come round until... until you'd had time to settle in back at home," he says, putting his arm round my waist. "I asked Immi, well, I asked her how you were doing and she said she thought you'd like to see me now and... well, here I am."

I close my eyes and rest my head on his shoulder, breathing in his Hugo Boss aftershave.

"It's OK, you don't have to explain anything," I say.

He draws me in closer and strokes my hair. I feel a wave of contentment.

"I was wondering," he says. "Would you like to go to the cinema on Saturday night? There's a film that I think you'd like about some bear cubs."

"Yes, I would like that very much." I say,

I realise that today is Wednesday, so according the rules he is asking me in good time for a Saturday night date, which means he really likes me. Seb is asking me out on a date, an actual date, I think.

"Oh good," he says, and he sounds relieved.

"Shall we go in?" I say, holding out my hand.

We walk inside.

Chapter 34

A T THE TOP OF THE FENNEL, at the ends where the flowers were, there are yellow seeds which the birds are eating. The baby birds have changed into their adult feathers and they are bright gold, green, and red, blue, black and all their colours glow bright and are lined with felt tip rather than blurring into each other and fading together. There are crisp lines between their different coloured bits.

I am listening to music. I want to be wrapped up in cotton wool. Maybe I already am. The mood stabiliser is holding me, and it is pushing me up, I am resting on cotton wool, a cloud of it. I think about Seb and at last I can feel excited that we are going out on a proper date tomorrow. At last we are seeing each other. It feels so good that something is happening with him. I think about him and feel all light and floaty and happy.

The fledglings are light enough to hang off the very ends of the flowers, upside-down, without even bending the stalks. Their parents are nearby – perching on the sides of the squirrel-proof birdfeeders which the squirrels have broken into of course. The adult birds watch their chicks – just far enough away for the fledglings to feel that they are now grown-up enough to go out catching sunflower seeds unsupervised, but just close enough for the parents to swoop in and wrap their wings round the fledglings and herd them to safety if the magpies or jackdaws were to drop in.

I am going for a walk with Immi again today, and I am already ready and waiting for her, not rushing at the last minute because I really, really, really don't want to irritate her.

A young jackdaw sits of the top of the other squirrel-proof feeder, behind the fennel. It sways under his weight – he's not quite able to balance properly, and keeps stepping from foot to foot, one foot at a time sliding down the curved metal arcs that the feeders hang from, and then he has to pull a leg up and then it starts again on the other side. The sense of balance must come later.

I scrawl tally marks next to the pictures of the birds I can see on the feeders on today's bird timetable. I mark the blue tits, great tits, coal tits and then goldfinches, greenfinches, jackdaws.

There's a flurry of activity around the bird feeders as someone swoops in and all the finches bomb back into the hedge. It's…it's….I can't believe it. It's a hawk of some kind. I check the *Complete Garden Bird Book* and realise that he must be a sparrow hawk. He has feathery knickerbockers and long custard yellow legs with huge talons.

I have my shoes on. I have my handbag with my purse, house keys, lip balm already in, and my handbag-sized umbrella, so I don't have to rush when Immi arrives. I am wearing indigo flared jeans and a long sleeved purple top with a lilac lace trim round the neck. I have put on some make-up – purple eyeliner, purple glitter at the corner of my eyes, lilac lip gloss; I look quite…pretty, I realize with a shock. I've even done some accessorizing.

The hawk is still in the garden. The whole garden has emptied. Anyone he would like to hunt has scarpered. There aren't any sparrows round here anyway – they are becoming scarce around here. He picks at the finch food that is loose on the tray with his killer's beak.

The doorbell rings. Both doorbells ring. We have a new one as well as the old one, I don't know why. It has only been here since I returned from hospital. I wonder whether it is spying on me to check that I… I don't know.

I run up to the door and I can see Immi outside, stepping from foot to foot in the cold. She looks perfect as usual: her auburn curls tumbling down her shoulders and a few diamante stars scattered throughout her hair, twinkling in the autumn sunlight. I unlock the door and slide it open. It is a bit stuck so I have to push it back along its railings.

"Don't worry, Tanya, let me do that." Immi says as I struggle with the door.

She wiggles it and it slides smooth along the groove.

"How'd you do that?" The door weighs as much as a herd of buffalo.

"It's not that difficult. You just have to be gentle and persuasive with it." She smiles a half-smile at me which says 'I have special powers.'

She does. They radiate out of her. A pink, purple, feathery aura of special powers.

"Ready?"

"Yes." I smile proudly.

"Feeling better?" Immi asks, with what sounds like genuine concern: rather than feigned interest.

"Definitely. How can you tell?" I ask her, wondering how she can be so observant when she hardly knows me yet.

"You're wearing make-up. You don't bother when you're low."

"There doesn't seem any point."

"Why not?"

"Because at those times anyone can tell that I'm depressed and…"

"No they can't; only people who know you. Anyway, I know that you've got something to be happy about," she says, smiling. "Seb told me that he's taking you out on a date tomorrow night."

"Yeah," I say.

"He really likes you," she says. "Be kind to him."

Seb really likes me, I think. Seb told Immi that he really likes me. A wave of happiness surges through my whole body.

"I will," I say, smiling back at her.

The colours leach back into my world. The background static stops crackling and I can hear what Immi is saying clearly, without interference. The roaring in my head has gone. My thoughts flow and I can finish my sentences.

We leave the house painlessly. I'm taking Immi somewhere special that I want her to see. We walk under the railway line. When I walk I can lift my feet, my feet lift themselves: I float. Once I found a dead bird in here. We emerge on the main road and the traffic buzzes past us as we walk along the road, cross and head down a path and then through a kissing gate and along a muddy path and then then into an orchard. It's very muddy, but Immi is wearing boots so it's OK. We round a corner and the field looks empty.

"Sometimes they're not here." I explain, squelching up to the fence.

"Who?" She stares into the distance, across the whole field, back to the woods far in front of us.

"The cows. Sometimes they're in this field, and sometimes they're not."

We walk along the hedge at the front of the field, and round the corner to cut through up the other side, and then I catch a glimpse of some ears sticking up, we turn the corner and there is a calf, he starts to walk towards us, and as we approach him I see that there are others, and then there are a whole herd of them.

There herd is a patchwork quilt of different coloured cows: some Friesians (black and white), some Jerseys (orange); some Hereford (brown and white) and some white ones which I'm not sure about.

They walk towards us until they are just in front of us right up by the hedge and we can stroke them.

"They are here because you believed in them." I say, resting my hand on the nose of a Jersey calf.

They are my best ones with their Tropicana coats and huge eyes with long ginger lashes. I hear the cows breathing. I feel the September sunlight and it is gentle. The grass is very green from the rain, and long, interspersed with cow parsley to match the cows, and nettles and brambles.

Immi looks at my cows. She takes pictures of them – she is a photographer along with her many other talents. Strands of her red hair fall in front of the lens and she pushes them back.

"Thank you for bringing me to see your cows," she says. "They are beautiful."

She strokes the nose of a Jersey calf. He looks at us through his long ginger eyelashes. His eyes are huge and liquid brown.

Here with my cows and Immi I feel calm. I feel that things are going to be OK, that the worst is over, that I am going to get better. I am so glad that my brother is going out with Immi and she likes me and wants to spend time with me and likes my cows and understands. I haven't felt well enough to visit my cows for ages but I'm so glad to be here now and to be showing them to Immi.

Later, I'm in bed, pretending to be asleep. In fact I'm lying awake worrying about, in no particular order: the structure and function of the kidney, the difference between transubstantiation and consubstantiation, whether the necklace that matches my plastic flower ring has been sold to someone else in the time I've been saving up for it, whether I'm going to be able to find a zip-up sweater to match my navy corduroy flares, what the role of the fool is in King Lear.

I start running through some possible outfits for my date with Seb tomorrow night, and feel a surge of excitement that I'm going on an actual date with Seb. From under my covers I hear the unmistakeable sound of mum tiptoeing in in her heels, which click click click muffled across the carpet. I screw my eyes shut but breathe in a regular manner, pretending to be asleep. She sits down on the edge of my bed and I feel her stroke my cheek and then kiss me on the top of my head. Then she gets up and walks out, leaving me wondering if that really happened at all. She used to do that when I was little.

Epilogue

"COME ON SWEETIE, if you want to go to the farm shop we need to get going now." Mum says, pushing her marking aside, into the middle of the dining room table, and sliding it into its plastic folder so that it doesn't get dirty.

"OK, in a minute, I'm just finishing this chapter." I say. "Henry VIII is about to tell Thomas More that he must sign the…"

"I've never been able to make head or tail of any of that history." Mum says. "Anyway, you can do it when we get back from the farm shop. There's no point in rushing this revision, Tanya. Your father and I want you to do as well as possible in your exams."

She means 3 As. We both know she does. I believe I can do it. If I can fight this illness I can do anything, after all.

"Just give me five minutes," I say, putting my goldfinch bookmark at the start of the next chapter.

"Of course, sweetie." Mum smiles at me, and strokes my hair as I walk off.

She looks happy and relaxed, I notice. She's put on a few pounds and doesn't look as scrawny as she used to. She is smiling a real smile: not a forced grimace.

My panther is lying on my bed when I enter the room; dozing, his chin resting on his huge paws. He opens his eyes and raises his head as he hears me come in, and bounds over to greet me, rubbing his cheek against mine and giving me a whiskery kiss. His cheek fur is soft as he rubs it against my skin.

"We have to go somewhere." I tell him.

He looks at me with his head tilted to one side, confused. A terrible pain sears through me, but I know I'm doing the right thing for him.

"Come in here." I say, opening my bag and pointing into it.

He sniffs the bag and puts a paw inside it and then, with a last glance at me, lifts his other paw so he can pounce into the bag, headfirst. His head disappears into the bottom of the bag, and then his front legs, and shoulders. He wriggles along the bottom of the bag and pulls his haunches in, until just the tip of his tail is sticking out of the top of the bag. I lift the bag up and he sinks deep into the bottom, weighing it down.

"Go to sleep." I tell him. "We'll be there soon."

I lift the bag and put my arm through the handles, so it hangs by my side from my shoulder.

Mum eyes the carrier bag as I lug it down the stairs.

"What's that? What've you been buying?"

"Nothing. It's a present I don't want." I say. "I'm going to take it back and exchange it

"I'll meet you back here in a few minutes." Mum says, as she locks the car at the farm. "I'm just going to the fishmonger to see what fish Ted can offer us for dinner tonight."

"OK. I'm just going to the Destiny shop." I say.

"Don't buy any of that rubbish they have in there." Mum says, smiling at me.

"I love you, Mum." I say.

"I love you too, sweetie pie." Mum says. "Come and find me in the fishmonger."

I push the door of the Destiny shop open. The wind chimes tinkle and fairy bells jingle and crystals spin in the spring sunlight. The smell of vanilla incense hits my nostrils as I see Amber Rose reading *Let Dolphins Heal Your Soul* at the front desk.

"Hey, Tanya," she says. "How are you? It's been a while," she adds, walking round the side of the desk to give me a hug.

She's added some henna highlights to her blue-black hair and she looks years younger and softer somehow.

"Your hair looks fab." I say. "It really suits you."

She smiles at me. "Thanks. You look great too. Haven't you grown up? What are you up to now?"

"I'm revising for my A-levels." I say, with a burst of pride.

"That's so exciting. When are they?"

"In June. Next month." I reply, looking at all the dragons and angels and fairies and waterfalls guarded by wizards that fill the shop.

I slowly slide the bag to the floor. She doesn't notice.

"Good luck," she says. "You'll do brilliantly. You're a clever girl."

"Thanks." I say.

I listen to the rushing of the waterfalls and the whale music that resonates throughout the shop and try not to think about what I'm doing. I turn to go, leaving the bag: my hand is on the door. My heart wrenches.

"Hey." Amber calls.

I stop dead. She lifts up the bag from where I've left it.

"Is this yours?"

My heart beats. Of course he's mine. Of course he is.

"Yes." I say.

I take the bag and walk out into the sunshine.

"Darling," Mum says, as she walks across the car park to meet me. "You were gone a long time. Did you take it back, whatever was in that bag?"

"No," I reply, putting my arm through hers. "I decided I did want it after all."

"Oh good," she says. "Shall we go home for tea?"

"Yes, I'm really hungry now." I say.

I lower the bag between us, just behind the handbrake. My panther's tail emerges between the handles and waves triumphantly.

"I could have sworn I just felt something stroke my cheek." Mum says, rubbing her cheek where my panther's tail is tickling it.

"It's probably your angel protecting you." I say, trying to keep a straight face.

Mum giggles, pulling me closer to her.

"Have you been talking to the girl in that silly new Age shop again? People shouldn't be allowed to talk such rubbish." She says, softly, starting the car.

Acknowledgements

Mum: for all her proofreading and copy editing and love and support.

Dad: For printing eight copies for me to work on and for all his love and encouragement.

Alexander: For all his helpful and constructive criticism over the years.

To Donna: my best friend and collaborator on many projects. Thank you for your amazing support over all these years and words can't express how much I love you and your depiction of the panther.

For Sissi and Sercha for all your support at work and your friendship.

Spitfire: For all his soft cuddles.

Lesley and Katy: for believing in me and IN BLOOM for all these years and for all the time you give me.

For the Megatripolis crew: thanks for being there for me. You know who you are but special mention for Luke, Ben, Zoot and FBI.

For Dr Robert Cohen: for all your hard work helping me deal with the panther over the past 20 years.

For my School: North London Collegiate – for letting me be myself for eleven years.

For the Sunday morning chat crew: Deborah, Matthew and Lisa.

For the Pilates and Barre crew: Sarah, Louise, Yasamin, Candi, Ruth, Terri and Tanya.

For the Far Side crew: Mark, Dave, Hayley, Julia and many others.

For my friends: Loren, Spencer, Tommy, Sunna, Solo.

For my aunts, uncles and cousins: thank you for all the help over the years.

For Angela who came into my life just in time.

For James H and James CC for all your encouragement.

For Paul, Gemma and all my other friends.

For Jane Thynne, Clare Mulley and Liz Hoggard – thank you for believing in my writing.

For Julia Bell at Birkbeck and all my writing group: Maggie, John, Dorothy, Linda, Kavita, Jamie, Amy, Robert and Sue – thank you for your comments on every draft.

For all my blog readers – especially Lauren, Marty and Linda.

For all my friends and family.

About the author

With a lifelong passion for literature, Cordelia Feldman showed a precocious talent for writing, penning her first (unpublished) novel – A Jilly Cooper-style romp called *Players* – at the very young age of 14.

She completed the first draft of *In Bloom* for a writing competition at age 26 and polished it further while studying for an MA in Creative Writing at London's Birkbeck University.

A straight-A student throughout her schooldays, Cordelia excelled in all academic subjects, particularly the arts, and went on to study Modern History at Oxford University, following a gap year when she worked as a volunteer in the Children's Zoo and Small Mammal House at London Zoo, whilst doing paid work in the Personnel and Marketing departments and even dressing up as a tiger, lion and penguin for Zoo events.

After graduating, she landed her first job with the Pollinger literary agency. Lesley Pollinger recalls that she was moved to interview and subsequently hire Cordelia because of the enterprise and humour she had shown in dressing as a penguin for her work at the zoo. After a year with Pollingers, Cordelia then went on to work for the authors' and actors' agency Eric Glass, where she stayed for fourteen years.

More recently Cordelia has been drawn to mystical and esoteric interests. She qualified as a Tarot Reader in 2019 and now provides readings on a professional basis. She is also currently studying for a three-year Diploma with the London School of Astrology.

A fervent lover of nature and all animals, Cordelia is a dog-walker in her spare time, pays regular visits to London and Whipsnade Zoos, where she is a member, and is devoted to her half-Ragdoll ginger cat Spitfire.

When not engaged in literary, professional, academic and doggy pursuits, Cordelia is an avid follower of professional tennis – a self-professed 'Rafaholic' – and is committed to a daily regime of physical exercise, including weightlifting, Pilates and barre.

She has endured a great deal more than her fair share of physical and mental suffering in her young life, having struggled with bipolar disorder since her late teens and being diagnosed with secondary breast cancer at age 34.

Now aged 41, Cordelia has her own apartment in North London, but since lockdown in March 2020 has been shielding with her loving parents Teresa and Keith in Hertfordshire.

Lightning Source UK Ltd.
Milton Keynes UK
UKHW020918180122
397329UK00006B/134